For John,
Don't be afraid to ask for help with the big words.

The Inheritance

Robert Gonko (signature)

By Robert Gonko

This is a work of fiction. All places, persons, products, and situations are either a figment of the author's imagination or used fictitiously. No resemblance to actual persons, living or dead, is intended nor should be inferred.

Cover art by Robert Brooks

Copyright © 2013 by Robert Gonko, all rights reserved

CreateSpace Edition

ISBN-13: 978-1482703047

For Angela

ONE

IT DIDN'T TAKE Sam Harman more than a minute to decide that being fired sucked.

As the security guard escorted him to the front door, Sam ignored the stares. People he'd known for years avoided making eye contact with him. Others whispered to each other.

"Isn't that Sam Harman?"

"He's been here forever."

"What did he do?"

"I can't believe it."

The security escort was standard procedure, he'd heard. The official reason was that a fired employee (or, in corporate-speak, terminated team member) was now a security risk and must not be allowed any opportunity to access privileged information. Knowing how this company operated, and the attitudes of some in management, Sam felt the real reason was to embarrass the victim and possibly send a message to those who remained. Either way, it sucked.

The guard showed him out the front door and suddenly Sam was on his own. His now-former boss had said she'd call him in a week so he could pick up his personal items. Not even allowed to clean out his desk. Fifteen years thrown out the door just like that. All because of a few mistakes...

Okay, maybe more than a few mistakes but his job was *hard*. Downen & Lowe (D&L for short) was one of the nation's leading financial companies and Sam had, until today, worked in its home mortgage division. In addition to generating its own business, the company made a lot of money buying up mortgages from smaller lenders and bundling them into security packages for investors. Sam's job was to review and setup these loans on the computer system. The problem was the level of detail involved had grown exponentially over the last few years and Sam had a hard time keeping up. The mistakes kept accumulating and despite his best efforts became too numerous for management to overlook.

Standing in front of the D&L building on 17th street, Sam suddenly felt very alone. Soon he would have to tell his wife what had happened. He'd been upfront with her about his troubles from the beginning, and, to her credit, Tracie had been nothing but sympathetic and supportive. She'd felt partially responsible since she'd helped him get the job in the first place.

As he walked to the parking garage down the street Sam wondered how they were going to pay for it all now. Oh, he'd go on unemployment until he found another job but that wouldn't replace all his lost salary. Then there were the medical concerns. Noah had had drainage tubes put in his ears three times since infancy and it looked like it would have to be done again soon. How was he supposed to pay for that?

He got in his car and just sat there, thinking. *Lord, I could sure use a way out of this mess.* This brief little prayer was genuine. For months Sam had prayed about his problems at work but things continued to get worse. He hadn't lost hope that God would make it all right, but he was more than a little discouraged.

Sam pulled his cell phone out of his pocket. He should call Tracie. No, that was a bad idea. Better to tell her in person. He would tell her tonight when she got home. He put the cell phone back in his pocket, started the car, and drove out of the parking ramp. His parking permit was good through the end of the month. It would come in handy when he came back downtown to go job hunting.

He drove across the river towards his part of town. Once he was across the bridge he reached a decision and put his Bluetooth headset on. He hit the speed dial and waited for the answer.

"Hello?"

"Marty? It's Sam," he said."They went and did it."

"Did what?"

"Fired me," he said.

There was a brief pause. "Sam, I'm sorry," he said. "Does Tracie know yet?"

"No," Sam replied. "I mean I just...I just don't know..."

"Where are you?"

"I just crossed the bridge," he said

"I'm at the church," Marty replied. "Come on over. We'll talk and we'll pray."

Already feeling better, Sam turned at the next light.

He had no idea that he was being followed.

Steve Bennett, a private investigator, hung a few cars back from Sam. Surveillance was pretty boring most of the time but every now and then something interesting would happen. Like this for example. Sam Harman worked 8 to 5 every day and only occasionally left the D&L building for lunch. Bennett, who had been watching him for a week now, was surprised to see him leave the building a mere half hour after arriving for work. Had Sam been fired, or had there been an emergency with one of his kids? He supposed he'd find out soon enough.

He was even more surprised when, instead of going to his kids' school or day care, Sam pulled into the parking lot of the Chester Avenue Christian Church. Bennett knew that the Harmans were members and had been for several years but why would Sam come here on a Tuesday? Bennett parked his firm's dilapidated Chevy Lumina, which they used for surveillance, down the street from the church and took out a pair of binoculars as Sam went inside. There was only one other car besides Sam's Dodge Avenger. Bennett read the tag number of the other car and checked it against the dossier he'd compiled of Sam's known associates. The car was registered to Martin Lovell, who Bennett knew was the pastor of the church. Curious, he made a phone call to a friend who worked at Downen & Lowe.

"George?" he said. "Steve. What's up?"

"The usual," George replied. "Something wrong? You never call me here."

"Need some information for a case I'm working,"

Bennett said. "You know Sam Harman, right?"

"Yeah," George replied, sounding surprised. "What going on with him? I heard he got fired this morning."

Word travels fast, Bennett mused. "You know that for sure?" he asked.

"As sure as anything is around here," George said. "This place has a rumor mill that would put Jefferson High to shame. But a couple of people I know saw him escorted out of the building so I'm pretty sure it's true. No idea why, though."

"That's okay," Bennett said. "You told me what I needed to know."

"What's this about?" George asked. "Why are you interested in Sam?"

"Can't tell you that," Bennett said. "He's not in any trouble, though, so don't worry. Give me a few days and I'll explain everything, okay?"

"Sure," George said. "I understand."

"And see if you can find out why he was fired," Bennett added. "It might be important."

Bennett said his goodbyes and hung up. Then he made another call.

"Yes?" A voice answered.

"It's Bennett," he said. "It looks like our friend just lost his job. I don't know why yet but I'm working on it."

"I see," the man replied. "Where is he now?"

"At his church," Bennett said.

The man at the other end chuckled. "If he only knew," he said. "I suppose we'd better move things up. Keep an eye on him, Bennett, and make sure he doesn't do anything stupid. I'll fly in tomorrow and then we'll have our little talk with Mr. Harman."

"Will do," Bennett said and hung up. He flipped open a laptop and paged through the file he'd accumulated on Sam Harman, including scans of the documents his client had provided. Boy, was this guy in for a surprise.

TWO

"SUSPECTING THIS WAS going to happen and having it happen are two really different things," Sam said, taking a sip of coffee. "And pardon me for saying this, but it really sucks."

Pastor Marty Lovell smiled. "I understand," he said. "Before I went into ministry I got fired a couple of times. You're absolutely right."

Sam sighed. "What am I going to do, Marty?" he asked. "What do I...how do I tell Tracie? This is going to ruin us financially. We could lose the house--"

"Whoa, slow down," Marty said. "It happened less than an hour ago. You need to keep a clear head if you're going to get through this. I know it seems like it but it's not the end of the world. God has a plan for you. I'm sure of it. He won't let you be ruined."

"I wish I could believe that," Sam said.

"You can believe it," Marty said. "You just don't want to right now because you're upset. That's perfectly natural. But as long as your trust is in God, He won't abandon you. And neither will I. You know if there's anything I can do you only need to ask."

Sam didn't doubt that for a minute. In addition to being his pastor, Marty was one of his closest friends. The man had led him back to God after being a borderline atheist for years. Sam trusted him almost as much as he trusted his wife. That was why he was here.

"You should call Tracie," Marty said. "Go ahead and tell her now. She has a right to know."

"I was going to do that at home, tonight," Sam said. "I thought--"

His cell phone rang. It was Tracie calling from work. "Well, I guess it was bound to happen," he said, hitting the answer button. "Hi, honey."

"Where are you?" Tracie asked. "I called the office but your phone went to voice mail."

"I'm at church, talking to Marty," he said. "They...honey, they fired me."

"Why didn't you call me?" she asked.

"I...I didn't know what to say," he replied. "I thought Marty might be able to help."

"Oh, Sam, I'm so sorry," Tracie said. "Do you need me to come over there?"

"No," Sam said. "I'll be okay. No sense in you making waves at your office. We'll talk about it tonight."

"You sure you're all right?" she asked.

"Just so long as you're not mad at me," he said.

"Honey, I'm not mad," she said. "We both saw this coming. We'll find a way to make it work, okay?"

"Okay," Sam said softly. "We'll have to tell the kids tonight."

"I'll pick them up," she said. "You stay there and talk to Marty, then go home and relax. We'll get through this."

"You're too good to me," Sam said.

"No, I'm not," she replied. "I've got to go. I'll call you when I go to lunch. I love you."

"Love you, too." he said.

"So she took it well?" Marty asked.

"Better than I did," Sam said.

"I knew you didn't need to be worried," Marty said.

"And you're about to tell me that I shouldn't worry about anything, right?" Sam said, half smiling.

"Well, Jesus said not to worry," Marty said, flipping open the bible on his desk and paging through it until he found the passage. "Matthew 6:31-34. Read it."

He handed Sam the bible. So do not worry, saying, 'what shall we eat?' or 'what shall we drink?' or 'what shall we wear?' For the pagans run after all these things, and your heavenly Father knows that you need them. But seek first his kingdom and his righteousness, and all these things will be given to you as well. Therefore do not worry about tomorrow, for tomorrow will worry about itself. Each day has enough trouble of its own.

Sam considered the passage. He understood the principle. Tomorrow would have problems whether he worried about it or not. But knowing the principle and being able to practice it were two different things.

"It's a matter of faith, Sam," Marty said. "You have to have faith that God will make it alright. He's got something special for you. I'm sure of it."

Sam stayed and talked to Marty for another half hour then went home, still unaware that he was being followed. He was still embarrassed and hurt, of course, but he was a bit more optimistic about the future. When he pulled up to the house at 1451 Knox Avenue, though, the doubts started to creep back. How long would they be able to stay there? Where would they go if they couldn't? It was like seeing the house and knowing how much they still owed on it destroyed whatever good feelings the time talking and praying with Marty had given him.

Something else from the bible came back to him at that moment. Get behind me, Satan! He thought. Marty always emphasized that worry and doubt came from the Devil. Sam wasn't sure that he always believed that but with the way things were going today he wasn't going to take any chances. He wasn't feeling particularly close to God right at that moment but then he remembered something else Marty said. Faith is not a feeling. God was always there. Sam would go on, and he'd work something out. He tried to keep that thought foremost in his mind. When he got into the house he grabbed every item he had with a D&L logo and threw it in the trash.

The kids took the news of his firing fairly well. Sam Jr., now eleven years old, understood the dangers better than the other two. For a child he was remarkably on top of the news. He knew about the unemployment problems and the problems in the housing market. The boy read the paper every day and spent time on the internet perusing news sites. Given his interest in current affairs Sam was willing to bet his oldest would be either a journalist or a politician. Sam hoped for journalist. He despised politicians.

Kristen and Noah, ages seven and four, didn't really

seem to understand what his being fired meant for the family. "Mommy still has her job, doesn't she?" Kristen asked. After being assured that this was the case Kristen seemed confident that everything would be alright. Sam wished he shared that confidence. The doubt had come creeping back again as he explained the situation to his children. He struggled to keep it out of his voice but he was pretty sure Sam Jr. had picked it up. The kid was really sharp.

Little Noah's response was the simplest of all. He gave his father a hug and said, "It's okay, Daddy, God will take care of us." Tracie nearly burst into tears.

Marty called later that evening and told Sam to talk to one of the church elders after services on Sunday. The man owned a car dealership and might have an opening. Sam wasn't sure he had what it took to be a car salesman. On the other hand he didn't want his family to starve. He promised Marty that he'd talk to the elder.

He would never make that call.

THREE

THE NEXT MORNING a Gulfstream IV private jet landed at John T. Mason International Airport. It taxied to one of the general aviation terminals where a limousine was waited. The aircraft carried two passengers. The first, an elderly man in a custom tailored suit, carrying a briefcase, disembarked and headed straight for the limo. An aide followed, carrying the old man's bags and his own. The luggage was quickly put in the trunk as the old man opened the door. After a quick look inside, he turned to the aide. "Ride with the driver," he said, his Texas drawl pronounced but his voice clear.

He got in and the limo drove off the tarmac. The old man turned to the man sitting next to him. Steve Bennett was dressed in a suit, specially cut to conceal the .40 caliber Beretta pistol he wore in an old-fashioned shoulder holster. Bennett seldom went unarmed. Not only was his work occasionally dangerous but as a former police detective he'd made enemies over the years, including a few who still wore badges. Port Mason wasn't the most dangerous city in America but it wasn't exactly the safest, either.

"How's our friend," the old man asked.

"Been holed up in his house since he got home yesterday," Bennett replied. "He's either moping around, polishing up his resume, or both."

"I think it's best if you make the initial approach," the old man said. "He should remember you, shouldn't he?"

"I think so," Bennett said.

"Good. Just get him to the hotel. I'll take care of the rest."

"He should have protection," Bennett said.

"I agree," the old man replied. "Hopefully we can persuade him. That is just one of the many decisions that poor man's going to have to make."

"Poor man?" Bennett said. "Interesting choice of words."

"I chose them carefully, Mr. Bennett," the old man said. "I'm not entirely sure we're doing him any favors here but my hands are tied. I have to do as I've been instructed. Sam Harman's about to be dragged into a world he knows nothing about. I'll try to give him what help I can but he's really going to be on his own."

An hour later, Bennett pulled up to the Harman residence. Sam hadn't moved too far away from his roots. He'd grown up a mere six blocks away. The house wasn't the nicest on the block but the family managed to take care of it. The grass was mowed, branches picked up and bushes reasonably well trimmed. On this warm spring Saturday morning the Harmans were outside. Sam and Tracie sat on the porch going over the morning paper as their children played in the front yard with a couple of kids from down the street. Still dressed in his suit, and feeling more than a little conspicuous, Bennett approached the house. When he set foot on the first step a dog started barking inside. Bennett saw the pooch through the front door, woofing away.

"Chloe, knock it off," Sam said. Then he took a good look at his guest. "Steve? Steve Bennett?"

"How are you, Sam?" Bennett asked, grinning.

"Wow, I almost didn't recognize you with that short hair and goatee," Sam said, getting up to shake hands. "Looks better than that mullet you had in high school."

Bennett cringed a bit at the memory. "Why do people always bring that up?" he asked.

"For reactions like that," Sam said. Then he remembered his wife. "Oh, Tracie, this is Steve Bennett. I played baseball with him in high school. Steve, my wife Tracie. Chloe, knock it off!"

The dog ignored the command. Steve and Tracie shook hands while Sam asked, "How are you doing these days?" Sam asked.

"Pretty good," Bennett said.

"You still a cop?"

"No I left the force three years ago," Bennett said.

"You did?" Sam replied, surprised. "I seem to remember you saying that was all you ever wanted to do. What happened?"

"Long story," Bennett said. "And one I really can't get into right now. I'm here on business. Can we talk inside?"

"Might as well," Sam said. "Chloe won't shut up until you go in to see her."

Sam opened the door. "Your wife might want to be

in on this, too," Bennett said.

The Harmans led Bennett inside. As soon as their guest was over the threshold Chloe, a mutt if there ever was one, started sniffing. Bennett held a hand out to her and after she'd inspected it he petted her on the head. That set her tail wagging and she cheerfully followed Bennett into the living room where they all sat down. Chloe rested her chin on Bennett's knee and whimpered slightly. Bennett resumed petting her.

"So what kind of business are you talking about?" Sam asked. "If you're here to give me a job, great. I got canned yesterday."

"I heard," Bennett said. "And I'm sorry."

"How did you hear?" Sam asked.

"Let me back up a bit," Bennett said. "After I was...left the force I went to work for my uncle at his detective agency and I've been doing that ever since. A few weeks ago I was hired by a lawyer out of Texas. His name is Anderson Braddock. High roller. He paid me a big retainer to find you and keep an eye on you."

Puzzled, Sam looked at his wife then turned to Bennett. "Why?

"I can't tell you that part," Bennett said. "Except that he knew you were born here and adopted here in 1973."

"Is that what this is about?" Sam asked. "My adoption?"

"Yes," Bennett replied.

"And this lawyer...is he..." Sam couldn't finish the sentence.

"No, he's not your father," Bennett said. "I'm not at

liberty to tell you the rest. Mr. Braddock arrived in town this morning. He has a suite at the Fairmont and he's very eager to meet you. He'll explain everything. I know it's been a long time and maybe you don't have any real reason to trust me but I can tell you this won't be a bad thing. Come with me to the hotel. Hear what this guy has to say. You won't regret it."

"And he knows who my birth parents are?" Sam asked. "You know too, don't you?"

"The terms of my deal with Braddock are clear," Bennett said. "He has to tell you everything."

"Can you wait here a second?" Sam asked. Bennett nodded. Gesturing to Tracie, Sam went into the kitchen. Tracie followed him.

"This is strange," Tracie said. "I don't like it. How long has it been since you've seen this guy?"

"Not since high school," Sam said. "We really didn't run in the same social circles."

"But can you trust him?" Tracie asked.

"I think so," Sam replied. "If this really is about my birth parents I can't pass up the chance. I think I'd better hear what this Braddock fellow has to say."

FOUR

FOR AS LONG as he could remember, Sam had known he was adopted and as far as he was concerned it was the smartest thing his parents could have done. He'd heard plenty about the turmoil kids went through upon finding out they were adopted after always assuming they were their parents' natural-born children and was grateful to have been spared it. The only thing that upset him was that he hadn't appreciated his parents' wisdom when they were alive.

At the same time, he'd always wanted to know where he'd come from. His desire to know, to meet his birth parents was in no way a rejection of the good people who'd adopted him. They were his Mom and Dad. They had taken him in, given him a name, given him a family, given him a life. Since becoming a Christian, Sam had come to believe that God had brought them together so he could have those things. But that didn't change his desire to know the truth. More than that, he also wanted medical information. What ran in his family? Cancer? Alzheimer's? Something else? Did his blood relatives die young or did they reach old age? Don't get ahead of yourself,

Sam, he thought. Hear the man out.

As Bennett's car approached the Fairmont, Sam bowed his head and quietly prayed for guidance and strength to face whatever was ahead. Bennett noticed but said nothing. Though not a religious man himself, the private investigator respected, or at least tried to respect, the beliefs of others. He knew one thing, though; if it was a miracle Sam was praying for he was about to get it.

The Fairmont was not only the finest hotel in Port Mason, it was the oldest, dating back to the city's founding in 1834. The hotel had been torn down and rebuilt several times. The current version had gone up in the 1920s. It boasted two gourmet restaurants and extensive conference and ballroom facilities. Sam had brought Tracie here for dinner on their first anniversary. After seeing the bill it was their last visit.

The door was answered by a young man in a dark blue suit. "Mr. Harman, a pleasure to meet you," he said, extending his hand. "My name is David Lambert; I'm Mr. Braddock's assistant. If you gentlemen will follow me?"

He led them into the suite. In the main room was white leather furniture, a grand piano, a widescreen TV that was too big for Sam's living room and a fully stocked bar. It also boasted a dining table that seated eight, a small kitchen and a sideboard. Though the doors were closed, Sam noticed a large balcony. He couldn't help but wonder what the rest of the suite looked like and, more importantly, how much this place cost per night.

"Nice, isn't it?" Bennett asked.

"You could say that," Sam replied.

Lambert went over to a closed door and knocked softly. It opened to admit a short old man, also wearing an expensive suit. 'Old' really wasn't a word to describe him, Sam decided. 'Ancient' seemed to fit better. He was slightly stooped over, walked slowly, and had deeply tanned skin which suggested he spent as much time outside as he did in an office. When he got a good look at Sam, he smiled.

"Well aren't you the spitting image?" he said with a pronounced Texas drawl.

"Spitting image of whom?" Sam asked.

"Oh, my," the old man said. "A Yankee accent coming out of someone who looks like you. I have to admit I wasn't expecting that. I'm Anderson Braddock, attorney-at-law. And you are Mister Samuel Brian Harman, born in Port Mason on May 11, 1973, am I correct?"

"Yes," Sam said, cautiously.

"Sit down son, sit down," Braddock said, heading for one of the sofas. Sam sat on the other. Bennett and Lambert remained standing.

"David, get an old man a drink, would you?" Braddock said. Though couched in the form of a request there was no doubt Braddock was, in fact, giving an order. Lambert hurried to the bar. "Either of you gentlemen want anything?" Braddock asked.

"Not when I'm working, thanks," Bennett said.

"Mr. Harman?"

"Uh, no, nothing for me," Sam said.

"Well we'd best get down to business," Braddock said after Lambert brought him his drink. He rifled through a briefcase on the coffee table before pulling out a file folder. "I suppose our Mr. Bennett here has told you that this meeting has to do with your adoption. Have you ever been interested in finding out about your...natural family?"

"Sure," Sam answered.

"Good, because you're about to find out," Braddock said. "Just out of curiosity, how much do you know?"

"Almost nothing," Sam said. "My mom and dad said all they were told was that my mother was very young and couldn't keep me so she gave me up for adoption. They didn't know anything about my father."

"That's how it was supposed to be," Braddock said. "All right, I'll give it to you straight. Your biological father's name was Henry William Curtis of Houston, Texas. I'm sorry to have to tell you that he died two months ago. He was eighty-two years old and a more cantankerous man you'd never meet.

"He liked to fool around," he continued. "Back in '72 he was working on a deal involving a couple of businesses based here. While he was in town he met your mother, had an affair with her and got her pregnant with you."

"I take it he was a married man?" Sam asked.

"Yes," Braddock said. "And I know this might sound strange but he did love his wife. They had three sons together. He just...loved other women too."

"I can't say I have a lot of respect for that," Sam said.

"I understand," Braddock said.

"What do you know about my mother?" Sam asked

"We'll get to the details in a bit," Braddock said. "I will say that Hank paid all her medical bills while she was pregnant and set her up with a small business after you were born. As I understand it, she originally wanted to keep you but her parents persuaded her to give you up.

"Anyway," he continued. "Despite the legal sealing of your adoption file, Hank knew exactly who you were and where you ended up. He kept tabs on you over the years through a series of private investigators, some of Mr. Bennett's competitors, I suspect."

"If he knew who I was, why didn't he contact me?" Sam asked.

"If you'll bear with me, I'll get to that," Braddock said. "Like I said, he kept tabs on you because he was genuinely interested in how your life turned out. He made sure you were taken care of but not in a way that would draw attention. Remember your dad's job with the trucking company?"

Kevin Harman had been a mid-level manager with the...the Curtis Freight Company. "He arranged Dad's job?" Sam asked.

"He was already working there when you were adopted," Braddock said. "And he was good at his job. His only failing, as I understand it, was his lack of internal political savvy. It's why he never rose higher than he did. Hank owned that company. It was one of his many businesses. He wasn't too involved with it but he made sure your dad was never fired or the victim of political maneuvering by more ambitious people. It was Hank's way of making sure you had a roof over your head and food on the table."

"And Dad had no idea, did he?" Sam asked.

"Not a clue. Hank saw to that," Braddock replied. "I'll be blunt with you. Hank was a very wealthy man. He made his big killing in the oil business down in Texas but he had his fingers in all sorts of things. He believed in being diversified. When he died he was worth over twenty billion dollars."

Bennett whistled. Sam was glad he was sitting down. "You sure you don't want that drink, son?" Braddock asked.

"No thanks," Sam said. "I need to keep my head clear."

"Well at least in that regard you're a bit smarter than Hank," Braddock said. "I seldom saw him without a drink in his hand. Got him into trouble more than once.

"Well, like I said, he always made sure you were taken care of," he continued. "He wanted to be your guardian angel. And he was. If he'd known about the troubles you were having at Downen & Lowe...well he was a major stockholder in that company. He didn't arrange your job there but he could have made sure you weren't fired. Sorry to hear about your trouble there, by the way."

"Thanks," Sam said. "But that doesn't explain why he never contacted me,"

"No, it doesn't," Braddock agreed. "The short version is that your turning up would throw his family into turmoil. None of them, especially his wife, knew about you. With the amount of money involved, can you imagine what might have happened? A divorce would have been devastating. His kids would have moved heaven and earth to make sure you didn't get a dime of his money. Bunch of greedy ingrates, I always thought. I'm afraid Hank wasn't all that good a father, in some respects. He spoiled those kids rotten."

"I take it you don't like them very much," Sam said.

"No I don't," Braddock said. "Hank worked hard his whole life to build his fortune. Those spoiled brats will ruin it all within five years, ten at the most. Mark my words, it'll happen.

"And all this brings us to you," Braddock said. "With Hank gone its left to me to carry out the terms of his will. As you've probably guessed, he remembered you in that will. Sam, Hank left you three billion dollars."

Again, Sam was glad he was sitting down. "Three billion?" he asked. "Billion with a 'B?'"

Braddock chuckled. "Yes, billion with a 'B.'"

"You've got to be kidding me," Sam said

"This is no joke, son. As of today, you are almost certainly the wealthiest man in Port Mason.

FIVE

WHEN HE FIRST became a father Sam had resolved to clean up his language. By and large he had succeeded. But there were times he just couldn't help himself. This was one of them.

"Holy shit," he whispered.

"In addition, he left you ten percent interest in his holding company, Curtis Enterprises," Braddock said. "It's a minority share but worth a lot of money."

Sam wasn't sure he was registering all of this. Three billion dollars from a birth father who was a Texas billionaire who fooled around on his wife and spoiled his legitimate children? Part of him wanted to dismiss this as some kind of trick, some kind of scam. But to what end? What did he have up to now that anyone would want to con him out of? Nothing. Heck, he'd just lost his job. Wait a minute...

"Your timing is...interesting," Sam said. "You show up the day after I get fired?"

"It's nothing sinister, I assure you," Braddock said. "Mr. Bennett's sources at Downen & Lowe informed him of your firing. That forced me to accelerate my plans so that you and your family won't starve. I realize this is a lot to take in, Sam, but it's all legitimate."

"Three billion..." Sam said softly. "What do I do with that kind of money?"

"Your options are virtually unlimited," Braddock said. "The first thing I suggest you do is get your own lawyer. I can't represent you because I'm the executor of the will but I can give you some names. Or if there's someone you know and trust you can seek their counsel. You'll also need a financial adviser. I'm sure you've heard about people who win the lottery and lose it all because they don't know what they're doing. I would hate to see you end up like that."

"Uh...yeah...so would I," Sam replied.

Braddock regarded him for a moment. "You really aren't sure what to make of all this, are you?" he asked.

"No," Sam said. "No, I am not."

"Certainly understandable," Braddock said. "You're probably not even sure you believe what I've just told you. In your position, I would certainly have my doubts."

"I'd call this a con job," Sam said. "But I can't figure out what I have that you'd want. I...I take it you can prove all this?"

"Yes, though it took some doing," Braddock said, handing Sam the file he'd been referencing. "Take a look through that."

Sam opened the folder. The first document was a photocopy of a birth certificate. In the upper left corner was a file number and Sam's name. The only information entered in the space for the child's name was the surname 'Orrick.' Henry William Curtis of

Houston, Texas, was listed as the father. Finally he allowed his eyes to fall on the mother's name, only then did he realize he'd been holding his breath.

It read 'Susan Marie Orrick,' gave her date of birth as August 18, 1952, and her address on a street Sam was pretty sure was in the welfare district. So that was it. After nearly forty years he finally knew the names of his biological parents. Then a thought occurred to him. "How did you get this?" he asked. "I was always told it was sealed by the court."

"Hank told me he found out who you were by way of some cash he had someone spread around the county courthouse," Braddock said. "Before the file was sealed. Obviously, we needed some official proof. Since Miss Orrick put Hank's name on the birth certificate I was able on behalf of the estate to petition the court to have the file unsealed and a copy made of the original birth certificate. After Mr. Bennett located you, we paid him to keep an eye on you until the family could be notified and the probate process begun."

"Probate can take a long time," Sam said. "I remember when Dad passed away it took me three months to get his affairs in order, and his estate was pretty simple."

"You're absolutely right," Braddock said. "Big estates like this can take years to sort out in the courts, even when everything is properly documented ahead of time. It will all depend on how much trouble the family decides to cause."

"So I assume there's no check I can go and cash on Monday," Sam said.

Braddock laughed. "Well, actually, there is," he

said, taking an envelope from his breast pocket and handing it to Sam. He opened it and saw a certified check for one million dollars drawn on a bank in Houston made out to him. He was very nearly profane again.

"As executor of the will I have the authority to disburse funds at any time," Braddock said. "That check is to help you and your family until we get the estate settled."

Still holding the check, Sam returned to the file. The next document was rather thick, almost half an inch. It was the last will and testament of Henry William Curtis. A paperclip stuck out from a page about a third of the way into the will. He turned to that page and saw the language that named him as an heir. Assuming he read it correctly, it willed Samuel Brian Harman three billion dollars and a ten percent stake in Curtis Enterprises.

"When you find a lawyer, have him review that will," Braddock said. "There's an appendix with the probate court information."

Sam put the file down, sat back, and closed his eyes. Lord, can this really be happening? He prayed silently. What am I supposed to do now?

"Sam you are about to be thrust into a world you know nothing about and which could destroy you if you let it," Braddock said. "Also, when word of this gets out, as it always does, you are going to become very popular. My best advice to you is to surround yourself with people you can trust, really trust. People who aren't going to hear cash registers the moment you tell them about this. When you hire a lawyer, hire one who's expensive and successful. Someone like that will understand what you need done. Hire an accountant, and then hire an auditor to keep an eye on that accountant. Don't hesitate to have background checks run on anyone you associate with."

"I can, uh, help with that," Bennett said, drawing attention to the fact he was still in the room.

"Mr. Bennett can also advise you on matters of personal security," Braddock said. "Take that advice seriously and act on it. Kidnapping is a very real threat to the wealthy. "

"How long do you expect this to stay secret?" Sam asked.

"Hard to say," Braddock replied. "The family found out about you after Hank died. His wife actually took it better than any of the others. Sallie's no fool; she knew he'd screwed around for years. I think she was half expecting something like this. Between you and me I'm surprised you're the only one.

"When his kids found out about the money and stake in the company they all went nuts," the attorney continued. "Threatened to sue. For now Sallie has got them under control but she's not in the best of health. Being married to Hank made for a stressful life."

"I'll bet," Sam said.

"At some point very soon you're going to have to come down to Texas and make an appearance," Braddock continued. "My guess is that's when this will hit the papers."

Sam's attention returned to the file and he looked at the birth certificate again. "What about Susan Orrick?" he asked. "Is she still alive?"

"Alive and well," Braddock said, handing him

another file.

"Does she know about me?" Sam asked.

"I talked to her this morning," Braddock said. "Her phone number is there, you can contact her any time you like."

Sam found the number and stared at it. He slowly reached for his cell phone. Everything he wanted to know was just a call away. In his hands was a million dollars with the promise of so much more. It had taken less than an hour for his life to turn upside down.

"You're going to call her now?" Bennett asked.

Sam thought about it for a moment. "No," he said. "Not just yet. I think I'd better get my wife down here."

Tracie arrived in the suite just as lunch, ordered by Braddock and charged to the estate of Hank Curtis, was being served. Being at a four-star hotel led Sam to expect some dish he wouldn't recognize and, most likely, be unwilling to eat. Instead room service brought up simple salads, a variety of cold cuts with assorted breads and cheeses, and a vegetable tray. "Never cared for what they call 'haute cuisine,'" Braddock said. Sam couldn't have agreed more. He was a 'meat and potatoes' man himself, despite Tracie's frequent entreaties for him to eat healthier.

Sam introduced Braddock to his wife. After that Tracie asked Sam to explain what was going on.

"Perhaps it would be easier if I explain, Sam," Braddock said. "But first let's get something to eat. I'm starved."

After everyone got their food and sat down at the

table, Braddock gave Tracie the short version of what he'd told Sam. For his part Sam didn't say anything but rather showed her the will and the check he'd been given. She sat in stunned silence long enough for Sam to become concerned. "Honey," he said. "You there?"

She slowly turned to look at him. "Is this for real?" she asked softly.

"As far as I know, yes," Sam said.

A small smile appeared on her face, followed swiftly by a shriek of delight as she threw her arms around her husband. "Oh, thank you God!" she exclaimed. "We can pay the bills, get rid of the mortgage--"

"And that's just for starters," Sam interjected. "That stuff will hardly put a dent in this first check. Can you imagine what we could do with the rest?"

"We should get a lawyer," she said.

"First thing Monday," Sam reassured her.

"Wow!" she exclaimed. "How could we be this blessed?"

"I don't know," Sam said. "At least this saves me the trouble of polishing up my resume."

"Now you'll have to learn how to read them," Braddock said. "You're probably going to be seeing a lot of them. Most of the services you require can be handled on a retainer or per Diem basis but you might want to start familiarizing yourself with the finer points of business."

"What kind of business?" Sam asked. "Like I said before, what does someone do with three billion dollars?"

"You could buy this hotel," Bennett said.

That brought a laugh. "And what would I do with a hotel?" Sam asked.

"Don't get too far ahead of yourself, Sam," Braddock cautioned. "Wealth comes with great responsibilities, not to mention occasional danger."

"Danger?" Tracie asked.

"Well I don't want to alarm you, Mrs. Harman," Braddock said. "But the fact is that the wealthy, particularly the newly wealthy, are frequently targets of all kinds of...nefarious schemes."

Tracie's look of delight quickly changed. "Who else knows about this?" she asked.

"Very few," Braddock said. "Aside from the people in this room, only Hank Curtis's other heirs are aware of the situation at this point. That will change, though. You won't be able to keep this secret forever. When that happens they'll come out of the woodwork. 'Long-lost' relatives, so-called friends you haven't heard from in years, all sorts of people who figure you owe them a living. You'll have to be ready to face that."

Tracie looked sobered by this. "How are we going to keep them away from us?" she asked.

"Mr. Bennett here can help you with your personal security," Braddock said. "In fact, he has already arranged temporary security around your home."

"My uncle is there, keeping an eye on things until the security people are in place," Bennett added.

"And the estate will pay for your security until probate is settled," Braddock said.

"Is there someplace my husband and I can talk privately for a moment?" Tracie asked.

"The office is right over there," Braddock said.

"Please help yourselves."

Sam and Tracie went into the office, which was as lavishly appointed as the rest of the suite. Once the door was shut Tracie turned to Sam. "Private security?" she said. "Floods of people after money? Sam, are you sure we should accept this?"

"How can I say no?" Sam replied. "I'm unemployed, you don't make enough to cover our bills and let's be honest we have a lot of bills. This is the answer to all our problems. Heck, this check alone will take care of everything hanging over us and then some. Do you seriously want me to walk away?"

"I don't know," Tracie said. "This is all happening so fast. We need time to think and pray."

"From what Braddock says it's going to be a while before we get the money," Sam said. "We'll have plenty of time to plan and pray. It's not like we have to start working on it today."

"You do know it's going to be a lot of work, don't you?" Tracie asked. "You don't just park three billion dollars in the bank and go rest on the beach."

"You don't?" Sam smiled. "Bummer."

"Be serious," Tracie scolded. "This is going to turn our lives upside down. And what about the kids? I don't want them growing up to be spoiled brats. How are we going to say no to them now when they want something? We're going to need financial advisers, lawyers, accountants and who knows what else. I don't know the first thing about having this kind of money and neither do you."

"Are you saying we shouldn't take the money?" Sam asked.

"Well...no," Tracie said with a guilty smile.

Sam chuckled and took her in his arms. "Honey, we'll make it work," he said. "Trust me."

Sam and Tracie came out of the office holding hands. "Mr. Braddock?" Sam asked. "What happens now?"

Before the lawyer could answer a cell phone rang. Everyone checked their pockets. Lambert found the call was for him. After a few whispered words he turned to Braddock. "Mr. Braddock," he said. "That was our pilot. The family jet has just landed at the airport. He says Mrs. Curtis was on board. He saw her get into a limo."

"Fat's in the fryer now," Braddock said. "Remember Sam, I said you were about to be thrust into a world you know nothing about? Well you're going to get your first look at it. Prepare yourself for Sallie Curtis."

SIX

BRADDOCK SUGGESTED THEY finish their lunch but neither Sam nor Tracie had much appetite suddenly. Sam didn't know what to think. First his birth father leaves him all this money, and now he was about to meet the man's widow who traveled by private jet. Was this roller-coaster ever going to end? Apparently not, if Braddock was to be believed.

Within twenty minutes there was a knock on the door. Braddock gestured for Lambert to get it. The assistant took a deep breath before opening it. In stepped an old woman who looked even more ancient than Braddock. To Sam's surprise, she wore a simple dress and shoes. Not what he expected from the widow of one of the richest men in the country.

Sallie Curtis may have looked old and frail but everyone in the room quickly realized that appearances were grossly deceiving. "Anderson Braddock, I might have known you'd take the best suite in the place," she barked. "And you charged it to Hank's estate, I'm sure."

"This is an estate matter, Sallie," Braddock said, respectfully.

"Hogwash!" Sallie said. "This is a family matter.

You should have told me you were coming to see him."

"I thought it would be better if I told him everything before he met you," Braddock said.

"You thought what my husband thought," Sallie said. "That I was too delicate to handle his fooling around. Now, which one of you is Sam?"

Sam took a small step forward. "I am," he said.

"Well come closer, boy, let me get a good look at you," Sallie commanded. And there was no doubt it was a command, just as Sam did not hesitate to obey. This woman possessed an even stronger will than Braddock.

She stared at him for several seconds. "Oh, my," she said softly. "Well there's no doubt about who your daddy was, boy. I had to see it for myself, though, you understand?"

Sam nodded.

"My Hank was a good man," Sallie said. "But he couldn't keep his pants zipped to save his life. Will somebody help an old lady to a chair?"

Sam offered his arm and guided Sallie to the sofa. "Well at least you were raised with some manners," she said. "Anderson? Get me a whiskey! Neat!"

To Sam's surprise, Braddock did as Sallie said rather than delegate the job to his assistant. Only when her whiskey was in hand, and a generous portion swallowed, did she speak again. "Now the first thing I want to say to you is that I don't hate you," Sallie said. "Nobody asks to be born and nobody can control what they're born into. The second thing I want to say is that I'm glad Hank did the decent thing and looked after you. Lot of men would have up and run.

"But what I mainly came here to say is that you're about to find yourself in a lot of trouble," she continued. "Hank and I have three children, all of them have large stakes in the company and all of them are drooling at the thought of taking over. If they're smart they'll make the company even bigger than it is now. The problem for you is that they don't want to share with anybody, even their half-brother."

"They won't be able to break the will," Braddock said. "It's airtight. Hank signed it in front of a dozen witnesses. Besides, I can show that Sam's been in every will Hank signed since 1973. The boys will waste a lot of money on lawyers, but in the end Sam will win."

"I don't want to see this happen at all," Sallie said. "I can be a spitfire and I don't take crap from anybody but I'm also a mother who loves her children. Seeing them behave like this makes me sick. It's not the way I raised them. It's Hank's fault, really."

"Mr. Braddock said they were spoiled," Sam said.

"The word doesn't even begin to describe it," Sallie replied. "We gave them a first-rate education. No sense in having money if you can't do that for your children. The problem is Hank couldn't say no to them on anything. Bill wanted a Ferrari? Hank bought it. Nick wanted to throw a party that cost $100,000, Hank wrote the check. I won't even start about Jerry. Hank wouldn't stop and now all three of them think they're entitled to everything."

"Why would he do that?" Tracie asked. "Didn't he realize what that would do?"

"Smart girl," Sallie gestured at Sam. "She your wife?"

Sam nodded. "Good. Make sure you hang on to her," Sallie said. "Anyway, my boys are fit to be tied over this will and they're going to try and break it. I want you to understand that."

"I think I understand," Sam said. "But I'm not too sure what I'm supposed to do about it. I don't know anything about having this kind of money."

"Luckily for you, I do," Sallie said. "And I'm going to help you."

"You are?" Sam asked.

"That surprises you?' Sallie asked.

"Well, yeah," Sam said. "I guess I figured you'd want me cut out too."

"Most people probably would," Sallie said. "But, as Anderson will tell you, I'm not most people. Hank left each of the boys more than he left you. But that's not enough for them. They want it all. Me, I see it differently. I think you were done a bad turn in life, and I think you deserve what he left you. Besides, you've already shown more manners and maturity in the last five minutes than my boys have since Hank died."

"So what should I do now?" Sam asked.

"You need to make your formal claim to your share of the estate," Sallie said. "This means you're going to have to come to Texas. When you do, I'll send my plane to come get you. You can stay in my house. When you go to court, I'll go with you. When they ask me if I'm going to help them fight Hank's will I'm going to tell them no."

"Mrs. Curtis," Sam began.

"Call me Sallie," she said. "I think we're going to be great friends."

"Okay, Sallie," he said. "I don't want to get in the middle of a fight between you and your sons."

"I appreciate that," Sallie said. "But you have to remember that these are your brothers, or at least your half-brothers. I want those boys to meet you, see how much you look like Hank. I want them to know you before they try to ruin you."

Until that moment Sam had thought this would be a relatively painless process. He'd sign some papers, maybe go to court, and get the money. Sallie's words proved that he was out of his depth. All of the revelations of the day were starting to get to him. "This is…all this…it's way too much to digest," Sam said. "Don't tell me any more right now. I've got to…I've got to get out of here."

He stood up. Tracie was at his side instantly, taking his hand. "Sam, let's talk to Marty," she said. "He can help us."

"Yeah," Sam said. "That's a good idea."

He picked up all the papers Braddock had given him including the check. He might have been freaking out but he wasn't stupid. "Mr. Braddock, how long are you going to be in town?"

"As long as I need to be," Braddock said. "You're right; you've been through a lot today. Go home, get settled, and let it all sink in. Call me here tomorrow and we can talk some more."

"I'll be here, too," Sallie said.

"Okay, thanks," Sam said. He left the suite quickly, followed by his wife and Bennett.

Braddock looked at Sallie. "In a way, I feel sorry

for that man," he said. "He's been hit with an awful lot today."

"Better he finds out now," Sallie said. "Anyway, this is nothing compared to what that money is going to put him through. Even if you're right about that will, he's still in for all sorts of trouble."

"Yeah, I know," Braddock said. "I mentioned that to Hank more than once, but he was adamant about leaving Sam a big chunk. You know how stubborn he was."

For the first time since arriving Sallie seemed to deflate a little. "I don't know why I loved that philandering old fool so much," she said. "But I did. Seeing that boy reminded me of when I first met him. You remember?"

"I sure do," Braddock said. He knew Sallie well enough to know that she had put on a brave front earlier. Beneath the surface she was a grieving widow. That front was gone now. Sallie started to cry.

"Maybe this wasn't the right time for you to meet him," Braddock suggested.

"At our age, Anderson, it's not a good idea to put things off," Sallie replied. "We probably don't have a hell of a lot of time left, you know. I'll be all right."

Braddock didn't believe it for a minute but also knew better than to press the issue. His thoughts were mainly with Sam Harman. What would he do once the full reality of his inheritance sank in? Normally an expert in predicting human behavior, Braddock was at a loss to answer that question.

SEVEN

TRACIE DROVE THE car out of the parking garage. Sam sagged in the passenger seat and put his hand on his head. "This is too much at once."

Tracie kept her eyes on the road, but inside her turmoil probably equaled her husband's. Like most people they'd occasionally talked about what they'd do it if they won the lottery. They even bought a ticket once in a great while. In all their private and shared financial fantasies, though, they'd never dreamed having lots of money would send them into a panic. But they both were panicking and, in their eyes, with good reason.

For her part, Tracie tried to take a positive view. This was a blessing from God, she reminded herself. They'd prayed for an answer to Sam's firing and this was it. Surely God wouldn't give them all this to destroy their lives. The God she believed in didn't work that way. There had to be a purpose in this, there had to be. *Father God*, she prayed, *please tell us what we're supposed to do.*

Sam called Marty, asking him to meet them at their house. Even though it was Saturday and he had a sermon to finish for the next day's services he agreed, knowing that Sam wouldn't have asked if it wasn't important. He promised to be there in an hour or two. They passed the rest of the trip home in silence, neither sure of what they were supposed to say.

If the truth were to be told, Sam was more afraid of the prospect of a fight with the Curtis brothers (his brothers, he reminded himself) than he was of having the money. Sam was not big on confrontation. He didn't even like to confront Tracie when he had a problem with something she was or wasn't doing. There had been times over the years when he regretted not being bolder with some people or in certain situations, but he was who he was and for the most part he was fine with that. He was just grateful he didn't have that problem with his children—yet.

His children. What was he going to tell them? He and Tracie had tried hard not to spoil their kids, while at the same time ensuring that they were happy and content. It wasn't always easy saying 'no' when one of them saw something they wanted on TV or in a store, but mostly they'd managed it. But now, with apparently limitless resources at their disposal, how were they supposed to say 'no?' Maybe he should turn down the money.

But in his gut he knew he wasn't going to do that. For one thing, he didn't want to go on working in jobs he hated, and he'd hated working at D&L. Who was to say that another comparable job wouldn't be the same way? Plus like many people, he had a dream of doing nothing and having a lot of money. Sam actually had a lot of dreams, virtually all of which were now accessible. That was something worth thinking about. And there was what he'd said to

Tracie earlier, all the good they could do for people with that kind of money.

Sam couldn't lie to himself. He wanted this money. He just didn't want all the trouble that was likely to come with it.

When they got home they found the kids playing with some of the neighborhood kids in their front yard. Chloe was barking like crazy from inside the house but Sam knew she just wanted to be outside with them. An SUV with the words 'Tyler Security' was parked in front of the house behind an old Ford Mustang which Sam took a moment to admire. It looked to be in beautiful condition and he was willing to bet it was either a '65 or '66. That was something to think about; he'd always loved looking at classic cars. Maybe that was something he could do. He'd need a bigger garage.

As he and Tracie came out of their garage, the owner of the Mustang got out and approached them, followed by two men from the SUV. Sam immediately knew the Mustang's owner must be Steve Bennett's uncle—the resemblance was obvious.

"I'm Charley Bennett," he said. "Steve had me come out a while ago."

"Thanks for keeping an eye on things," Sam said. "Everything quiet?"

"Everything except your kids," Charley said, grinning. "But no problems."

As if on cue their children broke off their game and ran over to them. "What's going on, Dad?" Sam Jr. asked.

"We'll talk about it later," Sam said. "Why don't

you go back to your game, so Mom and I can talk with these gentlemen?"

"Who are they?" his eldest son asked.

"They're, uh…"

"Here to install a security system," said the older of the two men from the SUV. "That's what you wanted, right Mr. Harman?"

"Uh, yeah, that's right," Sam said. "Go on, now. This will only take a minute."

Kristen and Noah accepted this explanation without question and ran back to their friends. Sam Jr. didn't seem to be buying it, but he obeyed his father and went back to the yard. Sam promised himself he would tell him the truth later. His son was too smart to be easily fooled.

"Thanks for the save," Sam said. "This wasn't a good time to tell him everything."

"I wasn't lying," the man said. "We are going to put in a security system. Just one of the many services we offer. I'm Stan Tyler and this is my son, Pat."

"Steve and I have done a lot of business with these guys," Charley said. "They'll take good care of you."

"And how are they going to do that?" Tracie asked.

"Well like I said, we'll put in a security system," Stan said. "We also offer armed twenty-four hour security if you want it."

"I'm not sure I want guns in my house," Tracie said.

"Why don't we discuss this inside?" Charley suggested.

The guests paid due respect to Chloe. She wagged her tail and followed the humans to the dining room where they all sat around the table. "Mrs. Harman, I understand your concern about guns," Stan said. "But our specialists are highly trained. We only hire people with law enforcement or military backgrounds who exhibit the highest degree of professionalism."

"And they're discreet," Pat said, speaking for the first time. "They'll wear plain clothes and stay out of sight if that's what you want."

"That'll be kind of hard here," Sam said. "As you've seen it's a small property. I imagine we'll…upgrade fairly soon, but for now this is still our home. I don't want to draw a lot of attention from the neighbors."

"How much do you know about our situation?" Tracie asked.

"I know everything Steve knows," Charley said. "All I told these guys is that you'd come into money and were worried about kidnappers and gold-diggers."

"Is there something else we should know?" Stan asked.

"I don't think so," Sam said. "But I'm still getting it all sorted out myself. What about the kids? I don't want them walking around the schoolyard with a bodyguard."

"Where do they go to school?" Stan asked.

"Sam and Kristen go to Chambers Elementary," Tracie said. "Noah goes to Mrs. O's daycare over on Peterson Avenue."

"We'll check them both out," Pat said. "The public schools actually have pretty good security these days, so I'm not too concerned about that. The day care might be an issue but I won't know until we have a look at the place."

"We can probably do with having a car near each facility whenever the children are there," Stan said. "Unless there's an immediate threat you're worried about."

"None that I can think of," Sam said. "What about the system for the house?"

"We'll put in motion detectors outside, alarms on all the windows and doors and they'll be linked to our operations center," Stan said. "It's manned twenty-four hours a day so if the alarms are tripped they'll have responders on the scene in minutes. And if our people are here too, you'll be even more protected."

"How soon can you have it installed?" Tracie asked.

"Today," Pat said. "We brought all the gear with us. If you like, I can get started right now."

Sam looked at Tracie and she nodded. "Okay, go ahead," Sam said. Pat left the room followed by Chloe, who immediately started barking when he went outside.

"Chloe, be quiet!" Tracie snapped. Chloe ignored her, as she always did. "If we're going to entrust our safety, and the safety of our children, to you, I think we have a right to know as much about you and your company as possible. Don't you think so, Sam?

"Absolutely," he agreed.

"That always a good idea," Stan said. "Well, like Charley, I used to be a cop. I took early retirement after I was shot chasing a suspect about, oh, fifteen years ago. I took the bullet in the knee and had to have a lot of reconstructive surgery. The knee works fine now but it isn't good enough for police work, so I called it quits, took my retirement savings, and started this business. At first it was just me and two buddies from the force. Now I have over thirty people working in various aspects of personal and business security. I can provide references. Some of our people work with members of the Vipers."

"Protecting them from angry fans?" Sam asked. Everyone at the table knew that Port Mason's major league baseball team had a bad habit of irritating their fans with their lousy playing. Sam sometimes wondered why he kept going to the games, but he'd never stopped going. There was another thought, he realized, season tickets.

"We provide personal security for visiting celebrities," Stan continued. "We also do more low-key stuff like home security systems and business security systems."

"Steve and I work with these guys from time to time," Charley said. "I know you don't know me but Steve and I will vouch for these guys. They'll do a good job, trust me."

"Are your people in position now?" Sam asked.

"Yes, that's what Steve asked for," Tyler said. "We have an unmarked car down the street and a man strolling through the neighborhood. Don't worry he won't attract attention. If anyone asks he's taking a political survey. Most people leave him alone when he says that."

"I wouldn't let someone like that in the house," Sam said.

That drew a chuckle around the table. Then Chloe announced Pat's return the house. "Mr. Harman, there's a Marty Lovell out here. Says he's your pastor."

"Let him in," Sam said.

Marty came in, a bewildered expression on his face. "What's going on?" he asked. "This guy at the door wouldn't even let me come up the front walk."

Sam looked at Tracie and smiled. "Here we go," she said.

"What?" Marty asked.

"Marty, remember yesterday when you said God had something special for me?" Sam said.

Marty nodded.

"You were right," Sam said. "Wait until you hear this."

EIGHT

ALL THINGS CONSIDERED, Marty took it well. He sat with them at the table, Charley Bennett and Stan Tyler having left to oversee the security. His hands lay flat on the table and for a brief moment Sam wondered if he was breathing. Then he spoke.

"Three billion?" he exclaimed. "Billion with a 'B?'"

Sam laughed, remembering his own question to Anderson Braddock. "Yeah," he said. "Can you believe it?"

"I'm not sure," Marty said.

"Neither are we," Tracie said. "That's why we wanted to talk to you. We need some guidance."

"Actually, we need a lot of guidance," Sam quipped.

"I don't know," Marty said. "This sort of thing never came up in Bible School."

"Help us through this, and you can write the book on the subject," Sam chuckled. "Really, we wouldn't mind."

"Sam, be serious," Tracie said.

"Talk about good timing," Marty said. "They tell you this the day after you lose your job. That's the Lord's work. I think we need to pray before we discuss this further."

"Good idea," Tracie said.

They joined hands and lowered their heads. "Father God," Marty began. "We thank you for this incredible blessing you've bestowed on Sam and Tracie. We know that this is your money that has been entrusted to their care. Guide them in their use of these funds so that everything they do will be to your glory. We give all thanks and praise to you, who are most worthy to receive it. In Jesus' name we pray."

"Amen," they said in unison.

"Well, at least we've started on the right foot," Marty said.

"Yeah," Sam said. "Now what?"

"I'm really not too sure," Marty said. "You've asked me for guidance but beyond praying for you, which I will do, I'm not sure what to tell you."

"We'll be giving money to the church," Tracie said. "As much as it needs."

"The tithe on that would be…three hundred million," Sam said. "I try to be good about tithing."

Marty couldn't contain his shock. "You'd actually give the church three hundred million dollars?" he asked.

"We might," Sam replied. "The board of elders could decide what to do with it."

"I don't know, Sam. When we started the church the founders agreed that we would stay a small community church. That kind of money could turn us into a mega-church. I'm not sure that's a great idea, and I don't think it's the kind of church I want to pastor."

"I don't want to see that either," Sam said.

"Maybe we should wait until we actually have the

money before we start discussing that," Tracie suggested. "Once we start doing things like that word will get out about us. We have to be ready for that before we do it."

"That is really smart, Tracie," Marty said, breathing a sigh of relief. "I think that's exactly what you should do."

"I've told you before, she's the real brains of this operation," Sam said, smiling at his wife. "There's nothing wrong with making plans, though, is there? You know, a list of stuff we want to do?"

"I don't think so," Tracie said.

"As long as you keep it to yourselves," Marty said. "Once people find out you have this kind of money, they're going to be breaking down your door."

"That's one of the things the security is for," Sam said. "But you're right. And I hate to say it, but I'm sure there are plenty of people at church who'll want to 'advise' us on what to do with the money."

"You're right, there will be," Marty said. "But I think you're going to run into that no matter where you are or who you're dealing with."

"True," Sam said. "Hey, look on the bright side. I can finally get those new golf clubs."

"There you go," Marty said, enthusiastically. One of the bonds of their friendship was a shared passion for golf. Hey...another thought. Maybe he could join one of those fancy country clubs with the really nice golf courses. He dismissed the idea almost immediately. Sure it would be fun to play those courses but he didn't really want to rub elbows with that crowd. The thought was a little intimidating

"You know, I just thought of something," Sam said.

"Are we going to be able to keep the same friends? I don't want to lose the people close to me because of this money."

"I've been wondering about that, too," Tracie said.

"I think you're going to find that your true friends won't care about the money," Marty said. "The ones who do...well they probably weren't very good friends to begin with. Have you told the kids yet?"

"No," Sam said. "That was something else we wanted to talk to you about. I'm not sure what to tell them. How do we keep them from turning into spoiled brats?"

"That I can answer," Marty said. "Keep raising them the way you've been raising them. Don't pass them off to nannies or babysitters while you go out and do...whatever you end up doing. Keep them, and yourselves, in church. Remember Proverbs 22:6: 'Train a child in the way he should go, and when he is old he will not turn from it.' Stay engaged in their lives, keep them rooted in God's Word, and don't let them come to believe that the money is the most important thing in life. Both of you would do well to remember the same thing."

After Marty left they decided it was time to tell the kids. They sat their children down in the living room and carefully explained the situation with Sam's birth parents. Sam Jr. and Kristen knew about the adoption and had for some time. In the past they'd tried to tell Noah about it, but he didn't understand. After explaining that their dad knew who his birth parents were and that he hoped to meet his birth mother soon, it was time to talk about the money. Sam and Tracie still weren't sure what to say.

Sam Jr. was the one who broke the silence. "We're rich now, aren't we?" he asked.

His father was taken aback. "What...what makes you say that?"

"You never said anything about getting an alarm system before," the boy replied. "And you just lost your job, Dad, so how could we pay for it? All of a sudden you find out about your real parents and we can afford a security system?"

Sam sighed. "Son, you are too smart for your own good sometimes," he said. "But you're right. My birth father left me money. A lot of money. We need the security now."

"Did you get a million dollars?" Kristen asked.

"Uh...more than that," Sam said. "I'm not going to talk about the details right now and we don't have most of it yet, anyway. But it looks like our lives are about to change, big time."

"I know you're going to be excited about having money to spend, but I don't want you bragging to your friends about it," Tracie said. "Your dad and I don't want you talking about it at all, actually. For right now it needs to be a family secret."

"Can we move to the country, by Grandma and Grandpa?" Kristen asked, referring to Tracie's parents. She loved their place, which was about thirty miles west of Port Mason, and had frequently asked if they could move out there.

"That's one of the things Mom and I have to talk about," Sam said. "We'll definitely be moving, but as for where...I'm not too sure yet."

"Daddy," little Noah said. "I like our house."

"I know," Sam said. "But you'll like a new house even better, I promise."

"Can I have a new Beyblade?" Noah asked.

Sam and Tracie laughed. "Not today," Tracie said. Noah asked for a new Beyblade toy at least once a day, never mind that he already had three of them. It was clear that he didn't understand, but they hadn't really expected him to. They had debated waiting until his bedtime before telling the other two but had decided against it. It wouldn't take Noah long to figure out something was going on. Besides, they had always tried to be upfront with their kids about things. They weren't going to change that now.

"There is one thing we're going to do," Sam said. "You guys get out of school for the summer at the end of the month, right? How would you like to go to Disney World for a week?"

Kristen and Noah reacted with glee. Sam Jr. seemed pleased too, though not as much. "Don't worry, we'll find stuff for us, too," his father said. "We'll take our clubs and play some golf. And we can visit the Kennedy Space Center. I've always wanted to see that, haven't you?"

"Yeah," his oldest said. They shared a passion for spaceflight. "Can we see a launch?" he asked.

"Let's check the internet and find out if they're having one soon," Sam said.

"That's one thing this will do for us, we can take more family trips," Tracie said. "But we're not going to get you everything you ask for just because we can afford it, okay? So don't start asking."

"But I want a new Beyblade," Noah protested.

Sam and Tracie laughed again. Kristen looked at

Noah crossly. "Will you stop talking about your stupid Beyblade?" she demanded.

"It's not stupid!" Noah shouted.

"Ugh," Kristen groaned. "You see what I have to put up with?"

"What you have to put up with?" Sam Jr. said. "What about me? I have to share a room with him."

"I think the family meeting's over," Sam said.

"Yeah," Tracie agreed. "I'll start dinner."

As they set about their evening routine Sam couldn't help but wonder how long this sort of thing would last. Would this tear his family apart? He just didn't know.

NINE

CONSIDERING EVERYTHING THAT happened that day, it was understandable that Sam didn't sleep very well that night. His mind was too busy. If he wasn't thinking about the money he was thinking about his birth mother. He'd called her after dinner and arranged to meet her at her home the next day. She had sounded excited over the phone but Sam was more than a little nervous.

Unfortunately, it also resulted in a restless night for Tracie, who couldn't sleep through all his tossing and turning and whose mind was also racing from the events of the day. They discussed the money, what they might do with it, and Sam's pending meeting with his birth mother. They held each other in the dark without talking for a while but neither could fall asleep. Finally, if only to release their tension, they made love with fervor they hadn't experienced in years. Only then did they fall asleep.

Sunday morning came far too early, but they had already decided that they would attend church the same as usual so they couldn't sleep in. Everything that morning seemed to take forever; at least that's what Sam thought. Breakfast, getting the kids and themselves ready, the drive to church; it was a test of his patience. Instead of paying close attention to Marty's sermon, as he usually did, he barely registered it.

When the service was finally over, Sam practically raced his family home to the point where Tracie had to caution him about his driving. He ate his lunch quickly then paced around the house impatiently until about 1:30, when he kissed his family goodbye and got into the car.

The Gables was an upscale development on the northeast side of Port Mason, well across the river from Sam's neighborhood. As he drove through the neighborhood Sam found himself musing that he could afford a home here now. He pushed the thought aside, though, reminding himself that this wasn't the time to be making plans like that.

He reached her house and parked in the street. In the driveway was a Mercedes. Clearly his mother had done very well for herself to be living in this neighborhood and driving that car. He slowly walked up to the door and rang the bell. Almost immediately the door opened and he laid eyes on his birth mother for the very first time.

She was short, shorter than Tracie, who was five foot seven. Her hair was silver, styled fashionably in a short bob cut. In truth, Sam didn't see much resemblance between them except for the eyes. Her eyes, he knew right away, were the same as his.

Susan Orrick had tears in her eyes and a big smile on her face. "He was right, you're the spitting image of Hank," she said.

"I...I'm not sure what to say," Sam said. "I've

waited my whole life for this and…and…"

Susan threw her arms around him, pulling him close. After only the slightest hesitation Sam returned the embrace. "I can't believe this is happening," he said.

"Neither can I," she replied as she pulled back. "I've missed you so much. They only let me see you for a few minutes after you were born, you know. And now you're all grown up."

Sam nodded, not sure what else he should say. "You look like you need to sit down," she said, taking his arm and leading him into the house. They went into the living room where she showed him to the sofa. She sat next to him and took his hand.

"I'm going to have to get used to calling you 'Sam,'" she said. "I always wanted to call you John, after my father."

"I guess you can call me that, if you want," Sam replied. "I could get used to it."

"No," Susan said. "No, I'll call you Sam. I think it would be better that way. Well, I suppose you have a lot of questions for me. I know I have a lot for you. You go first."

"Okay," Sam asked. "Braddock only gave me the basics of how...how I came to be born. If you don't mind, I'd like to know the whole story."

"I thought you would," Susan said. "You'll understand that even now, it's not easy to talk about. It's a part of my life that I'm not really proud of. The way I behaved in those days, I mean. But if anyone deserves to hear it, it's you.

"I was a student at the University," she said. "It was every bit the party school then just like it is now.

Back then everybody was doing everything, including me. I tried pot, drank quite a bit and, I have to admit, I'd starting getting…promiscuous. I'm not proud of it, like I said.

"I met Hank on my 21st birthday," she continued. "My friends and I made our first stop on what I thought would be a kind of pub crawl. I never made it past that first bar. Hank was there with some people. I thought he looked so funny. Cowboy hat, bolo tie, boots, all with a suit. You don't see much of that around here. Oh, was he a charmer. You can probably guess what happened later."

Sam nodded uncomfortably. He remembered feeling the same way when thought about his parents having sex. It was just…weird.

"I was very young and very naïve," Susan said. "I didn't know anything about birth control. Hank either didn't know or didn't care. It wasn't a one-night stand, either. He was here on business but every night he'd take me to dinner and then back to the hotel. That went on for about two weeks before he had to go back to Texas. I thought that would be the end of it, but he surprised me by giving me a telephone number and to call him if I ever needed anything. He must have really liked me. Anyway, about a month after he left I found out I was pregnant. That's when everything went nuts."

"Why...why did you give me up?" Sam asked.

Susan looked pained at the memory. "My dad was very old-fashioned," she said. "A pregnancy out of wedlock was not something to be open about. They didn't want the rest of the family, their friends or church to know about it. They didn't even tell my brothers, they just said I was going to school in Europe for a year. I tried to argue with them but my dad...he was a hard man."

"What did he do to you?" Sam asked.

"Oh he was never violent," Susan said. "But he was headstrong and did not take kindly to being told 'no' by his children. He made it clear that if I didn't do what he said, he'd cut me off from the family."

"That's...well, I don't know how to describe it," Sam said. "I can't imagine doing something like that to one of my kids, no matter what they did."

"It was a different time," Susan said. "They found a home for unwed mothers over in the welfare district and sent me there. After about a month I got up the nerve to call Hank and tell him what happened. I didn't know how he would react. He said he'd do whatever he could to help out with the expenses. He sent a very generous check. I suppose I could have left the home at that point but the women there were so supportive, so helpful. They understood what I needed and what I was going through. I'm still friends with some of them.

"My mom would come to see me occasionally," she continued. "She wasn't quite as firm about the situation. She was disappointed in me, but she still loved me. She couldn't come too often because Dad didn't want my brothers to know. I didn't tell them about you until after Dad passed away."

"Are both of your folks gone?" Sam asked.

Susan nodded. "They have been for a long time. I don't want you to get the wrong idea about my dad. He did what he thought was right. As the years went by and that sort of situation became more accepted, he softened up a bit. When he was in the hospital dying, he actually apologized for the way he treated me when I got pregnant with you. I'm glad we were able to make our peace."

"That's good," Sam said.

"Now, tell me about you," Susan said. "I want to hear everything."

"Well I'm not going to tell you about some of my college adventures," Sam said. "Too embarrassing."

They both laughed. "Seriously," Susan said. "Tell me about yourself. Anderson didn't tell me that much. Tell me about your parents. I understand they've both passed away?"

"Yeah," Sam said. "Mom died almost twenty years ago. Sudden stroke, she never recovered. She never even got to meet my wife, let alone see any of her grandchildren."

"I'm sorry," Susan said.

"At least it was quick," Sam continued. "I watched both of my grandparents on her side waste away from cancer. Mom never wanted that to happen to her. Dad died six years ago, about a year after my daughter was born. He went fast, too. He had a heart attack."

"I wish I could have met them," Susan said. "It might sound crazy but I wish I could thank them for raising you."

"They would have liked to meet you, too," Sam said.

"How many kids do you have?" Susan asked.

"You have three grandchildren," Sam said. "Sam Jr., Kristen and Noah."

"How old are they?"

"Eleven, seven and four," Sam said.

"Did you bring pictures?"

Smiling, Sam got out his cell phone and started showing her pictures of the kids. "Oh, how adorable," Susan said. "That one looks like you. Is that Sam Jr.?"

"Yeah," Sam said, switching to another photo. "And that one's Kristen. And here's one of Noah with Tracie, my wife."

"She's lovely, Sam," Susan said. "How long have you been married?"

"Fifteen years," Sam said. "I was…uh...married before but it didn't last long. It's not something I like to talk about."

"I understand," Susan said. "I don't like talking about my marriage either."

"Well we certainly have plenty of other things to discuss," Sam said, eager to get away from that topic. "So do I have any brothers or sisters?"

"I have a daughter," Susan said, smiling. "Ashley just turned thirty-three. She's married and has two girls. They live in California, though, so I don't get to see them too often. She knows about you and wants to meet you. They're coming out in June, so hopefully you two can connect."

"I'd like that," Sam said. "You know, it's funny. When I woke up yesterday, I was an only child and an orphan. Now I have a mother again. I have a sister by you and three brothers by Hank Curtis. Not to mention I'm apparently a billionaire. Did you hear about that part?"

"Anderson told me everything," Susan said. "Do you know what you're going to do yet?"

"Not really," Sam admitted. "Everything's happened so fast. Tracie and I didn't sleep too well last night from all the anxiety. I mean, I do have a couple of ideas but nothing concrete."

"Can I give you some advice?" Susan asked.

"Sure."

"Don't make any plans for a while," she said. "Try to take it easy and enjoy yourself a bit. There'll be plenty of time to figure out what to do with your money."

"Yeah, that makes sense," Sam said. "My pastor pretty much said the same thing. I can't stop thinking about it, though."

"No, I don't suppose you could," Susan said.

"You've done pretty well for yourself by the look of things," Sam said. "What do you do for a living?

"Interior design," she replied. "I've been in the business my entire professional life. Hank helped me set it up after you were born. Wouldn't let me pay him back, either. I guess that was his way of making things up to me."

"He kind of looked after me, too, I'm told," Sam said, explaining about his adoptive father's job.

"I didn't know he'd kept tabs on you," Susan said. "Or that he even knew who had adopted you. I wish he'd told me."

"I don't think the...means he used to find out were entirely legal," Sam said. "Maybe he didn't want you implicated."

"Maybe," Susan said, sadly. "I suppose it doesn't matter now. What matters is that you're here. I have my son back."

"Yes you do," Sam agreed. They embraced again.

Meeting her had been everything he could have hoped for.

TEN

TWO WEEKS LATER Sam sat in the passenger cabin of a lavishly appointed Gulfstream 550 jet as it waited for clearance to take off for Houston. He wore a brand new suit purchased downtown at Bridges' Clothier and Haberdashery, considered the finest men's' store in town. In his new luggage were two more new suits along with his regular clothes. The total for this excess was nearly $10,000, but he'd been assured by his new lawyer that appearances would help establish his credibility and he, along with Tracie, had reluctantly agreed. He hoped he didn't burn through the first million before the Curtis estate was settled. They had also paid off their house and car loans with the money. It felt really good to have those off their backs.

Once the check cleared things began to move quickly. The other heirs found out about Braddock's disbursement of funds to Sam and were outraged. A series of tense calls between their lawyers and Sam's lawyer ensued. In the end Sallie Curtis intervened, inviting Sam to Texas to meet with all of them and sending the family's private jet for him. He did not relish the prospect of doing battle with his half-brothers, but he knew it had to be done so he went.

His new lawyer insisted on coming along. Aaron Charlton was a senior partner at Leonard & Spengler, one of Port Mason's leading law firms. The firm was recommended to him by Anderson Braddock, who had dealt with them several times over the years. According to Charlton, the firm's senior partners resorted to a lottery to decide which of them would handle Sam and Tracie's affairs.

The flight attendant stepped out of the cockpit. "We're ready to take off, gentlemen," she said. "If you'd please turn off your mobile devices and buckle up, we'll be on our way."

Charlton spoke a few more words into his cell phone, then turned it off and put it away. Sam's was already off. "This is the way to travel," Charlton said. "A lot nicer than flying commercial, even first class."

Sam was inclined to agree, though he'd never flown first class, so he couldn't be too sure about that. The plane was gorgeous. He'd always been interested in aviation. He attended the local air show every year and loved crawling around the planes and talking to the pilots. As a young boy he'd wanted to become an Air Force pilot and eventually, an astronaut. Those childish wishes were quickly dashed when he discovered he didn't possess the math skills needed for such endeavors. And as he'd grown up he'd become interested in other things but his love of aviation and astronautics had never wavered. Maybe after all this was over he would finally take flying lessons. That would be fun.

As the engines revved up and the plane began to taxi

Sam took another look around the cabin. It was paneled in leather and highly-polished wood. It could seat 14, he'd been told, and boasted numerous amenities including a widescreen TV, air-phone service and wireless internet service. The seats could be folded down to double as beds and there were two sofas that could also be folded out. They also had access to their baggage at all times during the flight. Charlton was right; this was the way to travel. If he really got the three billion, Sam just might have look into getting his own plane.

That was, in his mind, still a big if. Sam and Tracie had burned up the internet over the last two weeks trying to learn as much as they could about the Curtis family, their business, and their family fortune. The more they learned the more Sam realized he was out of his depth with this whole business. Braddock had been right, this was a world he knew nothing about and, quite frankly, he wasn't sure he wanted to learn about it. Oh, the luxuries were all kinds of fun as he was rapidly finding out. But the kinds of people he would find himself dealing with—that gave him considerable pause.

Once they were airborne and the all-clear had been given, Sam pulled out his laptop and called up the file they'd assembled on the Curtis family. As Braddock had said, Hank Curtis was a self-made man. He'd made his first killing in oil, but his real genius had been in spreading out his investments and other businesses. Curtis Enterprises was a family-owned conglomerate with its fingers in manufacturing, real estate, shipping, aviation, commodities, commercial foods, agriculture and its founding business, oil.

Hank's approach had been to find small companies in these areas and turn them into big ones. He had succeeded brilliantly. Sam had been somewhat amused to learn that the business deal Hank had been working on when he met Susan Orrick was the purchase of what would become the Curtis trucking company, his dad's old outfit.

Sam put that aside and linked the laptop to the aircraft's wireless internet. He called up his email account and sent a quick message to Tracie, at work. You wouldn't believe this plane, he wrote. I might have to get one of these.

She wrote back. Don't get ahead of yourself. Besides, we agreed not to do too much traveling while the kids are in school

Spoilsport, he replied with a smiling emoticon. Okay, so maybe he wouldn't buy one of these planes. He might just hire them from time to time, though. That thought made him smile.

The plane landed at Ellington International Airport early that afternoon, local time. Once an air force base, it was now shared by the military, NASA, and general aviation interests. The Curtis plane taxied to one of the general aviation terminals where a limousine was waiting. Standing by the car, to Sam's surprise, was Sallie Curtis herself. When he got off the plane he was again surprised when Sallie gave him a big hug. "Thanks for coming down, Sam," she said. "Is this your lawyer?"

"Aaron Charlton, Ma'am," the lawyer said, offering his hand. She shook it, but only briefly.

"Get in, get in," she said as the driver opened the

door for her. "I don't like being out in the heat too long."

It didn't seem too warm to Sam, but he reasoned that at her age Sallie might be a bit more sensitive to temperatures, so he followed her into the limo. He took the offered seat next to Sallie while Charlton took a spot across from them. Charlton looked perfectly at home here but Sam wasn't. The only other time he'd ever ridden in a limo was at his wedding. Still, like the private plane, he thought he could get used to this sort of thing.

The car drove north towards downtown Houston. Sam had never been here before and had spent part of the flight learning about the city. He was surprised to find that Houston was the fourth-largest city in the United States and that it had a wide range of commercial interests. It was second only to New York in the number of Fortune 500 companies that were based there. Of course Sam knew that Houston was the home of the Johnson Space Center, and he hoped that there'd be time for a visit on this trip. From what he'd seen in the air and now on the ground, it looked like a beautiful city.

"We're going to have to get right down to business," Sallie said without preamble. "The boys are waiting at Braddock's office. Do yourself a favor and leave the talking to me at first. Those boys need to be put in their place and I'm the one to do it. Why'd you bring the lawyer?"

"I insisted on coming, Mrs. Curtis," Charlton said. "I represent Mr. Harman's interests in this matter. I can't do that if I don't know what's going on."

"Well this is a family meeting, not a legal one,"

Sallie said. "I'm trying to keep those boys from starting a legal fight over Hank's estate. You showing up sends the wrong message."

"We're meeting in a law office, aren't we?" Sam asked.

"Anderson's idea," Sallie said. "He thinks he'll be a mediating influence."

"But you don't think so, do you?" Sam replied.

"Not one bit," she confirmed. "It don't matter where this meeting is. Those boys, especially Jerry, are mad as hell about you and want to fight."

"I didn't want any of this," Sam said.

"I know you didn't," Sallie said. "But mad as I still am at Hank for his fooling around I think he did right by you leaving you that money. I want those boys to understand that you're not a gold digger."

Sam looked down at the new suit. "Maybe wearing this wasn't such a good idea," he said. Charlton suddenly looked uncomfortable.

"Wouldn't have been my first choice," Sallie admitted. "But it does look good on you."

"Thanks," Sam said. "Do you think your sons will listen to a reasonable proposal?"

"Depends on the proposal," Sallie said. "What did you have in mind?"

Sam told her.

ELEVEN

BILL, NICK AND Jerry Curtis were seated at one end of a long conference table when Sallie thundered in, followed by Sam. The lawyers were in Braddock's office, forbidden by Sallie to enter the room. The Curtis brothers stood up immediately and came over to greet their mother. When she introduced them to Sam, though, none would shake his hand. "I taught you boys better manners than that!" Sallie barked. "This man is your brother. You can at least shake hands with him!"

The first to do so was Bill, who politely but coolly introduced himself. They shook hands briefly. Nick was next and though he did as his mother commanded he didn't even look Sam in the eye. Jerry took Sam's hand and squeezed until it hurt, though Sam did his best not to show it. He'd read Braddock's file on all three of these men. Jerry scared the living daylights out of him. He was determined, though, not to give him the satisfaction of seeing it. He'd prayed over this and believed that God would protect him.

"So what makes you think you have any right to our daddy's money?" Jerry asked belligerently.

"Read the will," Sam replied.

"Wills can be broken," Bill said calmly. "As far as we're concerned you may be our biological brother, but you're not part of this family. You have no right to claim any of the family fortune."

"Hank Curtis seemed to think otherwise," Sam said. "As I understand it, each will he signed over the last thirty years included me as an heir. If you guys go to court, both Mr. Braddock and my own lawyer will use those wills to show that this was no sudden impulse."

"Bull," Nick said. "That whore who gave birth to you had Daddy wrapped around her finger."

"Watch your mouth," Sam said. "She's no whore."

"Be that as it may, our position is clear," Bill said. "You don't have any right to our family's money."

"Your daddy said different!" Sallie barked. "I'm madder than hell over what he did all those years ago, but none of this is this boy's fault. Hank wanted to make sure he was taken care of the same as the rest of you."

"Then Daddy was an idiot!" Jerry snapped back. "It should all be ours and that's that! What did this bastard ever do for the family or the company?"

Sam decided to overlook the 'bastard' comment but it wasn't easy. Strength, Lord, give me strength, he prayed silently. Calmly, more calmly than he thought possible, he said "I didn't know about you or your company until two weeks ago, so I guess I have good reason for not doing anything."

"That the best you got?" Jerry asked.

"If you're trying to provoke me, it won't work," Sam said.

"Oh yeah?" Jerry replied. "Then how about I beat

your worthless--"

"Jerome Wayne Curtis!" Sallie interrupted. "You will not touch a hair on this boy's head!"

Bill stepped between them. "Jerry, let me handle this," he said. Jerry stalked to the other end of the room. "Mr. Harman, I apologize. I would prefer we handle this with civility."

"So would I," Sam replied. "I didn't come here to fight with any of you."

"You just came to take what's ours," Nick said.

"I came because your mother asked me to," Sam said.

"Which brings me to something that puzzles me," Bill said. "Mama, why are you siding with this man? He's not your son. He's the product of Daddy's horsing around all those years. I would have thought that you'd stand with your own sons."

"I would if I agreed with you about the will," Sallie said. "Don't the three of you have any respect for his wishes?"

"Daddy cheated on you, Mama," Nick said. "He went and got some girl pregnant. How is that fair?"

"If it helps any, I don't approve of what he did, either," Sam said.

"Well isn't that nice!" Jerry barked from across the room. "Let's give him three billion dollars for that!"

"Your daddy left each of you four billion, plus your stakes in the company," Sallie said. "Sam here doesn't get as much as the three of you."

"He shouldn't get any of it!" Jerry barked. "It's ours!"

"It's mine too!" Sallie snapped back. "And I say Sam deserves his share!"

"Jerry, Mama, please," Bill interjected. "You two shouting at each other doesn't solve anything."

"I'm downright ashamed of you boys right now," Sallie said. "Your daddy did wrong, no doubt about that. But do you know what he did? He spent the rest of his life trying to do right by his son. And Sam is his son, whether you three like it or not. Look at him. He looks more like Hank than any of you. I accept that he's Hank's son and I'm the one who got cheated on. If I can accept it, so can you. This boy is your brother, for heaven's sake. Can't you see that?"

"Three billion dollars, Mama," Nick protested. "He's just going to waste that money. He doesn't know anything about handling it."

"No, I don't," Sam said. "But I'm surrounding myself with people who do. I'm going to learn."

"Boys," Sallie said. "I know you've gotten too big for me to simply tell you to do something and you do it. So I'm begging you. Yes, that's right I'm begging you to respect your daddy's wishes. Let Sam have the money."

"What about the share in the company?" Bill asked. "That concerns me greatly. Ten percent is a voting share. He doesn't know anything about our businesses. He couldn't even hold down a lowly office job at that mortgage company up there."

"Is it the company you're really worried about?" Sam asked.

"Frankly, yes," Bill said. "I have plans for this company, plans that your voting share could put in jeopardy, if only by your ignorance."

"I don't really have much interest in any of the businesses Curtis Enterprises is involved, in," Sam said. "And three billion will be more than enough for me. So I'm going to offer you gentlemen a deal. If you agree to recognize my claim to Hank Curtis' will and the money he promised me, I'll let the three of you have my share of the company. For nothing."

That took the Curtis brothers by surprise. Even Jerry seemed taken aback, his anger momentarily forgotten. "Sam," Sallie said. "I didn't say anything when you mentioned your idea, but are you sure you want to walk away from that? Your share of the profits from the company would run in the hundreds of millions of dollars."

"Sallie," Sam said. "Three billion dollars is more than I'll probably ever spend. Frankly, I've never understood what people like you do with all that money, anyway. I'll be just fine."

Bill looked to his brothers. "Give us a minute to talk it over," he said.

Sam nodded and went back into Braddock's office. He found Braddock and Charlton chatting over drinks at a coffee table. "Did they go for it?" Charlton asked.

"They're talking it over now," Sam said, plopping down in an empty chair. "I thought Jerry was going to pound the crap out of me for a minute there."

"If Sallie hadn't been there, he probably would have," Braddock said. "Aaron here told me what you had in mind. Sam, are you sure about this?"

"I've made up my mind," Sam said. "To be honest, big business isn't for me. Fifteen years at D&L proved that. I have some things I'm interested in. Some things I want to invest in. I'll have plenty of money for that. Who knows, I may actually increase my inheritance. With the right help, that is."

"For the record, I still think you're making a mistake," Charlton said. "You're walking away from guaranteed profits."

"Maybe so, but I don't care," Sam said. "I'll have all the money I need to take care of my family, and then some. I don't want a long, drawn out fight. That will only benefit you lawyers. No offense."

Braddock laughed. "None taken," he said. "I don't know what Hank would have made of you, Sam. But I think you've done a great thing here today. My hat's off to you."

Just then the door to the conference room opened. Sallie let her sons out of the room. She was smiling. "Mr. Harman...Sam," Bill said. "You've got a deal. We won't contest the will if you sign over your interest in the company."

"Good," Sam said. They shook hand, much more warmly this time. "I believe my lawyer has drawn up a preliminary agreement. What did you call it, Aaron?"

"A memorandum of understanding," Charlton said, taking the papers from his briefcase. "Gentlemen, this memorandum is simply a promise by all parties not to contest the will and for Sam to sign over his share of Curtis Enterprises when probate is complete, at which time the final papers formalizing the transfer of stock will be signed."

All four of Hank Curtis' sons signed the agreement, which was witnessed by the lawyers. Each man got a copy. "Well now that that's done, I'm starved," Sallie said. "I'm putting supper on at the house. I'd love to eat surrounded by all these handsome, well-dressed men. Even you lawyers."

That seemed to break the tension. "All right, Mama," Bill said. "We'll be there."

And with that, Sam Harman was on the road to billions.

TWELVE

SAM WANTED TO keep the inheritance quiet as long as he could. His hope was that since the whole thing was being probated in Texas, word might not even hit the Port Mason media. This was not to be. News of the probate settlement leaked to the Houston Chronicle and was quickly picked up by the rest of the media. Before Sam got home from Texas the vultures descended on them. He arrived home to find the media camped on his street. Tyler Security kept them off the lawn and away from the house, but one of the reporters recognized Sam as he got out of his cab. Sam had to literally shove his way through the mob of reporters to get inside.

After consulting with his lawyer, he decided to give a press conference in his front yard. It went well, or so he thought. Unfortunately, one of the photos from the press conference included the street number of his house. That particular picture ran on the front page of *The Port Mason Register*, the city's only newspaper. The paper later apologized for the mistake but the damage was done. Now that the whole city knew where he lived, the trouble really started. He woke up the morning the newspaper story appeared to find the police trying to move dozens of people off of Knox Avenue. Most of them were gawkers, here to see the new billionaire. The press had been mollified by the conference the day before so they were gone, but they were replaced by a small and vocal group of protestors carrying placards and shouting "No more billionaires" as they paraded in front of his house. Sam got his family into a hotel for a few days.

At that point he gave serious thought to telling the Curtis brothers to keep all the money and leave him out of it. Two things held him back. First, he hated the thought of bowing to pressure so easily. He might not have the biggest backbone in the world but he surely had the stamina to withstand at least some scrutiny. Second, and more importantly, he didn't want to give Jerry Curtis the satisfaction of having gotten to him.

He was convinced that the youngest Curtis brother had leaked the news. Before leaving Houston, Sallie warned him that Jerry had only gone along with Sam's deal because both his brothers pushed him to. He didn't like the settlement one bit and was, in Sallie's opinion, bound to try and pull something stupid in the near future. Since the only people who knew about the settlement were the brothers, the two lawyers, Sallie and Sam, the list of potential leak sources was short. Luckily for the Harmans, the attention of the public was somewhat fickle. They were off the front page almost as quickly as they'd appeared on it. Within a week the family was home.

The first Sunday after Sam got back from Texas gave him and his family a taste of what they would be up against in the months ahead. They arrived at

Chester Avenue Christian Church a little after ten in the morning for the 10:30 service. People stared at them as they walked across the parking lot. The lobby, filled with people leaving the early service and arriving for the late service, quieted considerably when the Harmans came in. People either stared openly or tried to avert their gaze.

"Maybe we should go," he whispered to Tracie.

"No," she said. "It'll be alright."

They took the kids to Sunday school. As they dropped each kid off to their respective classroom the hushes fell again. Sam did his best to ignore it but he found it really annoying. When they entered the sanctuary and took their usual seats, everything seemed normal. A few moments later, a couple who usually sat in the same row approached timidly and actually asked if they could sit there. Sam was flabbergasted. Was this how it was going to be from now on?

After Praise and Worship it was customary for the congregants to greet one another for a few moments. People seemed hesitant to approach the Harmans so Sam dove into the crowd, shaking hands with as many people as he could before being called back to his seat. He didn't want to be given special treatment.

The service itself went normally, but afterward Sam and Tracie found themselves on the receiving end of more deference. People actually got out of their way as they walked up the aisle to the exit. That had never happened before. Sam couldn't tell if this was because people wanted to be extra nice to them, or if they were becoming pariahs because they didn't fit in anymore. Either way, Sam didn't like it.

As they made their way back to get the kids they were intercepted by Owen Gorman. Sam was immediately on alert. A few years before, Owen had tried to get his signature on a petition to put a 'defense of marriage' constitutional amendment on the state ballot. Sam politely refused, explaining that he didn't approve of the mixing of politics and religion. Their interactions since had been cordial, though Sam never really counted him as a friend. He knew Owen to be very conservative in his politics and that he was an active member of Port Mason's Tea Party, an organization which Sam had little use for.

"Sam, Tracie, I was wondering if I could have a moment of your time," he said politely.

Sam looked at his wife, who seemed as apprehensive as he was. "Why don't you get the kids," Sam said.

Tracie made her excuses and left. "First, I want to say congratulations," Owen said. "God has really blessed you."

"Not to mention gotten me out of a jam," Sam replied, explaining about losing his job. "So, what can I do for you?"

"Not for me," Owen corrected. "For your country. Sam, I know you don't like to deal with politics at church but I didn't know how to get hold of you, so I hope you won't mind."

"This better not be about me contributing money to your Tea Party bunch," Sam said. "Because if it is, the answer is no."

"Sam, let me explain--"

"No, I don't think so," Sam said. He saw Tracie come back into the lobby with the kids and decided a quick exit was in order. At the same time he saw the perfect opportunity to send a message. "I'm not political," he said. "I don't like either of the two parties and if I can be frank, I'm not fond of the Tea Party, either. I've never contributed to candidates or to political action committees, and I don't plan to start now. I'm sure you're disappointed to hear that, Owen, but that's my final answer. Now, if you'll excuse me."

He joined his family and left the church without even stopping for coffee. He didn't see the enraged look on Owen Gorman's face.

THIRTEEN

WHEN THE KIDS finished school for the year, they took the promised trip to Disney World in Florida. They'd flown first-class and while Sam enjoyed it, the memory of the trip on the Curtis family's private jet stayed with him. The family had a wonderful week in Florida.

During the summer Sam kept busy around the house, getting the place ready to sell once they had the money and were able to buy a new home. He also spent time working on a private project he'd been thinking about before learning about his inheritance. But one of the greatest joys of this period was getting to know his birth mother, Susan.

She proved to be a delightful woman and was thrilled to be reunited with her son. Sam met her daughter, Ashley, in late June and they were starting to develop a relationship. Susan doted on her new grandchildren, and the kids quickly came to know her as 'Grandma Susan.'

For Sam and Tracie the next big decision would be where they were going to live once they got the money. Since money wasn't really going to be an object, they were seriously considering having a home custom-designed and built. Susan promised to put them in touch with some good architects she knew through her interior design business, if they decided to go that route.

The solution to the housing problem came from Tracie's parents. Carl and Mary Pruitt owned several acres of land about thirty miles west of Port Mason. It was farm country and at one time they had, in fact, farmed. Though most of that land had been sold off years ago, the Pruitts still owned some open land they weren't using, and they offered it to Sam and Tracie. Sam insisted on paying fair market value on the land and finally persuaded his in-laws to agree.

The parcel they bought was about a mile down the road from the Pruitt homestead. It was a five acre site bordering on some woods with a stream running through it. It was perfect. Tyler Security examined the site and pronounced it an excellent choice. More importantly, their children heartily approved of the plan to move out by their grandparents.

Sam spent a fair amount of time playing golf and doing research on potential investments. He supposed at least some of the money would go into traditional investments like stock and bonds and so forth. But he really wanted to get into other things. Commercial space flight was one of those ideas. Alternative energy creation was another. He wasn't what one would consider a hard-core environmentalist, but on the other hand he did believe in at least trying to take care of the planet. It was the only one they had.

He'd had some interesting conversations with some of his friends at church over these views. Many of them tended to be more conservative than he was, and this was reflected in their views on the environment. They considered global warming a product of questionable science. Sam privately thought that was propaganda from the right-wing playbook but held his tongue most of the time. As his dad had often said, "Never argue politics or religion. Nobody wins." One friend said he didn't recycle because Jesus was coming back soon and when He did, nothing on this earth would matter. Sam took a different point of view. In his eyes, the earth was a gift from their Father in Heaven. When a father gives a child a gift, he expects the child to take care of it. God may have given humanity dominion over the earth, but Sam had never read anything in the bible that gave man the right to trash it.

That fall school resumed for the Harman children. After much searching and prayer on the subject, Sam and Tracie decided to send their children to Blessed Savior's Christian Academy, about fifteen miles from where they would eventually be living. It was a Kindergarten through 8th grade school that was operated by Blessed Savior's Christian Church. The timing was actually perfect for this move. Noah had just turned five and was starting Kindergarten that fall. Enrolling in the school did not include a change in churches; the Harmans would continue to attend Chester Avenue Christian Church in Port Mason.

On the first day of school, Sam dropped off his kids and headed off for a planned golf date with Marty Lovell and a couple of other guys from church. As he drove to the golf course, he got the phone call he'd been waiting for. Anderson Braddock reported that the Curtis brothers had signed off on distribution of Sam's three billion dollars, minus the million he'd already been advanced, and he could come to Houston anytime he wanted to take possession. Sallie Curtis once again sent the private jet. Tracie agreed it was a lot more fun than flying commercial.

The family spent a pleasurable Labor Day weekend in Houston during which Sam signed the papers that officially made him a billionaire. He didn't encounter Jerry or Nick but did play a round of golf with Bill and Sam Jr. at a local country club. His oldest half-brother seemed to be making a genuine effort to build bridges, perhaps out of gratitude over the handling of the business with Curtis Enterprises. Whatever the reason, Sam appreciated it and thought that maybe at some point they could become friends.

When they returned to Port Mason from this trip, they hit the ground running. Sam and Tracie met with the architects, selected one, and got to work on the new house. Tracie handled most of this, which was fine with Sam. His only requests were for a 'man-cave' for him to retreat to whenever there was a ball game on or some reason he needed to escape the kids and a multi-car garage/workshop, where he could start collecting classic cars.

At this point Tracie finally decided it was time to quit her job. Though she hardly needed to, she gave two weeks' notice and worked diligently up until the last minute. Since it was the last day of an old life and the first day of a new one, Sam decided to get his wife a present.

When she walked out of her now-former employer's building on that last day she was shocked to see Sam standing there next to a brand new BMW X5 SUV. She very nearly fainted, then took Sam to task for the extravagance. It was, after all, an $86,000 car with all the options Sam ordered. When he'd persuaded her to at least give it a try, though, the objections melted away fairly quickly.

It had given Sam great pleasure to go out and buy something really nice for his wife. She'd gotten so little of that over the years. She never complained, to be sure, but it often bothered Sam that he couldn't afford nice things for her. Now that he could, he was determined to make the most of it.

It also meant that he could go out and buy a car of his own with no guilt whatsoever. The day after he presented Tracie with her car he returned to the dealership and ordered his own BMW, a 550i xDrive sedan. The total for this car came to just under $86,000. Still enjoying her own new car, Tracie only objected mildly to Sam's expenditure. Besides, they could afford a fleet of these cars. The only problem Sam had was the wait for the car to be delivered. When it was, he spent an entire Saturday driving around town and in the country trying the car out.

Since it would be nearly Christmas before their new house was finished, they spent the fall on Knox Avenue. The security people, now on his own payroll, were not happy about this but did the best they could to keep the family safe. There were no incidents. The police patrolled regularly to keep troublemakers at arms' length. Their neighbors welcomed the increased police presence, though they knew it would end when the Harmans left the neighborhood. That made Sam somewhat uncomfortable. Why did he deserve special treatment from the police? Okay, he had an incredible amount of money, but why should that matter?. He talked to Tracie about it one night after the kids were in bed.

"I'm not sure how I feel about the cops increasing the patrols just because of us," he said as they got ready for bed.

"I'm glad they're doing it," Tracie said. "The neighborhood isn't what it used to be."

"I know," Sam said. "But that's been going on for the last few years. They're only doing something about it now because we have a lot of money. That's not right."

"They're protecting everyone on the street because of us," Tracie said. "When you look at it that way it's not such a bad thing."

"But what about after we leave?" he asked. "You know they won't keep up that kind of presence. Everything will go back to the way it was before, and the neighborhood will suffer. That's not right."

"No, I suppose not," Tracie agreed. "What do you suggest we do about it?"

"What can we do?" Sam asked. "I'm not the chief of police."

"No, but you could probably get through to him right away if you called," she replied. "I'll bet every politician in this town is drooling at the prospect of getting our financial support. The added police patrols are probably our alderman's or maybe even the Mayor's way of saying they'll scratch your back if you scratch theirs."

"No way," Sam said. "I won't give money to politicians."

"I'm not suggesting that you do, honey," Tracie said. "I don't like them either. But maybe you don't have to. Maybe we should look into giving the city a grant of some kind to keep up the patrols in this area."

It was at that point Sam realized the scope of what he would be able to do to make Port Mason a better place to live. He and Tracie stayed up late, making plans.

FOURTEEN

ON A COOL evening in early October, the annual Black Tie charity dinner on behalf of the Atkins Foundation was held at the River Oaks Country Club just north of the city limits. It was an invitation-only event attended by the 'cream' of Port Mason society. Hundreds of thousands of dollars were collected here every year to support a variety of causes but its other purpose was for the wealthy to get together and, frankly, show off.

A parade of limousines and luxury cars drove up the country club's long drive to its main building, informally known as Atkins House after the family that founded the club in the 1920s. The passengers, resplendent in their tuxedos and formal dresses, formed a line to be greeted by the event's hostess, Priscilla Atkins, head of what until very recently had been the city's wealthiest family. Accustomed to being the center of attention she was puzzled when heads in the line began turning towards the door and portico. Sam and Tracie Harman had arrived.

The Harmans were elegantly dressed, he in a new Armani tuxedo and her in a red cocktail dress with matching wrap from Dolce and Gabbana. The doors to Atkins House were opened for them and people gathered around to pay their respects to Port Mason's new billionaires.

Keeping her hostess face on, Atkins strode through the crowd and approached the new arrivals. "Mr. and Mrs. Harman," she said, holding out her hand. "Priscilla Atkins. A delight to meet you both. Welcome."

"Thank you," Tracie said, shaking her hand. Sam merely nodded. He did not look comfortable here, which suited Atkins just fine.

"Of course we've all been following your good fortune in the news," Atkins said. "And we're honored that you've graced us with your attendance this evening. I trust you'll enjoy yourselves."

"I'm sure we will," Sam said. Atkins knew at once he was lying but said nothing. Instead she smiled and gestured for them to enter the lounge while she resumed greeting guests. To her irritation, much of the crowd followed them. She had invited them to the dinner out of curiosity. It wasn't every day, after all, that a nobody was transformed into a billionaire and she wondered what they were like. She hadn't counted on her other guests fawning over them.

Priscilla Atkins had been on top of Port Mason society for a long time, and she liked it that way. Her family controlled nearly half of the choicest real estate in the city and surrounding area, in addition to their other business ventures. She had been in charge of the family businesses for over fifteen years and had expanded their holdings considerably. Despite being born to privilege, Atkins had worked hard to get where she was. She wasn't about to let some nouveau riche upstarts come in and steal her thunder.

She did not let any of these thoughts and feeling show on her face as she finished greeting her guests and made her way into the lounge. Sam and Tracie were surrounded by well-wishers but looked like they'd both rather be anywhere else. Priscilla decided to take charge.

"Now, everyone, let's give our new friends room to breathe," she said pleasantly as she strode up to the Harmans. A waiter appeared with champagne and everyone took a glass. Priscilla noticed that Sam only sipped at his and made the slightest of faces as he did so.

Tracie, on the other hand, seemed to appreciate hers. "This is wonderful," she said.

"Dom Perignon 1996," Priscilla said. "I'm glad you like it."

Sam took a new look at his glass and took another sip. He still didn't seem to like it. What a waste, Priscilla thought. If he expected to find a beer here he would be disappointed.

"I must say yours is simply a fascinating story," Priscilla said. "I don't know if you're aware of this but I knew Hank Curtis rather well. His company and mine participated in a few joint ventures. Very successful ones, I might add."

"I didn't know that," Sam said. "What did you think of him?"

"Oh he was a delight," Priscilla said. "A real Southern Gentleman and a shrewd businessman. I hope you've inherited his talents."

"Well, we'll have to see," Sam replied.

"I'm curious, Ms. Atkins," Tracie began.

"Please, dear, call me Priscilla," she said.

"Priscilla," Tracie agreed. "What specific charities does your foundation support?"

"We help fund the homeless shelters and food pantries," Priscilla said. "There are also scholarship programs at the university we sponsor, along with other education programs. There's much more, of course, but you'll have to wait until my speech later to learn about them."

This drew polite laughter from the crowd. "Priscilla you're being too modest," an older gentleman said. "The Atkins Foundation is Port Mason's leading charity organization. They put over twenty million dollars a year into helping our city."

"That's...quite a bit of money," Sam said.

"Naturally, much of our work is funded by my family, but we like to encourage others to take part," Priscilla said. "That's why we hold this dinner every year. I trust you'll be launching your own foundation at some point?"

"Very soon, actually," Sam said. "We're laying the groundwork now. Tracie's actually going to be in charge of that aspect of things. I'll just write the big checks."

That drew some more laughter. "I look forward to seeing what you have planned," Priscilla said. "I'm sure it will be something special.

As the conversation broke down into small talk, Priscilla noticed that Sam's discomfort only seemed to grow. Yes, this man was definitely out of his element. His wife did a better job of hiding her discomfort, but to the practiced eye it was still detectable. Well, at least she didn't have to worry too much about them upstaging her tonight.

When it was time for dinner, Priscilla led the Harmans into the main dining hall and seated them at her table on the dais. As they sat down Sam surprised her by holding out her chair after seating his wife. After dinner the real festivities began. Priscilla took the podium and spoke about everything her foundation had accomplished in the last year. Then came the most important part of the evening—the collection of this year's gifts to the foundation.

One by one, her guests came up and handed her envelopes. She would open the envelope, see how much was given, and announce it to the crowd. Polite applause would follow each endowment. Sam found the spectacle sickening. These people didn't really care about the people they were claiming to help. They were showing off how much money they could dispose of and patting each other on the back for it. It was almost enough to make him get up and leave.

However, Sam agreed with all the things the Atkins Foundation was doing. He and Tracie planned to support many of the same charities once their own organization was launched. With that in mind, they'd decided to make a good first impression with their own gift. After seeing what others were giving he smiled to himself. They would make an impression, all right.

"And now we come to our newest friends, Sam and Tracie Harman," Priscilla said. "This is their first year with us so won't you join me in welcoming them? Sam, Tracie?"

She gestured for them to join her at the podium as the crowd applauded. They did so as Sam took their envelope from his pocket and handed it to the hostess. Priscilla smiled as she opened the envelope. When she saw what was inside her jaw dropped.

"L-ladies and gentlemen, I don't know what to say," Priscilla said softly, barely audible despite the microphone. "The Harmans have been...very, very generous. I'm holding in my hand a check for ten million dollars."

There was silence for a moment then the audience broke into thunderous applause and gave the Harmans a standing ovation. This time Priscilla Atkins couldn't hide her scowl.

"Do you think we went too far?" Tracie asked when they were in the limo and on their way home.

"Well, in our defense we didn't know they announced each donation amount to the whole crowd," Sam replied. "But since they did, maybe we showed them what charity was all about."

"She was not happy with us," Tracie said. "I think we stole her thunder."

"We did," Sam said, smiling.

"Why are you happy about that?" Tracie asked.

"Because I don't like snobs," Sam replied. "It's nice to see people like that taken down a peg. Now I'm glad I bought the tux."

"I doubt we'll be invited to join River Oaks now," Tracie said. "She owns it, after all."

"That's okay with me," Sam said. "I don't like mixing with those people. I hope that never changes."

"Me too," Tracie said, snuggling up to him. "You do look good in that, by the way. She noticed, too."

"Who?"

"Priscilla," Tracie said. "Before dinner she was checking you out."

"Really?" Sam said. "I didn't notice."

"That's because you were too busy being uncomfortable," Tracie replied. "And she was very subtle."

"Well don't worry, she's not getting anywhere with me," Sam said, kissing his wife on the forehead. "I think the next time we get an invitation like this we should turn it down."

"I agree," Tracie said. "I don't think I could do that sort of thing on a regular basis."

"Me neither," Sam said. "Besides, I hated the food."

"So did I," Tracie agreed.

"If we ever have our own charity event, we'll make it burgers and dogs," Sam said.

Tracie laughed then kissed him. They snuggled the rest of the way home.

FIFTEEN

THE FOLLOWING MONDAY Sam and Tracie officially opened the offices of Harman Family Enterprises, funded with 1.5 billion dollars of their new money. Their offices were located in the Nardulli building, right across the street from Downen & Lowe. Sam found the location quite pleasing. He could drive past his former employer every morning in his BMW, secure in the knowledge that he had more than landed on his feet after his unceremonious firing and would never have to set foot in the place again.

The purpose of Harman Family Enterprises was twofold. First, it existed as a means to invest huge sums of money and, hopefully, see a return on it. Sam was overseeing this part of the operation. Second, it would be the parent of a foundation dedicated to charity works. Tracie was overseeing this area. When it came to major monetary decisions, however, both would be involved. According to Aaron Charlton, the company would act as an umbrella for any business or charitable activity they chose to undertake. It would also help with the taxes, though Sam was dead certain he would never understand that part of things.

Three important events took place that first morning. The first was a surprise visit from Mayor Eric Hawkins. Sam and Tracie had not bothered with a formal ribbon-cutting or, for that matter, any ceremony at all for their opening day. They simply launched their website, sent out a press release, and hired a group of temporary employees to handle the initial flood of calls. Within an hour of this, the Mayor and his entourage showed up in the lobby and asked to speak to the Harmans. Sam and Tracie welcomed His Honor into the conference room, served coffee, and waited for him to make the first move. That move was not long in coming.

"Naturally, I've been following your story in the press," Hawkins said after heaping lavish praise on their offices and the quality of their coffee. "There are many in city government who are…curious about your plans. Your political plans, I mean."

"So they want to know, if I may hazard a guess, whether we're going to throw a bunch of money into politics and upset their precious status quo," Sam replied. "Or that maybe, just maybe, they'll be left out of the gravy train. Am I right so far?"

"Well, I wouldn't put it quite that way," Hawkins said, fighting the urge to cringe. "But I suppose that is a matter of concern to some members of the council who face tough re-election fights next year. You could have a powerful influence on things."

"I can set your mind to ease on that, Mister Mayor," Sam said as politely as he could. "Tracie and I agreed when we first found out about this that we were not, under any circumstances, going to donate to political causes. There's too much money in politics already. We're not going to make it worse."

"I see," the mayor replied, cautiously. He was clearly not pleased to hear this, but he knew he couldn't afford to offend people who could have a profound economic impact on his city.

"We're not trying to be belligerent," Tracie said. "But Sam and I aren't interested in political influence. We do have plans to help the city with some of its problems, but that's one area in which we are firm. No political contributions."

"Okay, you want to help the city," Hawkins said. "What exactly did you have in mind?"

"Our current home is just across the river in the 11th ward," Sam said. "Over the last few years crime has steadily gone up. There are even rumors that one of the drug gangs is trying to set up shop there. We know the police budget has been tight over the last few years and that it isn't easy to maintain an increased police presence in that area."

"We have beefed up patrols in the last few weeks," the mayor pointed out.

"We appreciate that," Tracie said. "And I know our neighbors do too but we're concerned about what's going to happen after we leave. We want to give a grant to the police department so they can maintain increased patrols and other anti-crime operations on that entire side of the river."

"That would have to be quite a grant, Mrs. Harman," Hawkins said. "I don't have the exact figures but what you're talking about means hiring more cops and buying more vehicles. Just how much were you willing to spend?"

"Well, we hope you can put us in touch with the right people in the police department who can tell us what they need to do what we're proposing," Sam said. "But if you really need a number we were thinking somewhere in the neighborhood of, oh, say twenty-five million."

Sam and Tracie would forever cherish the look on the mayor's face when they revealed the figure. "That's...well for once I don't think I have the words," Hawkins said. "You're serious about this, aren't you?"

"Yep," Sam said.

"We know you'd reap political benefits from this," Tracie said. "And in general we're okay with that. We actually voted for you. But don't mistake our wanting to help the city as any kind of endorsement."

"Uh, no, of course not," the Mayor said, calculating the possibilities.

"We also plan to give a five million dollar grant to the city library," Tracie said. "Funding for the library has dropped quite a bit in the last six years or so and we feel that only hurts the city. We're thinking of making that grant an annual thing."

"That is very generous of you," Hawkins said. What he didn't tell them was that he had been thinking of cutting the library even further to appease some of his base supporters who thought it a purveyor of filth and degeneracy for its open internet policies and some of the books in the collection. Those people wouldn't be pleased to hear of the Harman grant but he decided on the spot not to interfere with their plans. In fact, unless they did something really outrageous he planned to let them give the city as much money as they wanted.

Over the next hour the Harmans detailed their plans to put nearly $100 million in to various civic ventures. They planned grants to the fire department to update equipment and hire more firefighters; to the city school system to improve classroom technology, keep school libraries open and improve teacher pay; and bolster the city's free clinics. There was also a plan to build a brand-new homeless shelter and soup kitchen in the welfare district that would house up to a thousand people at a time in addition to supporting existing facilities. Mayor Hawkins was shocked at the breadth of their plans but saw nothing in them that was objectionable.

"How long do you think you can keep this up without blowing your fortune?" he asked.

"As long as we have to," Sam replied. "Remember we're going to be involved in business enterprises and we certainly expect those to make money. Those profits can be used to support further charitable activities."

"We believe we have an obligation to help make our community a better place to live," Tracie said. "And to help those less fortunate than ourselves."

"To put it another way, Mister Mayor, 'Charity begins at home,'" Sam said.

"I won't argue with that," Hawkins said. "You mentioned business enterprises, Mr. Harman. I assume at least some of them will help with economic development in the city?"

"I'm sure they will," Sam said. "We've been focusing most of our planning up to now on the charity side of the operation. Now that we're 'open for business,' I'm starting to look at that side of it."

Sam and Tracie could see that the Mayor was pleased, but they knew it was because of how their plans could benefit him politically. This had been anticipated. Politicians were pretty much the same in their shared opinion. If something made them look good to their supporters and the voters they'd go along with it. Bringing in that kind of money for the city would be a huge feather in Mayor Hawkins' cap but Sam and Tracie had decided to go through with it anyway. They really had voted for Hawkins nearly four years earlier but only because his opponent was far more repulsive. All parties left the meeting happy at the outcome.

The second important event that day was the signing of a preliminary agreement for Sam to put $50 million into a space venture called 'Lunar Exploration Technologies,' LET had been started by a group of wealthy space enthusiasts and former astronauts who felt that the moon had great potential for further space exploration. They planned to use a Russian rocket to send a cluster of small robots to the moon to prospect for metals, helium-3, and water. If the probes found what they were looking for, they would proceed to the next phase, determining if those resources could be exploited.

Sam was positively giddy about this project. The biggest problem in spaceflight, as he and many others saw it, was getting people and material from earth into space. It took powerful rockets and tremendous amounts of fuel to get even moderately sized payloads into low earth orbit. The great Saturn V of the Apollo program used the power of its first two stages just to get the small moon craft into earth orbit. Once there the amount of thrust needed to reach the moon was far less. The small engine used by the command-service module was sufficient to get the spacecraft back home. But once a spacecraft was in orbit, all it needed was an engine and fuel to go wherever it wanted. The problem was getting the fuel there.

LET was banking that, if there was water on the moon, it could be converted to hydrogen and oxygen (in other words, rocket fuel) and shipped either to lunar orbit or earth orbit without too much difficulty. If sufficient quantities of silicon, titanium, iron and nickel were there, they could build spaceships on the moon. Getting off the surface of the moon was much easier than lifting payload from earth. Sam knew it might be years or never before the results came in, but he didn't care. It was his money and he was going to put into things he believed in. The truth was he'd been prepared to go much higher on his initial investment but Tracie and Aaron Charlton talked him out of it. Sam's investment put LET over the top on its fundraising for the Russian Proton rocket launch.

The third major event of the day was…complicated. Since it was their first day of operation Sam and Tracie weren't besieged with appointments. So when a man came into the outer office and asked to see Sam, he obliged. The man handed him some papers and informed him that he'd just been served with a paternity lawsuit. Sam called his lawyer and went to see Tracie.

"She did it," Sam said, tossing the papers on her desk.

"Oh, no," Tracie said. "Did you call Aaron?"

"He's on his way," Sam said, sitting down on her sofa. Tracie came over and joined him.

"It's not like we didn't think this might happen," Tracie said.

"No, but it's still a hit below the belt," Sam said.

"Do you have…do you have any doubts about it?" Tracie asked.

"No," Sam said, testily. "The baby was born almost a year after I left her. It couldn't be me."

"I'm sorry," she said. "But you're going to be asked this again and again. You might as well get used to it."

"She can't win," Sam said. "But she can drag my name through the mud and make me look like a deadbeat if I refuse to help her at all. I don't know what I ever saw in her."

"You were just a kid," Tracie said. "Kids do stupid things."

"Yes, they do," he agreed. "And mine was a doosey."

SIXTEEN

WHEN AARON ARRIVED Sam gave him the papers, which he read quietly. When he was done he sat back and fixed Sam with a somewhat critical eye. "Is it true?" he asked.

"Not a chance," Sam said. "And a DNA test can prove it. I'll submit to it."

"I think you'd better tell me the whole story," Aaron said.

Sam didn't like talking about this chapter in his life. It was something he thought he'd put behind him. When he was twenty years old, he was dating a girl by the name of Becky Dunlap. They'd met at Port Mason University, where both majored in communication and often found themselves in the same classes. Working together on group projects led to private study dates. The study dates led to real dates. The real dates led to a deeply passionate, but mostly physical, affair.

Sam was convinced he was in love, and in spite of his parents' warnings that Becky was really no good, he proposed to her. Rather than wait until they graduated college, the young couple dropped out, got jobs, and eloped. Both families were furious. Sam's mom didn't speak to him for three weeks.

The next six months were exactly what Sam hoped they would be. He was making good money working in a bank. They had a nice apartment, and they spent most of their time together in bed, which was what he thought he'd always wanted. Becky was an enthusiastic and inventive lover and initiated sex as often as Sam did, if not more. He felt like he was in heaven.

Then reality came crashing down. One particular week he was scheduled to work on Saturday. Whenever that came up, the bank's policy was for those employees to leave early one day during the week so they wouldn't go over forty hours. That week he'd forgotten to tell Becky that he was on that schedule. When he came home early Wednesday afternoon he thought he'd surprise her. Instead, he was the one who was surprised. He went into their bedroom to find his wife straddling some guy he didn't know. To make matters even worse, Becky said that this had been going on for a month because she was starting to find Sam a little boring.

The guy gladly fled when Sam told him to get out. Sam then told Becky to get her clothes on, pack up her stuff, and get out of the apartment. She refused, saying it was as much her place as his and telling him that if he wanted to run home to his mommy he was more than welcome to. Sam pointed out that he was supporting both of them, since she'd lost her most recent job due to spending too much time on the phone. He again told her to get out. She again refused and said that he wasn't man enough to do anything about it, just like he wasn't man enough to keep her satisfied.

It was like he was seeing her for the first time, only she was completely different from the girl he thought he loved. For a moment, a very brief moment, he wanted to hit her. It must have shown on his face because she did back off a bit. Sam didn't say another word. He turned around, walked out of the bedroom, and left the apartment. He never wanted to see her or speak to her again.

Within days Sam had moved back in with his parents, who welcomed him home with open arms, and filed for divorce. Becky didn't counter-file, mainly because Sam wasn't worth all that much. Because of that, and because Sam cited infidelity as his reason for filing, the divorce proceeded quietly and without rancor. Becky was out of the picture, and Sam started putting his life back together.

He re-enrolled at the university part time while keeping his day job at the bank. Since his parents would never charge him rent he was able to pay his tuition. He slept at home, but spent very little time there. Even on the nights he wasn't in class, he was at school studying or getting lab time in. He didn't socialize much with his fellow students, mainly because he didn't want to fall into another bad relationship. For a time he swore off women completely, convinced he'd been such a bad judge of character that he didn't dare try again.

About a year after he'd caught Becky with that other guy, he heard she'd had a baby. This came as something of a surprise, because when they'd been together she'd always used birth control pills. At least that was what she told him. A few discreet questions here and there convinced him that he was not the father; the boy had been born eleven months after he left her. As far as he was concerned, that should have been the end of it.

For eighteen years it was. He barely thought of her during that time and hoped that his children wouldn't ever find out about his first marriage. Even after coming to Christ, he felt no guilt over leaving her. After all, Jesus himself said that infidelity was legitimate grounds for divorce. Becky Dunlap was the past. It should have stayed that way.

But when Anderson Braddock warned him about lawsuits, he immediately thought about Becky. It seemed to fit that she might pull something like this, and now she had. Sam was totally convinced that the child in question was not his and was willing to do whatever necessary to prove it.

"She a gold-digger, Aaron," Sam said when he finished his story. "Nothing more."

"Are you sure you want to fight this?" Aaron asked. "Even if you win, and prove this boy isn't yours, you could look bad for refusing to help her in her time of need."

"I've never really cared what other people think of me," Sam said. "Why should I start now?"

"Just consider this," Aaron said. "You are a public figure now. Public figures aren't held to the same standard as everyone else. I know that isn't fair, but it's true. Maybe if you negotiated a small settlement with this woman, say, a million dollars, the whole thing could go away."

"A million?" Sam asked. "Why not ten, or twenty, or fifty? Aaron, this is extortion, or at least a pathetic attempt at it. Okay, let's say I settle this one. What about the next one? And the one after that? Once I open that door, it will never shut again. No, I'm not going to put up with this. We're going to fight."

SEVENTEEN

THE SERVING OF papers was only the first salvo. The next shot was fired almost immediately. While Sam and Tracie discussed matters with their lawyer, Becky and her lawyer issued a press release detailing the lawsuit and calling a press conference for the next day. They even launched a website full of pictures of the boy, now seventeen. His name was Kyle Rodgers and according to the site, wanted to know who his father was and meet him. When he saw the pictures, Sam was more convinced than ever that the child was not his. Kyle didn't look anything like him.

Becky was represented by a lawyer named John Peterman. According to Aaron, Peterman was a disreputable ambulance chaser, who had very likely never seen the inside of the courtroom. His style was to file massive lawsuits, make a lot of threats, drag his target through the mud and then settle out of court. Though he'd originally been hesitant about fighting the suit, Aaron now relished the prospect of taking on Peterman. It would be fun to put him in his place. Sam thought about it and called Steve Bennett for some extra digging.

The Port Mason Register contacted him for

comment on the story. Despite Aaron's advice to refer all media contacts to him, Sam couldn't resist the opportunity to fire back. "This lawsuit is a sham," he said. "I haven't heard so much as a word from my ex-wife in eighteen years. Now I inherit a fortune, and look who shows up? It's a blatant, not to mention pathetic, attempt at extortion. I feel sorry for Kyle, though. No kid should have to be put through something like this." He thought the last statement was a nice touch. Tracie agreed.

The story appeared the following day: Sam felt he was treated fairly. They printed his quote in its entirety and raised the point that Kyle had been born eleven months after Sam first filed for divorce from his mother. The article also mentioned Sam's willingness to take a DNA test to find out the truth. After reading the story in the paper, Sam logged on to their website to see the reaction. Many of the comments he read seemed to favor his position, though a few thought he should be nice to his ex-wife now that he was a billionaire. A couple of people said Sam's decision to fight paternity was disgraceful, since he could easily afford to help the child.

None of the local TV stations carried the press conference live but one of them did provide a feed on the internet so Sam, Tracie and Aaron were able to watch from Sam's office. It was held in front of an old tenement building in the welfare district, which may have been one of the reasons only four reporters showed up. Even the police didn't go into that part of town lightly.

"Thank you all for coming," he said. "We've called this press conference, not only to detail our case against Sam Harman, but to put a human face on this sad affair."

"He's got a lot of nerve using the word 'affair,'" Sam said.

"Please allow me to introduce my client, Ms. Becky Dunlap and her son, Kyle Rodgers," Peterman continued.

The camera focused Sam's ex-wife. His first thought was the years had not been kind to her. She hadn't gained any weight but wore a ton of heavy makeup and her once-naturally blonde hair looked like it came out of a bottle. It was unquestionably Becky, but she looked awful. Her son looked like a typical teenager. He greatly resembled his mother, or rather what his mother had looked like when Sam was married to her. Becky looked excited to be where she was but Kyle had a 'deer-in-headlights' look to him.

"You were married to her?" Aaron asked.

"She looked a lot different then," Sam replied. "Look at that poor kid."

"He doesn't look like he wants any part of this," Tracie said.

Peterman began his pitch. "Eighteen years ago Sam Harman had the temerity to accuse this poor woman of adultery," he said. "He then abandoned her and her unborn child. Now that he is the wealthiest man in Port Mason, we demand he be as much of a father to Kyle as he is to his other children."

"Ambulance chaser," sneered Aaron.

"Thanks to poor legal representation at the time, Ms. Dunlap has not received so much as a dime in alimony and child support," Peterman continued. "We naturally plan to ask for that in addition to damages for spousal and child abandonment. There is also the matter of punitive damages--"

"Excuse me," said one of the reporters. "Amanda Clark, *Port Mason Register*. According to Kyle's birth certificate his father's name is Alan Rodgers. If Sam Harman is actually his father why use the other name?"

"My client was naturally quite angry with Mr. Harman over his leaving her," Peterman said. "She didn't want to give him the satisfaction of knowing Kyle was his. We have a signed affidavit from Mr. Rodgers attesting to this."

"And how much did you promise Mr. Rodgers for this affidavit?" Clark asked.

"I resent your implication, Miss Clark," Peterman said. "Let's take another question."

"Go get him," Sam said.

"Just a moment," Clark interrupted. "Mr. Peterman, how do you explain the fact that Kyle was born eleven months after Mr. Harman filed for divorce?"

"I'll answer that," Becky said. "I tried to reconcile with Sam after he left me. One night he seemed to reconsider and slept with me. That's when Kyle was conceived."

Sam was out of his chair. "That's a lie!" he shouted.

"Of course this was just another example of his mental cruelty," Peterman interjected. "We are confident that a court of law will see that my client is the wronged party here."

"Mr. Peterman," another reporter began. "According to your firm's website you normally represent accident victims against insurance companies. How is it that you're representing Ms. Dunlap?"

For the first time Peterman looked uncomfortable. Before he could answer, Becky took his hand and faced the cameras. "John is a wonderful lawyer," Becky said. "He works hard for little people. I trust him to get me justice."

"She's sleeping with him," Sam said

"How do you know?" Tracie asked.

"I know that look," Sam said.

"Ms. Dunlap, are you aware that your lawyer tries cases in court?" Clark asked.

"My opponents settle because they know I will not rest until I obtain justice for my clients," Peterman said, confidently. "They know I am relentless. If Mr. Harman is foolish enough to challenge our claims in court, I will wipe the floor with him."

"Just try it, you bum," Aaron said.

"So you're hoping for a quick settlement?" Clark asked.

"Naturally," Peterman said. "We believe that once the facts of this case are made clear Mr. Harman will do the decent thing and see that my client and her son are taken care of."

"He wants to rip you off, Sam," Aaron said.

"No kidding," Sam said.

"Excuse me, Mr. Peterman," Clark said. "If you are so convinced that Mr. Harman will do the right thing, why the lawsuit?"

Peterman looked dumbfounded by the question. "Suing people is his lifeblood," Aaron said. "He can't conceive of doing any differently."

Once again Sam's ex-wife came to the lawyer's

rescue. "What else could we do?" Becky said. "I've written to Sam, sent emails but he hasn't responded. I don't necessarily blame him, but he's been surrounding himself with people who keep him isolated. We had to get his attention."

"What a crock!" Sam barked. "We're having our own press conference."

"Hang on, Sam," Tracie said. "Let's hear the rest."

"...is represented by the top law firm in the city," Peterman was saying. "But I am not intimidated. Becky and poor Kyle, here, will have justice."

"Mr. Peterman," Amanda Clark began. Sam could see the lawyer's face tighten. "Can we ask Kyle some questions?"

"Uh, Kyle is a bit young for the rigors of facing the press," Peterman said. "He might release a statement later."

Clark must have been getting ready to ask another question because Peterman quickly signaled that the press conference was over. He hustled his clients back into a waiting car and the live feed went dead. Sam closed the browser and ran his hands through his hair. "Aaron," he said. "We've got to respond to that farce."

"You really need to find a press agent," Aaron said. "I know you've resisted that, but if you're going to fight this thing so publicly, you need the right people on your side."

"Yeah," Sam said. "I guess you're right. Any suggestions?"

"I know exactly who we need," Tracie said.

EIGHTEEN

AS USUAL, TRACIE'S plan was the right one.

Jenna Vanderberg was the daughter of one of their church's elders. She worked for a public relations firm only a few blocks from the Harmans' offices. In her relatively brief career, she had worked with a variety of high-profile clients and had contacts throughout the city. Sam wasn't crazy about having someone do his talking for him but he had to admit if he had to have a PR person, Jenna was the perfect person to hire.

The first thing she did was disavow Sam of the notion that she was a high-priced mouthpiece. "Talking to reporters is only a small part of my job," she explained. "I write press releases, arrange press conferences, help my clients frame their message and connect them with the right media outlets. You still get to speak for yourself. I just help with how you do that."

The next thing she did was nix Sam's press conference. "You won't beat this by playing their game," she said. "I suggest we find one reporter, either print or broadcast, and give a one-on-one interview. State your case, answer all the questions, and get in front of the story."

"What about that reporter from the paper," Sam said. "Clark?"

"Amanda Clark," Jenna said. "Good choice. She's tough but fair. You'll get grilled but she'll give you a chance to tell your side of the story."

"And I can thank her for the grilling she gave that ambulance chaser," Sam said.

"Just don't call him that on the record," Jenna said. "Name-calling won't get you any points."

"Works for the politicians," Sam quipped.

"True, but do you really want to sink to that level?" she asked. Sam immediately resolved to stop calling John Peterman an ambulance chaser, at least in public.

The interview with Amanda Clark took place the day after Peterman's press conference. Jenna was right, she gave him a grilling. The interview didn't just cover the lawsuit; it covered Sam's whole life. Naturally, most of the attention was devoted to the last six months. The only thing Sam declined to answer was the nature of his negotiations with the Curtis brothers that had staved off a court battle. His only answer to questions about that settlement was that it was fair to everyone concerned.

Their discussion of his first marriage was not as difficult as Sam expected. Clark asked hard questions, but he found that he had little trouble talking about it. He supposed having told Aaron everything loosened his normally tight-lipped approach to that chapter of his life. Either that, or the reporter was simply very good at getting answers. Most likely it was a combination of both. Sam vehemently denied being Kyle's father and stated his willingness not only to take a DNA test but to pay for it out of his own pocket. Then Clark got to a tough question.

"Mr. Harman, you have so much," she said. "Even if it is proven that you aren't Kyle's father, would it be so bad for you to give them some financial aid?"

"This isn't about the money," Sam said. "I could give it to them and never notice it's gone, but it's like I told my lawyer, once that door is open it will never shut again. If Becky had come to me directly, and she could have no matter what her lawyer says, maybe I would have been willing to do something. But the way she chose to do it is reprehensible. And she's dragging that poor kid of hers into it. That really makes me mad."

"Do you really intend to go to court?" she asked.

"If she wants to force the issue, sure," Sam said. "I'm not afraid of the truth. I am not Kyle's father."

When the story appeared the next day the local blogs were full of comments. Jenna, an expert in monitoring these things, reported that public opinion was split about 50/50. Sam was pleased with the tone of the piece; Clark had played fair with both sides. John Peterman issued his own press condemning Sam for starting a PR campaign to smear his client's reputation. "One interview is not a PR campaign," Jenna commented.

"He's the one conducting the campaign," Tracie said, a touch of anger in her voice. What made her angry was how this woman had hurt Sam. Because of that hurt it had taken Sam a long time to warm up to her. He'd told her the reason why, and she understood his reluctance, but it was hard to watch him struggle with the demons of his past. It didn't take Tracie long to fall in love with Sam, but it took him a while longer to act on his feelings for her. He was worth the wait to be sure, but she had more than a little animosity towards Becky Dunlap for the damage she'd done. She knew she shouldn't feel that way. Jesus taught his followers to forgive and not to hold grudges. In the case of Sam's ex-wife, however, doing that was not easy.

Early the next morning, another process server showed up with a new summons. Becky Dunlap was now suing both Sam and the Port Mason Register for defamation of character and libel for printing Sam's comments about her infidelity. She was asking for fifty million dollars in punitive damages. Aaron assured him that this lawsuit was just plain ridiculous.

That afternoon Steve Bennett came by the office with his report on Becky Dunlap and John Peterman. The private investigator had really done a thorough job, Sam thought as he paged through Bennett's information and he began to see a way out of this mess. He called Aaron and told him what Bennett had found out. The lawyer was elated and together they hatched a plan. Aaron would call Peterman and ask for a meeting to discuss settlements in both cases.

As they both expected, Peterman leaped at the opportunity. A meeting was arranged at Aaron's office for the next day. Tracie excused herself from the meeting. She didn't trust herself to stay calm after the way Becky had dragged Sam's name through the mud and had no desire to be in the same room with her in any event. Sam normally wouldn't, either, but in this case he made an exception. This was going to be sweet.

Sam and Aaron were waiting in one of Leonard & Spengler's conference rooms when Becky and Peterman showed up. Both were smiling. The lawyers introduced themselves. The former spouses said nothing. Coffee was served and then they quickly got down to business.

"So what kind of settlement did you have in mind?" Peterman said. "I'll warn you, you won't be able to lowball us."

"I'm going to let Mr. Harman explain the terms," Aaron said.

That took Peterman and Becky by surprise. They looked at Sam with expectation.

"It's really quite simple," Sam said. "I'm not going to give either of you a dime and you are going to drop your lawsuits. In addition, neither of you will ever file anything against me again."

"Sam, I always knew you were out there, but this is ridiculous," Becky said.

"I agree," Peterman said. "What makes you think you can get us to drop these cases for nothing?"

"The fact that if you don't you, Mr. Peterman, will lose your law license and you, Becky, will be publicly humiliated and possibly subject to arrest for welfare fraud," Sam said. "Shall I go on?"

Neither said anything, which Sam took as assent. He laid two folders on the table and pushed them to his ex-wife and her lawyer. "This is a report from Bennett Investigations," he said. "According to this, you two have been living together for the past three months. I'm no legal expert, but I'm sure the Bar

Association would take a dim view of you representing a client with whom you're romantically involved. They might also not like how you staged that press conference in the welfare district when, in fact, Becky has never lived there."

"I'm just staying with him, Sam," Becky said. "I'm not sleeping with him."

"Look in the side pocket," Sam said. They did and found color photos of them kissing in a bar and another of them in the parking lot with Peterman's hand up Becky's shirt. They stared at the photos in stunned silence.

"That's part one of the report," Sam continued. "Part two contains a timeline of Becky's welfare filings and her employment history. On at least three occasions she received food stamps and housing assistance, even though she was gainfully employed. The government, I'm afraid, is not going to be pleased. Shall I move on to part three?"

Without waiting for an answer, he continued. "Part three, Becky, is something you didn't bother to contest," Sam said. "My divorce petition. Since you didn't contest it, it's a legal admission that you were unfaithful to me. I can hardly be sued for defamation for telling the truth."

They looked at him with loathing in their eyes. "This is what's going to happen," Sam said. "You, Mr. Peterman, are going to go the courthouse and do whatever it is you do to drop these lawsuits. If you do, we won't say a thing to the Bar Association. You, Becky, are going to go away and never bother me again. As long as you do, I won't blow the whistle on your little welfare scam."

"You bastard," Becky spat. "What about Kyle?"

"He's not mine and you know it," Sam said. "I'll do the DNA test to prove it and release the results to the press. Is that what you really want?"

They both reluctantly shook their heads. "Aaron, if you and this…gentleman would step outside I need to have a private word with Becky," Sam said.

The lawyers rose to leave. Just then Sam heard a siren from outside. "Sound like an ambulance," he said to Peterman. "Shouldn't you be chasing it?"

Aaron couldn't wipe the grin off his face. Peterman mouthed an obscenity at Sam but left the room. Now, for the first time in eighteen years, Sam was alone with his ex-wife.

NINETEEN

FOR A MOMENT, Sam wasn't sure what he was supposed to say. No, that wasn't true. He had plenty to say. He just didn't know where to start.

Becky saved him the trouble. "What do you want with me now?" Becky said. "You won, isn't that enough?"

"Not quite," Sam said. "I'm not going to ask why you did it. That's obvious. But telling your son that I'm his father and dragging him into this was...well I don't know if I have the words."

"You want me to say I'm sorry?" Becky replied. "Is that it? You want me to apologize because I was wrong about everything? Well, I wasn't. You walked out on me, remember?"

"And you cheated on me, remember?" Sam said. "I had every right to walk out on you."

"Oh, yes, you're the wronged party, aren't you?" Becky said. "And now you have it made. New wife, kids of your own, and three billion dollars. Where does that leave me? Broke with a kid to support, that's where."

"And it never occurred to you to just ask me for help?" Sam asked.

"You wouldn't have done anything for me," Becky said. "And you know it."

"You're probably right," Sam admitted. "For you, I probably wouldn't lift a finger. After what you did, could you blame me? You were the one who, what was it you said? 'Got bored with me?'"

"You never tried to patch things up," Becky said.

"Why should I?" Sam asked. "After the things you said to me, what incentive did I have? None. I can put up with a lot of things, Becky, but not a betrayal like that."

"I thought you were a big-time Christian now," she taunted. "Aren't you supposed to forgive me and all that?"

"Yes I am," Sam said. "And believe it or not, I do forgive you. But that doesn't mean I have to let you try and harm me again. But with that said, there is something I'm willing to do."

"What's that?" Becky sneered. "Pray for me?"

"Well, that too," Sam said. "But that wasn't what I was talking about. I'm talking about your son. I know you've bounced from job to job since the divorce and that you've had a lot of trouble making ends meet. On your own it would be tough enough, but going through that and raising a child has to be a real strain."

"You could say that," Becky agreed. "I don't even know where we're going to sleep tonight. John'll probably kick us out now that he isn't going to get rich."

Sam sighed. Even after everything, he couldn't just leave her and her son in the lurch. "Okay," he said, taking out his checkbook and pen. "I'm writing you a check for ten thousand dollars. That may seem like a paltry sum, but I'm not going to give you a free ride. Use this money to keep a roof over your head, at least for now."

He wrote a second check. "This is for five hundred dollars," he said. "You'll get this every week until Kyle goes to college, if he chooses to. Use it for him, to feed him and clothe him and so forth. When he gets out of high school, come see me and we'll see what can be done about his education, if he wants to go to college."

He gave Becky the checks. "Now, I understand you're not working right now," he said. "I'm not going to give you a job working for me. For one thing, Tracie would kill me. For another, I'm still not crazy about the idea of being in contact with you. However I'm on fairly good terms with the company that owns the Curtis Trucking Company, the outfit Dad worked for. I'll see if they're hiring. If they're not, I'll see what else I can turn up."

"What's the catch?" Becky said.

"Tell Kyle the truth about who his father is," Sam said. "By the way, was it the guy I caught you with?"

Becky nodded. "He moved in after you left, then moved out when I told him I was pregnant. I don't want Kyle to know about that. Alan never so much as lifted a finger to help."

"You should have sued him instead of me," Sam said.

"For what?" Becky said. "Sam, can't you be a father to him? Would it kill you to do that?"

"I can't," Sam said. "It would be a lie and I couldn't live with that. And he'd find out eventually. Where would that leave him?

"One other thing," Sam said. "And then we're done here. I'll help you find a job this one time. If you can't hang on to it, if you goof off and get yourself fired, that's it. No more helping hands. What I'm giving you for your son won't be enough to live on, not in this town."

"Why are you being so tough about this?" Becky said. "You have so much now."

"Yes I do, but it's not about money," Sam said. "Not really. You've never been the most responsible person, Becky. It's high time that changed. This is the best deal you're going to get from me. Take it."

Becky thought about it for a moment before nodding in agreement. "Do you want me to sign something?" she asked.

"I probably should, but I'm not going to," Sam said. "I will keep an eye on things, though. And…Tracie's going to kill me but I'll give you my cell number. Only use it in emergencies."

"Okay," Becky said. "You know, if I'd known then what I know now…well, I sure would have done things differently."

"We all would," Sam said.

When Sam and Becky came out of the conference room Aaron was waiting for them alone. "Mr. Peterman was quite put out," he said, still grinning. "You, Ms. Dunlap, may have a problem. He said something about throwing your things into the street."

"Told you," Becky said to Sam. "I guess I'll see you sometime."

"Sometime," Sam said. "Take care of yourself, and

your son."

Becky nodded and left the law office. As she went, Aaron turned to his client. "Sometimes I wonder why you keep me on retainer," he said. "You solved that problem rather nicely. Maybe you should have become a lawyer."

Sam made a sour face. "I don't think so," he replied. "I'd tell you why, but I don't want you to think I look down on lawyers or anything like that."

Aaron laughed. "Sam, you are turning out to be one of my most interesting clients," he said.

"Thanks," Sam said. "Wait until you hear about my next idea."

"This ought to be good," Aaron said.

"It is," Sam said. "I'm going to make a movie."

TWENTY

SAM HAD A bachelor of arts degree in communication, focusing on television and film. While in school he'd worked for the university's television office. When he graduated he'd had high hopes of landing a job at one of Port Mason's TV stations or one of its independent production companies. What Sam hadn't counted on was the extremely cost-conscious nature of the television business. Two of the TV stations and three of the production companies wanted to hire him, but only on a part-time or per diem basis. No one was hiring full-time for production personnel, not when they could do it cheaper with part timers and freelancers.

Sam had been devastated and at first didn't know what to do. Starting a production company was out of the question. By his estimates it would take at least $50,000 to start out, possibly more. He didn't have that kind of money and between his student loans and credit cards he didn't think he could get financing. He also wasn't sure if he could successfully compete with the other production houses in town.

The university let him stay on as a part-time 'extra help' worker but he didn't make enough to live on.

The wedding was coming up and Tracie had been adamant that Sam have a full-time job before they got married. Ultimately, he took the job at Downen & Lowe, working there full time while putting in a few hours a week at the University, mostly editing video and doing a little production work. All in all, he didn't think it was that bad of an arrangement. He was able to do something he loved but he was also able to earn a decent living.

About three years later, though, the university faced a tough round of budget cuts and his job was one of the first to be axed. The director of the office really felt badly about it but the jobs had to be reserved for students first. Since Sam was unwilling and financially unable to go back for his master's degree, that was the end of it. He tried offering his services again to the local production operations, but they had all the help they needed. A couple of them promised to keep him in mind should anything come up, but he never heard from them again.

Sam knew what the real problem was: Sam himself. Television is an extremely competitive business but Sam seemed to lack the drive to fight his way into the industry. He wanted to do it his way or no way at all. He resigned himself to being out of the business and tried to concentrate on his full-time job but he couldn't get over his disappointment at how things turned out.

Sam loved movies. He loved going to them, he loved their artistry, the stories, the performances and the technical work that went into making them. Even before inheriting his fortune he'd had an impressive collection. But what he really wanted to do was make movies. Again, his unwillingness to leave Port Mason and his reluctance to take great risks came into play. He never tried going to Hollywood or anything like that. But he never stopped dreaming, hoping that somehow, someway he'd be able to achieve his dream.

A few years earlier a Christian film called *Fireproof* came out. Starring Kirk Cameron, the film had been produced on a budget of $500,000 and with a crew made up mostly of volunteers. Sam and Tracie went to a showing at their church and came away from it with some new perspectives. Tracie had gotten a lot out of the film in a spiritual sense. Sam came away seeing other possibilities. He'd never considered that a Christian film would have much appeal but Fireproof had done some fairly good business, especially considering its low budget. It got Sam thinking.

A couple of years later the church showed another film called *The Encounter*. Sam enjoyed this one more than *Fireproof* and again came away thinking about the possibilities. Maybe this was the way to go. Of course the biggest stumbling block was the money. He couldn't go to Marty and ask for half a million to make a movie. It was a small church, after all. He also needed a story.

The story issue was resolved the year before Sam inherited the Curtis money. The church had had a picnic at a park on the outskirts of the city. The park had some woods and after eating Marty led a small group on a nature hike. Sam, Tracie, and the kids tagged along. As he walked through the woods Sam found himself seeing things in terms of camera angles and moves. Then he had the craziest idea: what if for some supernatural reason they couldn't get out? He mulled it over and decided that while his idea might make for a good movie he didn't have the resources or the time to do it.

Then he met Anderson Braddock, learned of his fortune, and realized that the opportunity had dropped into his lap.

Sam had been planning this project ever since his first trip to Texas to meet with his half-brothers about the estate. The problem was that Sam was not a writer. He could articulate his idea for the film, which he called *The Path*, but actually writing a script on his own wasn't going to happen. He needed a writer. After a great deal of thought and prayer, Sam decided to start reaching out.

He found a Christian filmmaking forum on the internet and joined up. Then all he had to do was create a new discussion thread saying he was looking for a screenwriter and boom, the responses started pouring in. Rather than explain his idea, which he didn't want someone to steal, he asked for writing samples so he could make a proper evaluation. It seemed like a reasonable approach but he got over 100 submissions, many of which were completed screenplays.

One stood out. A young college student who went by the internet handle of 'faithwriter1992' sent him a screenplay for an untitled film about a soldier whose Christian faith is destroyed by his experiences in Afghanistan. The story seemed pretty straightforward but the writing was, in Sam's mind, exemplary. The writer created characters that got Sam interested and dove deeply into their flaws. When Sam showed it to Tracie, she wept when she was done. That settled it. Sam contacted faithwriter1992 and asked him to look at his idea. The writer agreed and Sam sent emailed his story treatment.

The response came back within an hour; faithwriter1992 loved the concept and couldn't wait to start work. Sam explained that he wouldn't be able to pay him for a while, though he didn't say anything about his forthcoming inheritance. The writer didn't seem to care. His love was his craft, not how much he made doing it. His real name was Scott Willably and he was an English Major at the University of Chicago. His life's ambition, he explained, was to be a Christian author, both of films and novels. He would start a first draft right away and spend his summer working on it. Even in an email his enthusiasm was obvious. Sam thought this could work.

About a month before Sam got his full inheritance the first draft of *The Path* was delivered. Sam loved it, although he made a lot of notes for revisions and new ideas he'd had. Once he had the money, he sent his notes to Scott along with his private cell number and a check for $50,000. The first time he actually spoke to Scott the young writer sounded aghast at the amount of money. The timing, he said, was perfect. He was having some problems with his scholarships and this money would more than close the gap. Sam already knew this, having had Steve Bennett do a background check on him.

Once the nasty business with Sam's ex-wife was concluded, he was able to turn his attention back to the film. Scott was hard at work on the second draft of the screenplay and Sam thought it was time to start moving forward with pre-production. The first thing he did was contact one of his former instructors from the University, who was now retired. Professor Bill Osbourne had been Sam's first production teacher and probably taught him more about the work than anyone else. Sam had taken three of his classes. The first two were required for his degree, but the third was an optional documentary course he'd taken largely because Osbourne was teaching it. He was the only instructor Sam had bothered to stay in touch with after graduating.

Osbourne had followed the stories about Sam's inheritance with great interest and was not entirely surprised when his former student contacted him about working on a project. He'd seen firsthand Sam's creativity and desire to do big things and was naturally disappointed when Sam didn't seem able to get things to come together. Sam sent him the first draft script, which he enjoyed reading and thought would make a really good movie.

The only problem was that neither of them had made a feature film before. Bill had extensive production experience, but that was in documentaries, TV news, shooting concerts and that sort of thing. Sam had made a few videos as a student, and while they were done in the style of films, it wasn't the same as the real thing. Nevertheless, Sam was adamant about directing *The Path* and Bill still had faith in Sam's talents. He agreed to come aboard as a producer. He would oversee the budget and hire crew for the film. Sam would direct and handle the creative decisions, though Bill would have input here as well. Bill was excited. Retirement was proving to be a bit dull and the chance to work on something big like this was a heaven-sent opportunity.

They agreed on a budget of five million dollars, though Sam was willing to put up a lot more. Bill argued that is made no sense to pump up the budget on a film like this. It wasn't like they were making a special-effects film. In fact, Sam didn't want to use visual effects at all. He preferred, for this project, to use camera and editing tricks to create the supernatural elements. He felt it would give it a more mysterious feel. Not only would the characters not understand what was happening to them, they wouldn't be able to see it either. If done right, Sam believed, it would heighten the tension. Bill liked the idea.

Sam was bearing all the financial risk on *The Path*, but in his view it was no risk at all. Compared to what he had, five million dollars was almost pocket change, though he'd never say that to Tracie who was determined not to take money for granted. Sam didn't want to either, but he also felt that there was no point in having it if they couldn't use it to achieve their dreams. Sam and Tracie had always tried to make decisions together and this was no exception. Tracie signed off on the idea and Sam, with his lawyer's help, launched a new subsidiary of Harman Family Enterprises called 511 Productions (the number was Sam's birthday).

By December, Scott delivered the second draft of the screenplay. Sam and Bill went over it, again made notes, and sent it back for further revisions.

They were both really happy with Scott's work and even discussed filming the screenplay that he'd submitted to Sam once they were done with *The Path*. Sam was positively giddy over the idea. He was really doing it; he was going to make movies. He thanked God every time he thought about the things he was able to do now. This whole thing, which had promised to be a nightmare, was turning into a dream.

Or so he thought.

TWENTY-ONE

WITH HIS PARENTS gone, Sam didn't have a lot in the way of close relatives. There were a couple of aunts and uncles and some cousins, but he'd never been particularly close to them and only saw them a few times a year. The one exception was his cousin Ted. Ted, his father's brother's son, was a couple of years older than Sam and had spent a lot of time with him growing up. He was the closest thing to a brother that Sam ever had.

As the boys grew older they spent less time together but always stayed close. It was Ted, the cool high-school freshman, who gave Sam tips on how to deal with his first crush when he was in seventh grade. The advice was good but Sam's execution was not and he wound up humiliated. Ted was there to comfort his cousin and help him pay back the kids who'd embarrassed him.

So it was Sam who was hurt the most when, at age 15, Ted was picked up by the police for possession of marijuana.

At first Sam refused to believe it. It couldn't have been Ted. Somebody else had to be responsible. His parents, nearly as shocked as he, privately wondered the same thing, but Ted's father had sounded certain over the phone. Sam wanted to talk to his cousin and find out what really happened, but Ted was not allowed to be on the phone with anyone.

After Kevin Harman hung up the phone, he went into Sam's room and started going through the drawers, the closet, everything. He even crawled under Sam's bed and rifled through his trash can. After he was done he sat his son down. "Now, I have to ask you something, and you'd better tell me the truth," Kevin said. "Has Ted ever offered you drugs?

"No!" Sam replied vehemently. "I never had any idea. I still can't believe it."

"I'll take you at your word," Kevin said. "Don't ever give me reason not to. I think it would be best if you and Ted didn't see each other for a while."

"Dad! No!" Sam protested.

"No arguments on this, either," was the reply.

No parental edict, no matter how forcefully delivered, could keep the cousins apart for long, though, and three nights later as Sam was falling asleep he heard a soft rapping on his window. Sam jumped out of bed and opened the blind to see Ted waiting for him. He quietly opened the window and invited his cousin in but Ted shook his head. "Can't stay long, man," he said. "My folks are sending me to rehab."

"Are you serious?" Sam asked.

Ted nodded "Yeah, they think me smoking a little weed makes me a full blown drug addict or something," he said. "Bunch of bullshit, if you ask me."

"So you do?" Sam asked. "You really smoke pot?"

"Sure," Ted said. "Just a little bit, here and there, nothing serious. It's cool, man. But you're part of the 'just say no' crowd, aren't you? That's why I never offered you any."

"Oh," was all Sam could say to that. He knew he would never have taken drugs from anyone else, but what would he have done if Ted was the one offering? He didn't know the answer to that question.

"How long are you going to be gone?" Sam finally asked.

"Thirty boring days," Ted said. "No big deal; beats being grounded at home. I'll sit there, listen to their crap, nod my head a lot and that'll be that."

Sam didn't tell him what he really thought. Even at thirteen he wasn't much for confrontations. Ted, though, knew him well enough to see that all this was bothering him. "Look, man, it's no big deal," Ted said. "It's not like smoking crack or shooting up heroin. It's just a little pot. Relax, everything's cool, okay?"

"Okay," Sam said, unconvinced, wondering if Ted was high right now.

"I made a stupid mistake and took some to school that day," Ted continued. "I won't be that dumb again. Trust me."

It was nearly two months before Sam had any further news of his cousin and, as he'd feared, the news was not good. This time Ted was caught with several other boys at a friend's house. It was, in its way, even more shocking than the original revelation. He'd believed that Ted was smart enough not to get caught again.

Sam's parents did their best to keep him away from

Ted during this time but he still showed up at Sam's window every now and then. Now that Sam knew the truth, Ted seemed to have no trouble talking to him about his drug use. It made Sam uncomfortable, but he was still glad to see Ted so he put up with the stories and, against his better judgment, didn't tell a soul. To his credit, Ted never offered anything to Sam.

As they both grew older Ted visited less and less and for the most part, Sam didn't mind. What little news he had of him through the family was usually not good. Despite his protests to the contrary it seemed like Ted had become a full-blown drug addict. He did another rehab stint in high school and was even transferred to a Christian high school in the hopes that it would be a good influence on him. It had the opposite effect. Ted stood out more and got more attention, which he loved. He barely scraped enough passing grades to graduate.

Once Sam was in college, though, the pendulum began to swing back. Port Mason University required freshmen and sophomores to live on campus, so Sam began his freshman year in one of the dorms. In truth, he didn't mind too much. As he'd gotten older he'd begun to chafe at the restrictions imposed by living at home and was ready to have some fun.

About a month after his first semester started, he was stunned when Ted turned up at his door one Friday night with a case of beer. Sam welcomed both his cousin and the beer as the usual Friday night party began to warm up on his floor. Though not a student, Ted fit right in and pretty soon was doing shots with some of Sam's friends. Sam stuck to the beer and parents, Sam went outside to tend to his cousin. By the time he got there Ted was sitting on the ground, shaking and sweating. "Ted, what did you take?" Sam asked.

"Nothing," Ted said. "It's been a few days...aw, shit."

With that he threw up. Sam got Ted into his car and drove him to the nearest hospital. "Heard you fucking got married," Ted said.

"And divorced," Sam replied. "It was a stupid thing to do."

"Shit, man, I could have told you that and saved you a lot of trouble," Ted said. "But you were too...fucking good for me, weren't you?"

"What are you talking about?" Sam asked.

"Can't have anything to do with the drug addict," Ted said, ignoring him. "Ted's no good. Ted's a bad boy. Fuck Ted."

"That's bullshit and you know it," Sam said.

"Did...did you ever try to track me down?" Ted asked. "Ever...ever come to fucking see me?"

Sam had nothing to say to that. Ted continued. "Like I said. Fuck Ted."

"What did you want me to do, Ted?" Sam asked.

"Ah, shit, I don't know," Ted said. "Hey, we're going about this all wrong. I just need a fix. I know a guy over on--"

"No way," Sam said. "You're going to the hospital."

"All right," Ted said.

That incident set the pattern for the relationship between the cousins for the next several years. Ted always seemed to be able to find Sam when he needed help, a handout, a place to stay when the girlfriend of the moment dumped him. Sam never knew where his cousin lived, which he suspected was a deliberate move on Ted's part, so Sam wouldn't have to lie if the police ever came looking for him.

Ted managed to stay out of trouble with the law but Sam could tell it was only because his cousin tried to keep a low profile. He couldn't seem to hold down a steady job and bounced from home to home so often that it was the first thing Sam asked about whenever he showed up. Ted had virtually no contact with any of the rest of the family, though he did show up for the funerals when each of Sam's parents died. Sam would see Ted three or four times a year.

When Sam found out about his inheritance, it didn't take long for his thoughts to turn to his wayward cousin. Sooner or later he'd show up, and Sam would have to make a decision. He knew he could afford to send Ted to the best rehab centers in the country but at the same time he knew that it would do no good if Ted didn't want to go. On the other hand, there was no way Sam was going to support Ted's drug habits. Letting him stay the night once in a while was one thing, paying for his habit was something else. What was he supposed to do?

As he grappled with the question, he decided to find out about Ted's current circumstances. Steve Bennett found him doing six months in the county jail on a misdemeanor possession charge. According to the court records, Ted was facing felony charges when he copped a plea and turned in two marijuana growers in exchange for a light sentence.

He was halfway through the sentence when Sam

went to see him. When a guard led him into his side of the visitors' cubicle, Sam saw that he looked healthy. There were a number of new tattoos on his arm and his hair had been buzzed off but he still looked good.

"Hey, this is a surprise," Ted said when he picked up the phone. "How'd you find out I was in here?"

"Private investigator," Sam replied. "I...uh...I guess you heard my news?"

"Yeah, my cousin the billionaire!" Ted said. "So what's it like?"

"Crazy," Sam said. "Everyone wants to be my pal all of a sudden."

"That'll happen," Ted said. "So did you move into a mansion or what?"

"We're building a house out by Tracie's folks," Sam replied. "It'll be a nice place but it isn't a mansion. I don't want to live in one of those."

"Why the hell not?" Ted asked. "Man, you need to live it up, now that you can."

"Oh we're having some fun," Sam said. "But you know, we're trying to help out, too."

He outlined some of their charity plans. Ted was suitably impressed. "I guess you really are walking the walk," he said. "When you went all religious, I kind of wondered how long it would last, you know?"

"It would do you a world of good, Ted," Sam said.

"Don't go there," Ted said. "I get my fill of that when the prison preachers show up. They do every now and then. I'm not interested."

"God is," Sam said. "In you, I mean."

"Damn, man, give it a rest," Ted exclaimed. "I'm not interested, okay?"

"Okay," Sam replied, sorry to hear it. "I had to try, you know."

"Right," Ted said, clearly wanting to change the subject.

Sam obliged him. "I really did come here to talk about you," he said. "What are you going to do when you get out of here?"

"I dunno," Ted said. "I'll worry about that when the time comes, you know?"

Sam sighed. "I realize this is probably going to sound like another attempt to win you over, but have you considered trying to do something more...constructive with your life?"

"Don't fucking lecture me," Ted said.

"I'm not trying to," Sam said. "But I worry about you. I know I don't do a very good job of showing it, but what happens to you matters to me. For one thing, I don't want to see you end up in here again."

"Neither do I," Ted quipped.

"Then do something about it," Sam said. "And I'll do what I can to help."

"How?" Ted asked.

"Get some help," Sam said. "Professional help. I'm talking rehab, therapy, the works. I'll pay for the whole thing, but you've got to want to do it, you know? If you get yourself cleaned up, and stay that way, I'll get you a job and a place to live. You can have a decent life. What you've had up to now is anything but."

Ted didn't say anything. Sam pressed on. "You look good, Ted," he said. "Been sober since you got here?"

"Yeah," Ted said. "It's easy to stay sober when you

can't get any shit."

"Then why not stay that way?" Sam asked. "When you get out, you'll have two choices. Either go back to what you were doing before, or try something new. I'll help with that, I swear I will. You won't have to ever see the inside of this place again."

Ted looked cold, distant. Nothing like the boy Sam grew up with. "See you around, Sam," he said. He hung up the phone, knocked on the door, and was escorted out.

TWENTY-TWO

SAM WAS DEEPLY hurt by Ted's refusal. He moped around for a couple of days before Tracie had enough and told him to get over it. "Only Ted can decide he needs help," she said. "Nobody, not even you, can do that for him."

"I feel like I've failed him," Sam said.

"You haven't," Tracie replied. "Ted's failed himself. You gave him a clear choice and he walked away. What more could you have done? Keep praying for him, but don't let it overwhelm you. You did everything you could."

Though he still felt awful, Tracie spurred him to get back into the swing of things. Sam spent a morning in late October scouting locations for *The Path*. After a quick lunch and change of clothes, he went in to the office for the afternoon to catch up on the latest returns from his various investments and to take part in a conference call with Lunar Exploration Technologies about their planned launch in the spring. He reflected that he was busier now than he'd ever been, but it was worth it because he was doing things he wanted to do. It was a great feeling and not even the situation with Ted could take that away from him.

This is what was on his mind when he went into his outer office to check with his Executive Assistant, Sandy Ward. Sandy was one of his oldest friends, having grown up just down the street from him. They'd never been romantically involved, though Sam harbored a secret crush throughout high school, but were more like siblings. In fact, Sandy often called Sam her 'little brother.' Though she had a good job at D&L, when Sam came into his fortune she eagerly took the job he offered her.

She was no secretary, though she did handle his scheduling and took calls when he was out of the office. Sam already knew she was great at multitasking when he hired her but seeing her organize his office and set up a system for weeding out crackpots out for a quick buck, while making sure people with legitimately good ideas got in to see him left him in awe and he considered increasing her salary. Sandy also worked well with Tracie and quickly expanded her role into helping both of them. Only three weeks into the operation and already they knew she was their best hire so far.

But Sandy, who was normally cheerful, did not look happy today. "Sam, did you by any chance listen to Bill Dodd's show on the radio this morning?" she asked.

"I don't listen to talk radio, Sandy, you know that," Sam said. "Why?"

"Well I do, and he's usually one of my favorites but he talked about you this morning and it wasn't very nice," she said.

"What did he say?" Sam asked.

"Maybe you'd better hear it yourself," Sandy said. "It's on the station's website as a podcast. I sent a link to your email."

"That bad?" Sam asked.

"I thought so," Sandy said. "Just listen."

Curious, Sam went into his office and brought up the podcast on his computer. Before listening to it, he went to the homepage for *The Bill Dodd Show* to refresh his memory about the host. Bill Dodd, who had hosted his AM talk show for over twelve years, leaned to the far right of the political spectrum. Frequently called Port Mason's own Rush Limbaugh, he was a darling of the local GOP establishment and was allegedly on first name terms with the Governor. Sandy indicated that Dodd's comments came about twenty minutes into the show so Sam dragged the audio player's slide bar to that point and let it play.

"...and now we come to Port Mason's new billionaires, Sam and Tracie Harman," Dodd said. "They have said publicly that they don't contribute to political campaigns, and I have it on good authority they have already rebuffed the Port Mason Tea Party. Sam is the illegitimate son of the late Hank Curtis, a Texas billionaire, and of course, we all followed the story of Sam's ex-wife, Becky Dunlap, who dropped her lawsuit almost as abruptly as she filed it. We like to be thorough, so we had one of our reporters do some digging into their background and what we found explains why they didn't help our friends in the Tea Party.

"They say they don't want to participate in politics but the truth, friends, is that they want to control it," Dodd said. "According to our usual excellent sources in city hall, the Harmans are planning to announce over one hundred million dollars in donations to the city and several of its local charities. Included in this massive giveaway is twenty-five million to expand police presence on the west side of the river, another twenty-five million to the fire department for new fire trucks and firefighters, twenty-five million to the school district to improve teacher pay and classroom technology and five million to support the public library. The other twenty million is going to soup kitchens, breadlines, homeless shelters and, unfortunately, the free clinic in the welfare district that promotes promiscuous behavior by giving out free contraception.

"Any fool can see that this will bring huge political benefits to Mayor Eric Hawkins, who faces a tough primary fight next February against a real conservative, Tea Party member Barry Morgan," Dodd continued. "If this plan works and Hawkins is re-elected, he will be in the Harmans' back pocket, along with several of the alderman whose wards stand to benefit from this massive outlay of money. Now, friends, I'm going to tell you why this is so dangerous for our city. All you have to do is look at Sam Harman's background.

"He comes from a working-class family that adopted him shortly after he was born," he said. "His late father, Kevin Harman, was a Democrat, as was his wife, Deborah. Kevin Harman was, in fact, a democratic precinct committeeman. Now it's true that Sam Harman has never declared a political party and, indeed, has never voted in a primary election, but the fact remains that he comes from a pro-union liberal background and that combined with billions of dollars is a dangerous combination indeed."

"That son of a--" Sam started to say as Tracie came in, having been alerted by Sandy.

"And what's just as troubling is his lack of openness about his wealth," Dodd said. "I mentioned the lawsuit filed and then abruptly withdrawn by his ex-wife. We were able to get in touch with her, but she refused to comment on why she suddenly dropped her paternity suit. It should be noted, however, that she recently moved in to a new apartment in Oakmont, and has enrolled her son, whom she claimed was also Sam's, in a private school. Looks like some money changed hands there, folks, but both Ms. Dunlap and Sam Harman have been curiously silent on the matter. Why?

"Then there's how he got his inheritance," Dodd said. "We have friends in Texas and they reported that Hank Curtis' heirs were all set to fight their father's. Sam Harman and his lawyer go to Texas to haggle it out and boom! They reach a secret settlement. Why keep the terms of this settlement in the dark? What does Sam Harman have to hide?

"We also found out that Harman is a space nut," he continued. "He invested fifty million dollars in some crazy scheme to mine for metals on the moon. Fifty million dollars! Sure, it'll put some people to work, and I don't have anything against that, but when this thing blows up in his face, those people are going to be out on the street and they'll have Sam Harman to thank for it. Waste of time and money, folks, nothing more. We'll be back with your calls right after this break."

Sam shut off the playback. "Can you believe this guy?" he asked. "What did I ever do to him?"

"You inherited three billion dollars and refused to give any to his cause," Tracie replied. "I've already called Jenna. She's on the way over."

"We should try to hire her away from that PR firm and put her on our payroll," Sam said. "Has she heard this yet?"

"Yes," Tracie said. "I'm not sure what she has in mind to deal with it, though."

"I guess we'll find out," Sam said. "I want to listen to his callers, see what they have to say."

"You may not like it," Tracie warned.

"Could it be any worse?" Sam asked. He resumed the playback.

"We're back," Dodd said after the commercials. "And we're taking calls about billionaire Sam Harman and his questionable politics. Our first caller is...John, one of our regulars. Go ahead, John, you're on the air."

"Thanks, Bill," John said. "You know, Harman is pretty new to the money game. I'll bet once he gets his tax bill for this year he'll change his colors pretty quick."

Dodd laughed. "Thanks, John, you make a good point. Our next caller is a first-time caller...Marie. Go ahead, Marie."

"Hi, Bill, love the show," Marie said.

"Thank you," Dodd said.

"I just wanted to say I feel sorry for his kids," Marie said. "They're going to grow up spoiled rotten and God only knows how they'll turn out."

It went on like that for almost five minutes. Not a

single caller tried to take issue with anything Dodd said. Of course his core audience wouldn't; they would hang on every word Dodd said. He wondered if the call screener would let a call through that disagreed with Dodd. It was only at the end of the segment that a call got Sam's full attention.

"We have time for one more before our next commercial break," Dodd said. "And we must be expanding our audience because this call comes from Houston, Texas. Jerry, welcome to the Bill Dodd Show. What do you have to say about Sam Harman?"

"He's throwing away money that shouldn't even belong to him," a familiar voice said. "I'm not surprised that he's a left-leaning wimp. I could tell that when I met him."

"How do you know Sam Harman?" Dodd asked. "And what makes you say that the money doesn't belong to him?"

"I'm Jerry Curtis," the caller said. "Sam Harman is technically my half-brother. He and his whore mother swindled my daddy out of three billion dollars and he's getting away with it. I doubt he's listening to a good show like this but on the chance that he is I want him to know I haven't forgotten the con job he pulled on my brothers to get my daddy's money."

"Folks, I had no idea we were going to get this call," Dodd said. "But I'm sure glad we did. Jerry, I was talking about the mysterious settlement between your family and Sam Harman that resulted in his getting the three billion. Can you tell us anything about it?"

"No, I'm sorry I can't," Jerry replied. "Harman's lawyer put a non-disclosure clause in the agreement.

If I tell you, I might hurt my family's company and there's no way in hell I'm going to let that happen. He conned my brothers and they pushed me into the deal. He's got no right to any of my family's money. I'm not surprised to hear that he's trying to buy your city. I don't know what he's really after, but it can't be any good."

Jerry hung up. "Wow," Dodd said. "What a way to end that segment. We're going to move on after the break, but if you still want to call in about the Sam Harman segment go right ahead. And if Sam Harman is listening, which I doubt, give us a call and we'll put you on the air right away. More after this."

Sam stopped the playback. "Well, I knew Jerry wasn't going away," he said.

"I think I'm glad I didn't get to meet him," Tracie said. "He sounds...I don't know...dangerous."

"He is," Sam said. "Let's hear what Jenna has to say. And a word with Anderson Braddock might not be a bad idea, either."

"If making nasty remarks on a radio show is the worst Jerry does, you'll be getting off lucky," Braddock said over the phone.

"I suppose you're right but I still thought you ought to know," Sam said. "What do you think I should do?"

"Ignore him and that loudmouth on the radio," Braddock replied. "Maybe issue a press release but let it go at that. Jerry's trying to get a rise out of you, that's all."

"Sound like what I'd tell my kids," Sam said. "But I suppose you're right. I don't think he's just going to go away, though."

"Neither do I," Braddock agreed. "Keep your eyes open, Sam. Jerry can be violent. Don't neglect your personal security for anything."

"I won't," Sam promised. "Thanks, Mr. Braddock."

"Call me anytime," the old lawyer said.

As Sam hung up he thought about Braddock's warning. Just what else was Jerry Curtis capable of?

TWENTY-THREE

THE HARMANS ARRIVED early for services that Sunday with the intent of talking to Marty about Sam's upcoming film project. Sam noticed that the new roof he'd paid for was now finished and that work had begun on a storage building at the far edge of the church's property. Once that was done he hoped to have some of the building's nagging electrical problems taken care of. In the spring the parking lot would be resurfaced. In truth he wanted to finance a whole new church building but he wasn't sure if Marty and the congregation were ready for that proposal.

They'd done their best to keep their donations to the church quiet. Marty readily accepted their request not to announce what they were doing; he wasn't comfortable with the idea anyway, and the board of elders agreed. Of course, their fellow members were not stupid and understood exactly who was paying for the improvement. A few close friends offered discreet thanks and compliments. Most everyone else didn't say anything either, though they did smile at the Harmans more often. These reactions confirmed to Sam that they'd done it the right way.

After dropping off the kids for Sunday school, Sam and Tracie went to Marty's office to talk to him about the movie project. On the way they were intercepted by Glen Dubetz, a good friend of theirs and one of the elders of the church. Dubetz owned the car dealership Marty had suggested Sam call after he lost his job. "Good morning," he said, shaking hands with both of them. "Do you two have a minute?"

"We were going in to see Marty," Sam said. "But I guess that can wait a minute. What's up?"

"Let's talk in private," Dubetz said.

He led them to the small room next to Marty's office that doubled as a library and conference room. Once the door was shut Dubetz explained what was going on. "Owen Gorman is trying to stir people up against you," he said. "He's in Marty's office right now asking him to kick you out of the church because your beliefs don't conform to the bible."

"That's crazy," Sam and Tracie said together.

"I agree and so does Marty, but Owen's been making a lot of noise," Dubetz said. "I mainly wanted to give you a heads up about it. Nobody is going to ask you to leave the church."

"I appreciate his...zeal for his views," Sam said. "But it sounds like sour grapes over the whole Tea Party thing."

"That's exactly what it is," Tracie agreed. "I wonder what his wife thinks."

"Actually, Amy's in there with him," Dubetz said. "Before either of you get any ideas, though, I'm supposed to keep you out of Marty's office. He doesn't want you folks getting into a confrontation. For one thing it would be all over the radio tomorrow."

"Bill Dodd?" Sam asked. Dubetz nodded. "Figures."

"Marty also wants to keep this quiet," Dubetz said. "The last thing we want is for the congregation to start taking sides. That might split the church and nobody wants that."

"Including us," Tracie said firmly. Sam nodded in agreement.

Unfortunately, a confrontation was exactly what took place. As everybody was settling in the sanctuary to begin the service, Owen Gorman rushed up to the podium and grabbed a microphone. "Could I have everybody's attention for a minute?" he asked. Sam stiffened in his seat but did nothing, mainly because Tracie grabbed his arm with both hands.

"I'm sorry to have to do this before services start but my conscience won't allow me to stand idly by while Sam Harman buys off this church," he said. "We all know he's paid for the roof, the storage building, the upcoming electrical work and the new parking lot next spring. I'm sure he's got plenty of other stuff in mind, too, but I ask you, can we accept the money of a man who doesn't follow God's teachings? A man who does not embody good conservative Christian values? I say to you now that we must exhort him to repent and be reconciled to what our church teaches."

Despite Tracie's attempt to restrain him, Sam got to his feet and went up to the front. "Just what values have I failed to embody, Owen?" he asked. "The last time I checked refusing to make political contributions isn't a sin."

"This isn't about that," Gorman replied. "It's about

what you have been doing with your money."

"That's not really any of your business," Sam said. He could see Marty coming up the aisle.

"It is when you set a bad example before the church," Gorman said. "You gave ten million dollars to the Morganstein free clinic in the welfare district."

"Yes, we did," Sam said. "So what?"

"Did you know that they provide free contraception?" Gorman asked.

"Yes."

"Free contraception promotes promiscuity, Sam," Gorman said.

"Oh, please," Sam said.

"It's the truth!" Gorman declared.

"Free contraception is a public health issue," Sam said. "We're trying to check the spread of AIDS and other diseases."

"You're giving people license to sin," Gorman replied. "And that's not all. That so-called 'clinic' provides referral services for abortion clinics."

"Which our funding does not support," Sam said. "Our donation was intended to provide free health care for the poor. We specifically told them not to use our money for abortion referrals."

Owen was undeterred by this. "You have associated yourselves with these sinners," he said. "Repent of this now! Be reconciled to the church! Turn away--"

"That's enough," Marty said, taking the microphone. "Owen, I explained it before. There is room enough in this church for everyone. "

"Especially if they have three billion dollars," Gorman replied.

"I have told you that isn't the case," Marty said,

starting to sound a little angry. "If you're so upset that Sam and Tracie are still here, then maybe you should leave."

Owen reacted as if he'd been slapped. "You really mean that?" he asked. "You would side with this sinner over the Word of God?"

"I'm not going to argue with you, Owen," Marty said. "Please, either sit down or leave."

"Why aren't we arguing about it?" a new voice said. Everyone turned to see Art Bryant, one of the founding members of the church and a leading voice on the Board of Elders, rise and walk up to the front. "I for one would like to know why Owen is being asked to leave. He's pointing out the truth and rebuking a sin. We are commanded to do this by scripture."

"I haven't done anything wrong," Sam said. "Is it a sin to help take care of the poor?"

"No, but it is a sin to promote sin in others," Bryant replied. "And that's what you've done by supporting that clinic. You've admitted supporting free contraception, which promotes sin. Your money would be better spent on abstinence programs."

"I disagree, Art," Sam said. "You want to debate this, fine. My answer is that handing out free condoms is an effort to prevent disease and unwanted pregnancy. People are going to have sex regardless, isn't it better that it be done safely?"

"No," Bryant said. "The wages of sin is death. If some adulterer catches a disease, that's God's punishment."

"You're serious," Sam said. "I always thought you were more reasonable than that."

"Sam, this money has turned you away from the teachings of the church," Bryant said. "Either turn away from this destructive path or leave this church."

"Please, everybody, stop this," Marty pleaded. "Nothing is going to be resolved this way."

"Marty, you've been our pastor since the beginning," Bryant said. "But if you don't rebuke this sin now, if you give in to greed and corrupt influences, the board of Elders may have to reconsider your call to be our pastor."

And at that point Sam knew that, despite his intentions, the church was about to be split. Owen Gorman was a hothead who could easily be dismissed, but Art Bryant was another matter. If he was questioning Sam's actions, others would too. He looked out into the congregation. Many people were looking at him with questioning eyes. He looked at Marty. The minister seemed at a genuine loss. Finally he looked at Tracie.

She'd brought him here in the first place. Over the years, this church had become home. Now he saw that those days were over. He could see in her tearing eyes that she understood that. Without another word, he extended his hand to her and left Chester Avenue Christian Church.

TWENTY-FOUR

MARTY LOVELL CALLED later that day with news. The board of elders had held an emergency meeting and asked both Art Bryant and Owen Gorman to leave the church. The vote was not unanimous and the two who voted with Bryant chose to leave of their own accord. Marty didn't yet know how this would affect the congregation but he believed the church would survive. He told Sam that he had no problem with the Harmans returning next Sunday. Sam told him he'd think about it.

In truth, Sam wasn't all that motivated to go back. It wasn't that his faith in God had been shaken; it hadn't. What was shaken was his faith in others. One of the board members who'd voted with Bryant was a good friend, though apparently not as good a friend as Sam thought. Naturally Sam felt betrayed. He couldn't help but wonder what the congregation as a whole thought of him over this mess.

He found that prospect troubling, which surprised him. For a long time, he maintained that he didn't care what other people thought of him. Even after coming to Christ and joining the church, he never worried about his reputation. He felt that, as long as he was right with the Lord, the rest would take care of itself. The only people whose opinions of him mattered was his family. Now that he was becoming something of a local celebrity, he found himself paying more attention to what people said about him. He found that he did care what other people thought of him.

On reflection he shouldn't have been surprised that the topic came up on that Monday's edition of The Bill Dodd Show on WXLR. Again alerted by Sandy Ward, Sam and Tracie listened to the podcast after the show went off the air.

"Once again we come to the subject of local billionaire Sam Harman and the havoc he is wreaking on our city," Dodd said. "This time he's split his own church in two over some of his 'charitable' acts. Yesterday three members of Chester Avenue Christian Church's board of elders and several of its members left because Pastor Marty Lovell, a good friend of Sam Harman's, refused to rebuke him for donating money to the Morganstein clinic, an organization we all know promotes contraception and abortion.

"We have as our guests two of the gentlemen at the center of the controversy," Dodd continued. "Former Elder, Art Bryant, and former church member, Owen Gorman. Thank you both for joining us this morning. Let's start off by establishing what actually happened at the church yesterday. As I understand it you, Owen, got up in front of the congregation to call Sam Harman to task, is that right?"

"Yes," Gorman replied. "I felt it was my duty as a Christian to rebuke Sam over his sins. I did it publicly because he has a tendency to avoid me at church. He's been that way ever since he inherited his money. Since I couldn't talk to him privately and since Pastor Lovell refused to do it, I felt I had no choice but to publicly call him out over his sins."

"Let me add that Owen consulted me before taking this action," Bryant said. "As Christians, we are called to rebuke one another when sins are committed. This isn't done to embarrass anyone, but rather to call them to repentance and, ultimately, to the forgiveness that comes from God."

"What happened then?" Dodd asked.

Owen told his side of the story which, naturally, didn't cast Sam in the best light. To hear Owen tell it, Sam became belligerent, rather than admit he was wrong and walked out when he didn't get his way. Then, Bryant got into the act and accused Marty of having been seduced by Sam's money and generous contributions to the church. Sam's blood began to boil.

"It's a sad story, gentlemen," Dodd said. "But, we often hear how the newly-wealthy make poor decisions and alienate those who were once good friends. In Sam Harman's case, the sheer amount of money makes matters even worse. Whether he realizes it or not, Harman has become a powerful man, and it seems to me that it's going to his head. We'll be back with your calls right after this break."

"I can't believe the gall of that man," Tracie said.

"Which one?" Sam asked.

"Dodd," Tracie replied.

"He's just in it for the ratings," Sam said. "He makes his living saying things like that about people who don't agree with him. I wish I'd been listening when they were on the air. I'd call in and give them a piece of my mind."

"Jenna said that wasn't a good idea," Tracie said. "Getting into a war of words with Bill Dodd will only bring him more attention and drag you down to his level."

"But it would feel so good," Sam said as the break ended and Dodd started taking calls.

"He has a right to do what he wants with his money," the first caller said. "Who are you guys to tell him otherwise?"

"We are his fellow believers," Bryant replied. "And as I said earlier, we have an obligation to correct one of our own when he strays."

They went to the next caller. "God bless you both for standing up for what's right," a woman said. "Are you going to be starting a new church? If you are, I'll join."

"We don't know where the Lord is leading us yet, Ma'am," Bryant said. "But thank you very much."

The third caller was firmly on Sam's side. "I was there when this all happened yesterday," the man said. Sam realized it was Terry Sturgis, a good friend and golfing buddy. "And your guests have left out a very important fact. When Sam gave the money to the clinic, they signed an agreement saying none of the money could be used for abortion referrals. It's strictly to provide health care for the poor."

"Then let him set up a Christ-centered clinic for that," Gorman said. "One that doesn't provide such sinful services."

"Get off your high horse, Owen," Terry said.

"Sam's not funding that part and you know it."

"Bless you, Terry," Sam said, making a mental note to call him later.

"I know that's you, Terry," Gorman said. "And I should have known you'd rush to Sam's defense. You're as bad as he is."

"Really?" Terry replied. "Bill, did you know that Owen's had it in for Sam ever since he tried to get him to support the Tea Party? Sam told him no, and he's been nursing a grudge ever since."

"I'd say that's just further proof that Sam Harman is a dangerous man," Dodd said. "Before we move on to our next caller I want to again extend an invitation to Sam Harman. You can call in or come down to the station and I'll put you on air right here in the studio. Now, next caller."

"Hi, Bill, my name is Gary," the caller said. "I have an empty building in Hartstown. If your guests need a place to start a new church, they're welcome to it."

"Thank, you. God bless you," Bryant said.

"Friends, our next caller is really going to get things going here on The Bill Dodd Show," the host said. "We have Dr. Greta Hobson, medical director of the Morganstein Clinic. Good morning, Doctor, welcome to the show."

"I hear Sam Harman getting beat up on your show and I don't like it," Hobson said. "We barely stay open thanks to dwindling government support and fewer private donations. But even though that money goes away, the poor don't and neither do their health care needs. Thanks to the Harmans, we'll be able to stay open for the next five years and not have to worry about how we're going to cover the basic bills."

"But your 'clinic' provides abortion referrals," Dodd said. "That's what my guests and I find so objectionable."

"Like your earlier caller said, we have an agreement with the Harmans that their funding won't be used for that purpose," Hobson said.

"How many unborn children have you had a hand in killing?" Gorman asked. "And how many more have to die before you see the incredible evil you are doing?"

"Amen," Bryant said.

"We provide health care," Hobson said.

"Abortion is not health care," Bryant said.

"How about it, Doctor," Dodd said. "Can you answer Owen's question?"

"I won't dignify it with a reply," Hobson said. She hung up.

Dodd laughed. "Typical liberal," he said. "Can't even defend her position."

Sam had heard enough. He stopped the playback and looked at his wife. "We can't let this stand," he said.

"Turn the other cheek, Sam," Tracie said. "I know you don't want to, but I think it's the right thing to do. And we need to pray."

Sam sighed. "You're right," he said. "I wish...what I really wish is that we could get away from all this for a bit. You know, just hire a jet and fly off for a few days. But there's too much going on here."

"Why don't we take the rest of the day off?" Tracie suggested. "We can go have lunch, see a movie and just relax."

"That sounds like a great idea," Sam said. "It's nice

being the boss, isn't it?"

TWENTY-FIVE

BRIAN VOGEL WAS a local activist most recently involved in Port Mason's chapter of the 'Occupy' movement. Over the last few years he'd led protests in the financial district with hundreds of people camping out in front of the large banks and the city's mercantile exchange. As in other cities, the authorities were tolerant of the protests at first but as time went on and the blockades didn't end, Mayor Hawkins decided enough was enough and sent in the police to clean the protesters out.

Dozens of arrests were made, accompanied by many complaints of police brutality. Vogel himself was admitted to the hospital after taking a blow to the head from a police baton. He claimed he was struck without warning and without provocation. The police claimed he was resisting arrest. This claim met with skepticism in the press, especially when amateur video emerged showing police firing pepper spray at handcuffed protesters.

Though the Occupy Port Mason movement started losing steam in the spring, Brian Vogel was a zealous as ever. He'd been an activist since his college days in the early 1990's when he got involved in various protests at Port Mason University. He had a long arrest record for civil disobedience but no felony convictions. A true believer, he'd been branded a communist, socialist, anarchist and general nuisance by conservatives like Bill Dodd and Mayor Hawkins. Vogel wore these labels with pride, firm in his beliefs and always ready for a new fight.

Sam Harman's inheritance was like a gift from heaven to someone like Brian Vogel. Protesting corporations and banks was pretty good, but as far as he was concerned having one person as the face of everything he was against sharpened his focus and would bring new attention to his cause. He'd led the small group of protesters outside the Harman residence shortly after the news broke but he had bigger things in mind even then. Now he was ready to move with nearly a hundred people to protest the billionaire.

The protestors arrived shortly before Sam and Tracie left the office for their impromptu date. Vogel divided his forces, covering the building's main entrance and the entrance and exit to the parking garage so that they were guaranteed a chance to confront the Harmans personally. Thorough in his research, he recognized Tracie at the wheel of her BMW the moment it appeared at the foot of the ramp. "Here they come!" he shouted. The protestors formed a human chain, blocking the exit.

At first Tracie thought that if she got close enough to them, they'd make way for her. When that didn't happen she came to a stop. Sam recognized Brian Vogel from his university days. They'd never met personally, but Vogel had made the campus newspaper enough times that Sam knew who he was. "So now I've got the conservatives and the liberals mad at me," he said. "Wonderful. That's what I get for being a centrist."

The lone security guard had absolutely no luck in getting the protestors to disperse. He came over to the SUV. "I'm sorry, Mr. Harman," he said. "They just showed up. We called the police."

"Let's see if we can defuse this before they get here," Sam said.

"You're not getting out, are you?" Tracie asked.

"Why not?" Sam replied. "That's Brian Vogel. He was at the university during my first go-round. He always claimed to be non-violent. I'll be okay."

Before Tracie could argue, Sam got out of the car and approached Vogel, who was getting ready to start speaking through a bullhorn. Sam offered his hand. Vogel didn't take it. "You could at least have some manners," Sam said. "I'm not here to start a fight."

Reluctantly, Vogel shook Sam's hand. "Now, what have I done to tick you folks off?" Sam asked.

"You're part of the one percent," Vogel said. "Your wealth comes at the expense of the rest of us. You sit up there in your fancy offices with your billions having a good time. What are you doing for the people who don't have anything?"

"I was hoping you would ask that," Sam said, snatching the bullhorn away from Vogel. "Will you give me a chance to answer?"

"Go right ahead," Vogel said, thinking that nothing Harman said would change his people's minds.

Two police cars and a police van pulled up. Cops dressed in riot gear started to get out but Sam rushed over and asked them not to do anything. He was able to persuade them to give him ten minutes to peacefully disperse the crowd before they started making arrests. Sam went back to the protestors. "They're not going to move on you for ten minutes," he said.

The crowd reacted skeptically. These were veteran activists who'd clashed with the police before. As far as they were concerned the police were the enemy, the armed tool of the wealthy and powerful. It didn't surprise Vogel at all that Sam was able to call them off. "So if we don't listen to you, you'll sic the cops on us?" he asked.

"I didn't call them," Sam said. "I'd like to resolve this peacefully."

"Yeah, right," Vogel said. "Okay, say what you have to say."

"Hi," Sam said into the bullhorn. "Do you folks think we don't do anything for people less fortunate than ourselves?"

"Yes!" the crowd shouted.

"It's not true," Sam said, to a chorus of boos. "Hear me out! We weren't going to announce this until next week, but my wife and I have already started our charitable foundation. Over the next year we plan to give five hundred million dollars to various local causes and national charities. We're going to build a new homeless shelter in the welfare district that will house up to a thousand people at a time. We've doubled the size of the Brown Food Pantry and made sure the Morganstein free clinic will stay open for the next five years. Is that good enough for you?"

"No!" Vogel shouted. "You'll make millions more

from your business activities from the sweat of the ordinary workers who barely earn a living!"

"Seriously?" Sam replied. "Just what kind of businesses do you think I've put my money into?"

"It doesn't matter," Vogel barked, taking the bullhorn back. "You're missing the whole point! Nobody should have as much as you do! Nobody! No more billionaires! No more billionaires!"

The crowd took up the chant. The cop in charge came up to Sam. "Nice try," he said. "But these people don't listen to reason. You'd better get out of here, Mr. Harman. We're going to run them all in."

"I'd really rather you didn't," Sam said. "They have their rights."

"They're a bunch of stupid hippies," the cop, a sergeant whose nameplate read 'Hill.' "We'll probably find pot on at least half of them. Go on, Mr. Harman, we'll handle this."

Sam walked back to Tracie's car. He heard Hill order the crowd to disperse but he knew it wouldn't happen. He was about to open the door when he felt something hit the back of his head.

Everything went black.

TWENTY-SIX

SAM WOKE UP in the emergency room of St. Mary's Hospital with a monster headache. The first person he saw was Tracie. "What hit me?" he asked.

"A bottle," she said. "Nobody saw who threw it."

"Of course not," he groaned. "Oh, my head."

"I'll get the doctor," she said.

Sam had absolutely no inclination to get up. He tried to remember what happened but it was all a blur. When he turned his head to look around a wave of dizziness hit him. He gripped the sides of the bed as the room tilted. That was when Tracie and a nurse came back in. Sam could feel the bile rising in his throat. Fortunately, the nurse was a veteran who recognized the look on his face and held a pan under his chin while he threw up.

The dizziness eased and Sam relaxed a bit. His head was still killing him and his stomach felt queasy but he thought the worst had passed. "Sorry about that," he said.

"Honey, you couldn't help it," Tracie said.

"Vomiting is pretty common after taking a hit to the head," the nurse said. "I'll give you a clean pan in case it happens again. The doctor should be with you in a minute."

That minute turned into forty minutes. Sam didn't get sick again but he sure didn't feel like getting up. Tracie pulled up a chair and sat with him, holding his hand. "How did I get here?" he asked.

"I brought you," she said. "The guard lifted you into the seat and buckled you in. I didn't want to wait around during a riot for an ambulance."

"Riot?" Sam asked. Then he remembered. "Oh, no. I didn't want any trouble."

"It wasn't your fault," she said.

He could see something in her face, something bad. "What happened?" he asked.

"One of the protestors was shot by the police," she said.

"Oh, no," Sam said. "How did it happen?"

"I don't know," she said. "It must have happened after I drove off because I didn't hear anything. It was Brian Vogel who was shot."

"Lord have mercy," Sam said. "Is he going to make it?"

"I have no idea," Tracie said. "I recognized him when the stretcher went by and I overheard someone say that a cop shot him. That's all I know."

At Sam's suggestion they prayed over it. They asked God to heal Brian Vogel and to be with the medical professionals attending to him. Tracie prayed for a good report on Sam's injury and for his healing. Then, they asked for the strength and wisdom to cope with what happened. They were still praying when the doctor came in. "Uh, Mr. Harman?" she asked.

"You the doc?" Sam asked as he and Tracie raised

their heads.

"Doctor Prasad," she said. She looked to be of middle-eastern descent but her accent was decidedly American. "I understand you had some vomiting after you came to,"

"Yeah, but I feel a little better now," Sam said. "So what's wrong with me?"

"You were hit in the head by a bottle, that's what," Prasad said. "I'd like to do a CAT scan to be sure but you're showing the symptoms of a concussion. I don't think it's too severe but we should watch things for a few days."

"Do I have to stay here?" Sam asked.

"Probably not," she said. "I would take it easy for a few days, though. Concussions can have lingering effects."

"What about the man who was shot?" Sam asked.

The doctor ignored the question. "The police are outside," she said. "They want to have a word with you. I can tell them to wait if you don't feel up to it."

"No, that's okay," Sam said.

Two plainclothes officers entered. "I'm Inspector Kugler and this is Detective Weddle," the older of the two said. "You had quite a morning, Mr. Harman."

"Call me Sam," he said. "There really isn't a lot I can tell you guys."

"We'll be the judges of that," Kugler said. "We already have the report from the officers on the scene. We'd like to hear your side of it."

"My side?" Sam asked. "After I got hit with that bottle I don't remember a thing. All I can tell you is that I tried to reason with those folks and they wouldn't listen. When I tried to walk away I was hit in the head. Next thing I know I was here."

"So you weren't a witness to the shooting?" Weddle asked.

"No," Sam said.

"Neither was I," Tracie added.

The two policemen seemed disappointed. "I don't suppose either of you knows who threw the bottle," Kugler said.

The Harmans shook their heads. Again, the cops looked disappointed. "What's going on?" Sam asked. "What happened after we left?"

"We're still trying to piece that together ourselves," Kugler admitted. "All we know for sure is that the protest leader was shot by one of our officers. Now he's dead and--"

"Vogel was killed?" Sam asked, in shock.

"Yes," Kugler said. "Did you know him?"

"No," Sam said. "I knew who he was, but we never met before today. I always thought he was non-violent."

"So did we," Weddle said. Kugler silenced him with a look.

"What did Vogel do to provoke your guy?" Sam asked.

"So far no one who was there has been able to tell us how it happened," Kugler said. "We were hoping one of you might have seen something."

"I drove away before it happened," Tracie said. "I never even heard a gunshot."

"You're sure about that?" Kugler asked.

"Yes," Tracie replied.

"I don't know if you guys know this," Sam said. "But the building has security cameras. Maybe they picked something up."

"We're having the tapes checked," Kugler said. "I suppose that's all we have for now. Thank you for your time. If you remember anything else, here's my card."

Sam looked at the card. It said INTERNAL AFFAIRS.

The CAT scan confirmed that Sam had a mild concussion but it wasn't serious enough to warrant keeping him at the hospital, so he was sent home with pain medication and instructions to see his own doctor as soon as possible. With the press coverage of the shooting and the injury to Sam, there was no hope of slipping out of the hospital quietly so Tyler Security sent a car and a detail to pick them up. The guards formed a circle around Sam and Tracie as they conveyed them to an SUV parked as close as possible to the hospital exit. Reporters shouted questions, but Sam didn't feel like talking. The convoy drove away quickly.

"There's already a crowd at your house," Stan Tyler said. He was riding shotgun for his son, Pat, who was driving. "I'd suggest hunkering down somewhere else, at least for tonight."

"Where are the kids?" Sam asked.

"At Mom and Dad's," Tracie said. "I called them after we got you to the hospital."

"Let's go there," Sam said. "I want to see them. Stan, what do you know about an Inspector Kugler?"

"John Kugler?" Stan replied. "Top notch guy. Heard he got moved over to Internal Affairs last year. Wasn't too happy about it, either."

"Why not?"

"Cops don't like to investigate other cops," Stan explained. "Most detectives have to pull a tour in IA, but they generally don't like it. Why are you asking?"

"He's on this case," Sam said. "The protest leader was shot and killed by an officer."

"That explains it," Stan said. "Well, John's as honest as the day is long. If there was anything hinky about that shooting, he'll get to the bottom of it."

When they arrived at Carl and Mary Pruitt's house they found three very worried children and two very worried in-laws waiting for them. The kids rushed to Sam and hugged him as soon as he got out of the car. Luckily, the press didn't know where they had gone so the reunion was unobserved. To be on the safe side, though, Stan Tyler would have a detail on the premises overnight.

Both Tracie and her mother fussed over Sam until he was seated in Carl's favorite recliner in the living room. Sam protested that he was fine, but the women would hear none of it. Mary draped a blanket over him while Tracie fixed an ice pack for his head. The first evening news show started just after he sat down so he had Carl turn up the volume and hushed the kids so he could hear the report.

"A protest in downtown Port Mason turned deadly today, leaving one man dead and police under fire for what many are calling an unnecessary use of force," Channel 4 anchor Craig Butler said. "For more we go to police headquarters and Channel 4's Don Romack. Don?"

The shot cut to a man standing outside the police headquarters building. "Craig, police have yet to

183

issue a statement regarding the shooting death of Brian Vogel at the hands of a Port Mason police officer during a protest in the financial district. Vogel was apparently leading a protest aimed at local billionaire Sam Harman, whose offices are located in the Nardulli Building. According to witnesses, Mr. Harman personally spoke to Vogel and the other protestors. Mr. Harman was leaving the scene when he was struck in the head by a bottle. He was treated and released at St. Mary's hospital.

"Police moved in to disperse the protestors," Romack continued. "Witnesses say they went in swinging batons and using pepper spray without warning. A gunshot was heard and Vogel was found wounded. He was rushed to St. Mary's hospital where he died in the emergency room. Police have refused comment, citing an ongoing investigation. Craig?"

"Don, have the Harmans released a statement?" Butler asked.

"Not that we're aware of," Romack replied. "As I mentioned before, Sam Harman was released from St. Mary's a short time ago but has not appeared at his home or at his offices. Calls to his office have not been returned."

"Thank you, Don," Butler said. "I've just been told that we have just received amateur video from the protest. Let's look at that now. We'll warn you the images may be disturbing to younger viewers."

"Kids, go in the other room," Sam said. "Now!"

The image was jerky and Sam could tell instantly that it had been shot by a cell phone. He could see Tracie's BMW pulling away from the building as the police moved in. The audio quality was poor but he thought he heard someone yell "Go get them!' as the police attacked the protestors. The police dove into the crowd swinging batons. Protestors crumpled to the pavement. Several started to flee, but officers chased them down and tackled them. Vogel was standing on a lightpost, waving his sign. He heard the gunshot and saw Vogel fall to the ground. Unfortunately he couldn't see any sign of the gun but it didn't matter. Brian Vogel was dead and from what Sam could see, he'd done nothing but wave a protest sign.

TWENTY-SEVEN

IT WAS A shaken and troubled Sam Harman who arrived at the office the next morning. He had no intention of sitting around at home in the middle of this controversy. When Sandy Ward saw him she rushed up, gave him a hug, and promptly reprimanded him for coming in when he was in this condition. Sam, who'd already endured the same speech from Tracie, simply smiled and asked for his phone messages.

There were several. The media inquiries were referred to Jenna Vanderberg. The Mayor, the Chief of Police and Sam's alderman all called. There were also several calls from members of Chester Avenue Christian Church. Sam called the Mayor first.

He was put through to Eric Hawkins right away. "Mr. Harman, thank God you're alright," the Mayor said. "We've all been very concerned."

"I'm more concerned about a man who was gunned down for waving a protest sign," Sam said. "What do you have to say about that?"

"Chief Huston promised me a thorough investigation," Hawkins said. "He put his best Internal Affairs Inspector on the case."

"Yes, I met him yesterday," Sam said. "What I want to know is why the cops had to go in swinging their clubs? Those people weren't violent. I know, I was there."

"I'm waiting for an explanation myself," Hawkins replied. "I saw the video on the news last night, and I'm as outraged as you are. When they find out who did this I'll make sure they're prosecuted to the fullest extent of the law."

"I hope so," Sam said.

His next call was to the Chief of Police, Alan Huston. Sam wanted to be diplomatic with the man, after all he hadn't been there, but his anger over the death of Brian Vogel was rising with each passing second. Huston echoed Hawkins' sentiments of relief that Sam was all right, but Sam wasn't in the mood for platitudes.

"Chief, I'm going to have a hard time justifying giving twenty-five million dollars to a police department that shoots unarmed protestors," he said without preamble. "I'm sure I sound harsh but after what happened yesterday I think I have a right to be."

"I understand your anger, Mr. Harman," Huston said. "But you have to give us a chance to find out what happened. Nobody saw the weapon being fired, so how can you know it was a police officer who shot him?"

"Oh, come on," Sam said. "Who else had guns? The protestors? Not likely."

"I agree, it looks bad," Huston said. "But there are things about this case that you don't know."

"Like what?" Sam asked.

Huston was silent for a moment. "Can I trust you to

keep this quiet for now?

Sam wasn't big on secrecy but he supposed that this one time he could go along with it. He was really curious. "Okay, I won't say anything," he replied.

"For starters," Huston said. "We examined the sidearms of every officer involved in what happened yesterday. Not a single one of them has been fired recently. All of their ammunition was accounted for. We've checked the security tapes from the building cameras as well as that video that was on TV last night. None of them caught the actual shooting. Finally, we have a preliminary report from the coroner. Vogel was shot with a .38 caliber round. Our officers all carry .40 caliber Glocks. Now tell me, who shot Vogel?"

Sam was silent. "I know how bad it looks, Mr. Harman," Huston continued. "But the evidence we have says that it wasn't one of our officers. We're investigating everyone who was there yesterday. Maybe one of those people isn't as peaceful as he claims."

"Maybe," Sam said. "But what about the events leading up to the shooting? Your guys went in swinging. Was that really necessary?"

"That's being investigated also," the chief sighed. "I admit; we started taking a hard line on protests after the whole 'occupy' business last year, but even then we never used force until we met with actual resistance. We've suspended the sergeant in charge of the detail, but until the results of the investigation are in there's nothing more I can do."

"I see," Sam said. "All things considered, Chief, I think we're going to have to postpone the official announcement of our grant until you get a handle on what happened yesterday. I'm not canceling it, but I am waiting. I want to be clear on one thing: those people were peaceful. There was no reason to go crazy on them like that and there certainly was no need to shoot Brian Vogel. That's my position and I will say so publicly, if asked."

"I respect your position, Mr. Harman," Huston said. He sounded tired. The man had probably been up all night. "Thank you for returning my call."

He hung up. As he put the phone back in its cradle, Sam wondered if maybe he'd been too hard on the man. Steve Bennett once told him that there was plenty about police investigations that never made it into the press. He'd based his tirade solely on what he'd seen in the press. That was a mistake. He resolved to call back in a little while to apologize.

After returning the rest of his calls, he logged on to his computer and checked his emails. There were many from well-wishers and a couple who said he'd been foolish to try and 'reason with those hippies.' There was one without a return address. How did that get past the spam filter? Curious, Sam opened it. It read: "You got what you deserved yesterday, Harman. It won't be the last time."

Sam stared at it a moment, then started making calls.

An hour later Sam and Tracie watched as Debbie Chriswell, the police department's top computer expert, and his own IT chief, Tim Druse, examined his computer. Chriswell was accompanied by Detective Jay Redman. Sam had also summoned

Steve Bennett. The private investigator regarded Redman with disgust. Sam had never seen that look on Bennett's face before.

"No good, boss," Druse said. "It came through too many nodes for us to trace back."

"How does someone do that?" Tracie asked.

"There are anonymous emailing services designed to keep senders' identities secret," Chriswell said. "They work with the sender's email program to route the email through at least a dozen internet servers to mask the origin point. Some even use a time delay, so the sender can have an alibi for the time the email was sent. The sites ask their users not to do anything illegal with them, but it happens all the time."

"I don't understand all this computer stuff," Redman said. "But my guess is that it's either someone just trying to mess with you or someone with a legitimate grudge. Is there anyone you can think of who might have a motive to send you threatening messages."

"My half-brother comes to mind," Sam said, explaining about Jerry Curtis.

"Well we'll try to look into it, but since he lives out of state I don't want you to get your hopes up for an arrest," Redman said. "I'm sure he'll have an alibi."

"I'm sure too," Sam said. "But I'd appreciate anything you could do, Detective."

"We'll do what we can," Redman replied. "We need to do anything else with that computer, Debbie?"

"No, I'm done here," Criswell said. "There's nothing I could do back at the lab that would tell us who sent it. If you get any more, Mr. Harman, do let us know."

"I will," Sam said. "Thank you."

"We will run down that thing with your half-brother," Redman said. "And Inspector Kugler asked me to tell you that they checked the security footage from yesterday. They didn't get a shot of who threw that bottle at you, but they were able to determine that it was thrown from about twenty feet from where you were standing. That means it wasn't one of the protestors."

"That's interesting," Sam said. "Thank him for me, will you?"

The detectives made their goodbyes and left. "You need me for anything else, boss?" Druse asked.

"No thanks, Tim, you can get back to work," Sam said. Druse left leaving Bennett with the Harmans. Bennett still didn't look happy. "What is it, Steve?" Sam asked. "You looked like you wanted to haul off and slug that detective."

"I did," Bennett replied. "I don't like him, and I don't trust him."

"Is he corrupt?" Tracie asked.

"Not that I've ever been able to prove," Bennett said. "But that's a long story, and one I really don't want to get into right now. What did you want me here for?"

"I didn't think the police were going to take as much of an interest in this as they did," Sam said. "I thought that I might need you to investigate it."

"If the computer geeks can't find who sent that email, there's no way I could," Bennett said. "Anything else I can do for you, Sam?"

"I suppose not," Sam said. "At least for now. I'm sure I'll have some more background checks for you soon, though, so don't get too comfortable."

"Will do," Bennett said. "See you both later."

After he was gone Tracie spoke. "I wonder what is between him and that detective?" she asked. "He seemed so...intense about it."

"I've never seen him like that," Sam said. "He was always such an even-keel kind of guy. It must have been something pretty bad. Maybe someday he'll tell us."

"Maybe," she agreed. "In the meantime, you're going home."

"I have work to do," Sam protested.

"No, you don't," she said. "You're going to go home and get some rest. I'll drive you myself. No arguing."

Sam used the two words he'd learned early on were the key to getting along with his wife. "Yes, dear," he said.

As she drove him out of the parking garage he saw a makeshift memorial that had sprung up where Brian Vogel was shot. Who had shot him? And why? He wanted the answers, but it was not to be. The killing of Brian Vogel was not solved for a long time.

TWENTY-EIGHT

ASIDE FROM A few snide remarks on *The Bill Dodd Show*, none of the fallout from the death of Brian Vogel touched Sam. That did nothing to assuage his guilt, though. Everyone around him said it wasn't his fault and the press seemed to agree, but Sam couldn't shake the sense that he was somehow responsible.

Though he still wasn't ready to go back to his church, Marty was counseling him and praying with him about Vogel's death and Sam's involvement. The only thing that seemed to help was his clandestine funding of Vogel's funeral. He'd had Aaron Charlton contact the family and offer to pay the expenses on the condition that nobody found out about it. Sam wasn't looking for public recognition. The family accepted the offer. As it turned out Vogel had a twelve year-old daughter. Sam set up a trust fund for her as well.

The protestors didn't return and Sam gave interviews where he essentially endorsed their right to protest, whether he agreed with the message or not. He was restrained in his characterization of the Port Mason police. For its part they determined that the

Sergeant in charge at the protest, one David Hill, had overstepped his authority in ordering the use of force. Hill, who turned out to be Steve Bennett's former partner, was demoted to patrolman and put on desk duty.

In the second week of November, Sam and Tracie officially announced their grants to the city and to private organizations. They held a joint press conference with Mayor Hawkins and the heads of the various departments and agencies they were helping. Sam was decidedly uncomfortable with all the attention but managed to put a brave face on it, even joking with the reporters. Had it been up to him he would have simply issued the checks and let it go at that but the politicians had to have their moment in the sun. Sam supposed he was going to have to get used to that sort of thing but he didn't have to like it.

During November Sam made frequent trips to the site of his new home to check on the builders' progress. By the standards of the Curtis family, who maintained opulent homes in Texas, the new Harman residence was pretty modest. It was a one-story (at Tracie's insistence) dwelling that, though large, could hardly be considered a mansion. Working with an architect, they had designed a structure with a core ranch-like section and two angled wings. Tracie liked the idea because from the front it looked like the house had its arms open, waiting to embrace all who entered. Sam wasn't nearly so poetic. He liked it because he would finally get his long-desired 'man cave.'

Sam's birth mother directed the interior design though Tracie and Sam (meaning, basically, Tracie) had final say over everything she did. Sam offered to pay for her services but Susan wouldn't hear of it. As far as she was concerned, her work was a gift to Sam in lieu of all the birthdays she had missed while he was growing up. Susan and Tracie got along famously throughout the process and the end result was pleasing to all.

In addition to the main house they also put up a five-car garage where Sam could store the classic cars he wanted to buy and, much to the delight of their children, an in-ground swimming pool with an inflatable dome that would enable them to swim during the winter months.

In all, Sam and Tracie spent nearly a million dollars on their new home. When Sam totaled things up and saw how much they'd spent he began to wonder if he was going too far. New cars, huge new house, fancy clothes, offices downtown; was it too much? He didn't really have an answer to that. What he did know was that he thoroughly enjoyed providing his family a fine new home to live it. It would be a huge change from Knox Avenue.

One afternoon, about a week before Thanksgiving, Sam got a call from the main contractor on the house, Blake Campbell. "Sam," he said. "We've got a problem. A couple of sheriff's deputies just showed up and asked to see our permits. They said they weren't valid and ordered us to stop work. I asked them what was wrong and they told me to shut up and stop work or they were going to arrest me. Sam, there is nothing wrong with those permits. I think you'd better get out here."

Sam had a pretty good idea what the problem was

and it infuriated him. Some people could be so petty. He made a few phone calls, then got into his car and drove out to the work site.

When he arrived Sam was pleased to see that his phone calls had borne fruit. News crews from channels 4 and 7 were there, as was Amanda Clark from *The Port Mason Register*. They were trying to interview Blake Campbell, who was in handcuffs and in the process of being put into a squad car by the two deputies. This was worse than he thought. The work crew had gathered around and looked ready to fight to get their boss out of the deputies' clutches. Agents from Tyler Security held them back, but to Sam it didn't look like their hearts were in it. As Sam parked his car, he saw Aaron Charlton's car pull onto the property.

Sam approached the scene and the reporters ran over to him. He took Amanda Clark's question first. "Mr. Harman why is your foreman being arrested?" she asked.

"That's a very good question," Sam replied. "Let's find out."

He approached the deputies, who had by now gotten Campbell into their car. "Gentlemen," he said. "I'm the property owner here. I understand there's been a problem with our construction permits. Would you mind explaining why you have my foreman in custody?"

"Disorderly conduct," one of the deputies said.

"Seriously?" Sam asked. The deputies nodded. "Blake, have you been a naughty boy?"

This drew a laugh from everyone surrounding the

squad car. Before Campbell could respond one of the deputies shut the car door. "He looks sober enough," Sam commented. "What did he do?"

"It'll all be in the arrest report," the deputy said.

"He told those morons that he wasn't going to stop work without a court order," one of the construction workers said.

The deputies started to move towards that worker when two more cars pulled up. One was a nondescript Chevy Impala. The other was a slightly more ornate version of the car the deputies drove. It was driven by another deputy, but it was the man in the passenger's seat who interested Sam. Sheriff John McCreary had been the county's top lawman for twelve years. Most of his tenure had been tranquil, politically, but the last year had been rough. DEA agents working a sting operation arrested two of McCreary's deputies for selling drugs out of the evidence room.

Hoping to cop a plea, one of the arrested deputies revealed that not only had this been going on for several years but that a group of deputies was taking bribes from area methamphetamine dealers to turn a blind eye to their operations. This revelation brought in the State Police to investigate. As a result fourteen deputies had already been indicted and several more were still under investigation.

While none of the corruption was directly tied to McCreary, the political damage was done. His allies on the county board ran for cover and every other politician in the area refused to have anything to do with him. McCreary resisted efforts to pressure him into resigning, insisting that he'd done nothing wrong and that he shouldn't be punished for the actions of others.

His party refused to endorse the lifelong Republican for re-election. They put up a retired State Police captain to run against him and, of course, the Democrats put up their own candidate. McCreary ran as an Independent, but the campaign was brutal. The final blow had been the sudden resignation of the chief deputy who alleged that McCreary had been warned of the illegal activities but refused to investigate the allegations.

In mid-October McCreary, facing near-certain defeat, came to Sam Harman and begged him not only for a campaign contribution but for a personal endorsement. As Port Mason's new favorite son, the Sheriff reasoned, his word would at least help his chances. Sam and Tracie stuck to their strict 'no politics' policy and turned him down. The Sheriff was soundly defeated by the Republican candidate and would have to leave office in the first week of January.

McCreary went red at the sight of Sam Harman surrounded by reporters. He also scowled at the occupant of the other county vehicle, county building inspector Trevor Anders. Stopping in his tracks, McCreary waved his deputies over but they were followed by the press and Sam. McCreary held up his hands. "If I could have a moment to confer with my deputies," he said. "Then I'll talk to you folks."

He request was granted. Sam waved over the building inspector. "Anything wrong with our permits?" he asked.

"No," Anders replied. "John's just not going to go

quietly."

"So it would seem," Sam said. "You'll tell the press what you just told me, right?"

"Sure," Anders said. "I never liked John anyway."

Sam smiled and waited for McCreary to make the next move. After conferring angrily with his deputies, the Sheriff came forward to address the reporters. He was flanked by one of the deputies while the other went over to the car and released Campbell. "Ladies and gentlemen," he said. "This has all been a big misunderstanding. We had received a report that work was being done here that went outside the boundaries of the permits issued for this property. My deputies may have acted somewhat hastily in arresting the foreman, but as you can see I've ordered his release."

"Sheriff!" one of the TV reporters interjected. "Is this retaliation for Mr. Harman's refusal to support you for reelection?"

"Absolutely not," the Sheriff replied. "And I resent the implication."

"Who made the allegation about the building permits?" Amanda Clark asked.

"It was a confidential source whose identity I cannot reveal," McCreary said. Sam resisted the urge to laugh out loud. McCreary looked like one of his kids when he caught them in mischief. "Naturally, we had to investigate."

"Isn't the building inspector supposed to handle these matters?" Clark asked.

"Yes, I am," Anders said, stepping into the fray. "For the record, there is nothing wrong with Mr. Harman's permits. Also, my office has received no reports of improper work being done on this site. I inspected this site personally yesterday and everything was in order."

Upon hearing this, the reporters turned to face McCreary again. His face had turned another shade of red and once again Sam had to resist the urge to laugh. "What an idiot," Aaron Charlton whispered. "He actually thought he could get away with this."

"From what I hear the rural part of the county has been his playground for years," Sam said. "He's about to lose it. I guess he's having a hard time with it."

"No kidding," Charlton said.

Flanked by his deputies, McCreary beat a hasty retreat. As their cars backed out some of the workers waved good bye as they laughed. Without the sheriff to go after, the reporters turned back to Sam. "Mr. Harman, what's your reaction to all this?" Amanda Clark asked.

"Nothing I'd care to see in print," Sam replied. "So I think I'd better stick with 'no comment.'"

"Mr. Harman," the reporter from channel 4 said. "Why don't you contribute to politicians?"

"My wife and I have come to believe that campaign financing is nothing more than a system of legalized bribery." Sam said. "We won't participate in a system like that. We're not looking for political favors. All we want to do is run our new businesses in peace and to help our community."

Once the crew was back to work on the house and the press gone, Sam sat in his car for a moment to collect his thoughts. This petty retaliation by itself wasn't a big deal but he could see where this sort of thing could become a serious problem in the future. Anderson Braddock had warned him about people with their hands out. Now he was seeing what the old lawyer had been talking about. The world of wealth wasn't just a parade of luxury; it was as troublesome, if not more so, than anything he'd ever gone through at D&L. The death Brian Vogel remained on his mind.

TWENTY-NINE

FROM THE MOMENT he first learned of his inheritance Sam wondered what it would do to his social life. Up to that point, his circle of good friends was relatively small. There were occasional cookouts or potlucks and the periodic birthday party, but that was the extent of their social activities.

By Christmastime that first year, Sam began to realize that those days were drawing to a close. Oh, he still had his old friends and they all still saw each other but there was a distance in some of those relationships. The money was creating a barrier. He wasn't sure how it did that, but people who would have teased him about this or that a year before were much more deferential now. He knew having the money was making him a local celebrity, but he hadn't counted on his good friends treating him like one. He wanted them to treat him like they always had.

What drove this change home to him was the housewarming party they had just before Christmas after they moved into the new house. Including Tracie's parents they had about a dozen guests, all from their pre-money social circle. Like most of their old gatherings, this one was a potluck. Nobody seemed to mind the arrangement, since this was what they had always done, or so Sam thought. At one point he'd gone to the bathroom and when he came out he heard one of the couples talking, unaware that he was behind them.

"I can't believe we had to bring food," the husband, Justin, said.

"With all their money, I'd expected it to be catered," his wife, Tanya, said.

Sam waited a bit before revealing himself so they wouldn't know he'd eavesdropped. Part of him wanted to ask what their problem was? They'd always done potlucks. Why should things be any different now? Simply because the Harmans could afford a fancy caterer didn't mean they had to have one, did it? Sam came away from the overheard conversation more than a little upset. Was this really what was going to be expected of them from here on out?

They had tried to keep things as normal as they could under the circumstances. When one of the kids was invited to a birthday party they kept to the same spending limits they always had for the present. They weren't trying to be cheap; they were just trying to keep things as normal for their kids as possible. Had they been naïve to think they could try to have normal lives as billionaires?

The rest of the evening reaffirmed Sam's suspicion that some of their old friendships were changing because of the money. One of the features of the new house was a nice playroom in the basement for the kids. The night of the housewarming party they'd invited their friends to bring their kids along for the evening. The older kids went with Sam Jr. to his new room while the others went downstairs. Sam hadn't heard much from the basement for a while, so he went to see if everything was okay. As he got to the door he found himself eavesdropping again, this time on the children.

"How come you guys don't have more video games?" Sam didn't recognize the voice.

"My folks won't let us have a lot," Kristen said.

"But you're rich," the boy protested. Now Sam recognized the voice. It was Nolan, a boy about Kristen's age. "You can have all the video games you want, can't you?"

Kristen sounded a bit uncertain. "I don't know," she said. "Mom and Dad said no."

Sam wasn't sure if he should walk in or not. Then Nolan went on. "But you have the money," he said. "Don't you get an allowance?"

"I get five dollars a week for helping Mom," Kristen said.

"That's it?" Nolan replied, surprised. "Your folks are cheap. If my parents were rich I'd get everything!"

That was enough for Sam. He walked in. "Everything ok?" he asked, as though he hadn't heard their conversation.

Nolan was startled. "Uh, hi Mr. Harman," he said.

"Mr. Harman?" Sam replied. "You've always called me Sam. Why the change?"

"Well...you're rich," Nolan said.

"So?" Sam said. "We're still the same people."

"You are?" Nolan asked, sounding skeptical.

"Sure," Sam said.

"Daddy," Kristen said. "Why don't we have more video games?"

"We've been over that, sweetheart," Sam replied. "Your mom and I don't think you should have too many games. All you'd do is play the Wii. That's not good for you."

It was an honest answer, but the look on Nolan's face told Sam that honesty wasn't going to persuade him. Not knowing what else he could say, Sam let the subject drop and left the room to head back upstairs. He passed his 'man-cave' and again found himself eavesdropping, this time on two of his golfing buddies, Lucas and Gabe.

"This is sweet," Lucas said. "I can't wait to come over here during baseball season."

"You think he's still going to invite us over to watch baseball?" Gabe asked. "I bet this is the only time we'll get to see the inside of this room."

"Why do you say that?" Lucas asked.

"Come on, man, rich people don't mix with the likes of us," Gabe said. "You manage a grocery store. I'm still at D&L. We're doing fine for ourselves, but we're nowhere near Sam's league. He can join any country club he wants. We'll never see him on a public course again."

"Sam didn't say anything about joining a country club," Lucas pointed out. "In fact, he once told me that even if he was rich he'd never do that."

"That's when he was broke," Gabe said. "It's easy to say things like that when you're just dreaming about having money. He'll join the country clubs, and then he'll be too good to play golf with us. You just wait and see, Lucas."

"I can't see him doing something like that," Lucas said.

"Wait until spring," Gabe said.

That night, as they were getting ready for bed, Tracie broached the subject. "I think things are changing," she said. "People weren't as…open as they used to be."

Sam told her about everything he'd overheard. "I thought we were doing this the right way," Sam said. "Now, I'm not so sure."

"I'm not, either," Tracie said. "Marty and Jan were fine and Mom and Dad were the same as they always are. But some of the others were kind of distant."

Sam lay down on the new king-size bed. "What are we going to do?" he asked. "I don't want to lose our friends."

"I don't either, honey," Tracie said. "Maybe...maybe we should try to include them more. You know, in the kinds of things we're dealing with now. Maybe you could take the guys on a golf trip."

That set off a light bulb in Sam's head. "That's fantastic!" he said. "I could get a plane and fly us down to Florida!"

"I could take the girls for a spa day," Tracie said, warming to her own idea. "Or maybe a shopping trip."

"Do both," Sam said. "And just to prove Gabe wrong, I'm having them over for opening day. Maybe the Vipers will actually win. Who knows?"

THIRTY

THE VERY NEXT day Sam started calling the guys to see if they'd be interested in the golf trip. The response was enthusiastic and Sam spent the rest of the day making the arrangements. They agreed to go in January. Sam was excited not only because of the time he'd get to spend with his buddies but also because he was going to play some of the best courses in the world. Now, Sam would be the first to admit that he wasn't exactly the world's best golfer so he bought several boxes of golf balls. Best to be prepared.

Before that, there was the matter of Christmas. This was the first in their new home and they were determined to make the most of it. At first they were going to treat it like any other Christmas, which they'd always kept manageable, from a budget point of view. But as the holidays grew closer, they both began to have second thoughts. They had all this money. Why shouldn't they enjoy it a little? By the third week of December, they had thrown their old rules out the window and splurged both on the kids and on each other.

Sam bought Tracie a diamond necklace. It

contained a 10 carat diamond surrounded by white gold in a teardrop shape. Tracie squealed with delight when she opened the package marked as being from Santa and noted that the jolly old elf had gone to Jared. Sam Jr. rolled his eyes at this, but a look from his father kept him from saying any more; Kristen and Noah still believed.

Sam was absolutely thrilled with his gifts. First, as he'd half-expected, was the complete James Bond collection on Blu-Ray. The only reason he hadn't bought it himself before now was because Tracie wouldn't let him. The second, though, was a real surprise. In keeping with the Bond theme, she bought him an Omega Seamaster wristwatch.

The kids made out pretty well, too. Sam Jr. was starting to really get into music so his parents got him a 32 gigabyte iPod touch with a docking station and speakers. They threw in a $100 gift card for the iTunes store. Kristen got an American Girl doll along with a matching bed for the doll, five outfits, five matching outfits for Kristen, and other accessories. She and the doll were inseparable for the rest of the day. Noah was starting to appreciate his father's *Star Wars* movie collection, so they bought him an Imperial Walker toy, an X-Wing fighter, several action figures and a Darth Vader helmet complete with voice-changer and prerecorded phrases. In addition, Santa brought each child an iPad Mini. Sam and Tracie got each other full size iPads, something they laughed over as neither was aware of what the other was doing.

Though they didn't go to church (Sam was still touchy on the issue) they kept family tradition by having Christmas dinner and gifts at Tracie's parents' house, the same one she and her brothers had grown up in. There would be a full house at the Pruitts this Christmas Day. Besides Tracie's parents, both of her brothers had come in with their families. Also in attendance were Carl's brother, Paul, and his wife, Diane, whose own children, a son and a daughter, weren't able to attend this year. In all, eighteen people would crowd around the table for Christmas dinner. With the passing of his own family years before, Sam had quickly come to cherish Christmas at the Pruitt home.

With help from Tracie and Diane, Mary put on a splendid feast and, as usual, Sam ate too much. By the time they congregated in the family room for presents he was ready for a nap. Instead, he sat down as the kids handed out the gifts. They were most efficient and within ten minutes everything was handed out. Before they started opening, Sam took a handful of envelopes out of his jacket pocket and handed them to Sam Jr. "Hand these out, too," he said.

The envelopes were quickly opened, followed by gasps of delight and disbelief. Each of Tracie's nieces and nephews got a brand-new $100 bill. Tracie's brothers and their wives and her aunt and uncle each got an all-expenses paid weekend in Las Vegas with $1000 in spending money. In addition, each of the women got a spa day, and the men got tickets to a monster truck rally coming to Port Mason in February. The kids were, of course, thrilled. Tracie's brothers and their wives protested that it was too much but they didn't protest very long. Diane was very quiet, and Paul looked downright hostile. Sam was about to ask him if something was wrong when his iPhone rang. He exchanged a few words with the caller and hung up. "Good news," he said. "Carl and Mary's gifts are here. Santa dropped them off outside."

He led the curious group out to the driveway. Sitting there was a brand-new Ford F-250 Super Duty 4X4 pickup truck with a big bow on the hood. Carl, a reserved man if ever there was one, let out a gasp as his jaw dropped. In the truck bed were two large boxes which, upon further examination, proved to be a new sixty-inch widescreen TV with home theater system. "Mom," Tracie whispered, "Why don't you take a look inside?"

"Registration and keys should be in it, Carl," Sam added.

"Wow, Grandpa," Noah said. "You must have been really, really good this year!"

"I don't think I've been that good," Carl said.

Sam watched in delight as his stunned in-laws approached the truck. Mary opened the passenger door and found two jewelry boxes in the seat. Each contained a diamond ring Tracie had picked out. Tracie had also thrown in a year's worth of spa treatments. As for the truck, Carl had talked about trading his in for a while, but he hadn't gotten around to it yet. Sam originally planned to take him to a dealership and letting him pick out what he wanted but Tracie pointed out that her father would probably not cooperate. This way was better. Besides, it was more fun.

Carl slowly got behind the driver's seat and took in

the interior. It was more truck than he would have ever bought on his own, and he had a pretty good idea how much had been spent. His first inclination was to refuse the gift, but when he saw the look of delight on his daughter's face he knew he couldn't do it. Besides, he really liked it. He saw Sam standing at the open driver's door. "Thank you, Sam," he said softly. "You really shouldn't have done it."

"Carl," Sam replied. "You and Mary have done so much for us over the years. I mean you helped us out of some real tight spots. You've been more generous to us than we deserve. We're not doing this to show off our money. We're doing this because we want to do something for you and I know you'd never let us simply give you a pile of money. Enjoy the truck and the TV. You deserve it."

Sam still didn't notice the scowl on Paul Pruitt's face.

After all the gifts were opened and the mess cleaned up, they returned to the dining room for dessert. It seemed like chance that Sam sat next to Paul, but it quickly became clear that this was not the case.

"You have fun buying everyone off?" Paul asked.

"What?" Sam replied.

"You heard me," Paul said. "What's the point of the rest of us buying gifts when you just swoop in with your money to buy us off?"

"What are you talking about?" Sam asked.

"I'm sure it doesn't mean anything to you to give people trips and cash," Paul said. "But to some of us that's serious money. You're throwing it around, and I don't like it."

"Well, I'm sorry you feel that way, Paul," Sam said, trying to be diplomatic. "We're not trying to 'buy' anyone."

"You're sorry I feel that way?" Paul said, indignantly. "You've been throwing your money around ever since you got it. Millions of dollars for the city, millions of dollars for charity, millions of dollars for some crazy space scheme. Nice new house with a swimming pool you can enclose in winter? Then you come here and try to buy us off with expensive gifts. What do you want from us, anyway?"

"Uncle Paul," Tracie said. "What's wrong with doing something nice for your family?"

"That's what you call this? Doing something nice?" Paul asked. "I call it showing off and I don't like it one bit."

"You know them better than that," Carl said to his brother.

"That's not how you and I were raised, Carl," Paul said. "They didn't earn their money like you and I did. But you got a nice new truck, didn't you? That all it takes to get you to go along with this?"

"I didn't ask for that truck," Carl said. "And you know it. Sam and Tracie did that on their own."

"And had to show it off in front of everybody," Diane said, speaking for the first time.

"It's Christmas," Sam protested. "It was a Christmas present."

"And you paid somebody to take part of their Christmas to drive it out here," Diane pointed out. "You think you can buy anyone and anything, don't you?"

"That's not true!" Sam barked. "If I wanted that kind of influence, I'd be giving money to the politicians. As for the guy who brought the truck down, he volunteered to do the job. I didn't ask him to do it and I didn't pay him a dime."

"Sure, he wants your future business," Paul said.

"Uncle Paul, that's enough!" Tracie snapped. "We tried to give everybody things we thought they would enjoy. We don't have any ulterior motives. We just thought you'd like it."

"Well I don't!" Paul said, shoving his envelope into Sam's hands. "Las Vegas? Really? I never wanted to go there."

"Then we can get you a trip to someplace you'd like to visit," Tracie said. "That's the whole point."

Sam could see that his wife was close to tears, and if there was one thing that set him off, it was people who made Tracie cry. He stood up from the table. "I didn't come here to insult or offend anybody," he said. "I think most of you understand that. I came here to celebrate Christmas with my family. Yes, I said my family. You've treated me like one of you ever since the first time Tracie brought me here. You've all been uncommonly generous to me and I have never forgotten that. This year for the first time I had a chance to return that consideration. To be as generous to you as you've all been to me. But if you'd rather be offended, just because I have money, there's nothing I'm going to say that will change your mind. So I think it would be best if I just went home. Tracie, I'll walk. It's not far. You and the kids stay. Merry Christmas, everyone."

With that, and despite many protests, he left the

house.

THIRTY-ONE

WHAT SHOULD HAVE been the nicest Christmas in Sam's life turned out to be the worst. As he walked home, he wondered what he'd done wrong. Okay, maybe presenting the truck in front of the whole family wasn't the brightest idea he'd ever had. But still, he'd meant well.

He didn't understand Paul's and Diane's hostility. They'd never acted like that before. Should he have gotten everyone a new car? He'd thought about it but in the end decided that would be going too far. Shoving his wealth into people's faces was the last thing he wanted to do.

At Sam's insistence, his security team had taken Christmas Day off so no one was waiting when he got to the end of his driveway. He used a specialized application on his iPhone to enter his security code, which deactivated the motion detectors on his property and allowed him to approach the house without the Sheriff's office being informed. Personally, he thought this much security was excessive but Stan Tyler insisted and he hadn't felt like arguing at the time, especially after he'd been hit in the head by that bottle.

He was maybe fifteen feet down the long driveway when he heard a car pulling up behind him. It was a rusty old Chevy that sounded like it was about to die. Sam was surprised to see his cousin Ted behind the wheel. He hadn't heard from Ted since his visit to the county jail. As the car came to a stop, the engine sputtered and conked out. A grinning Ted got out of the car. "I actually made it," he said. "I thought this thing was going to die about ten miles back. Merry Christmas!"

"Merry Christmas," Sam replied, without much feeling.

The cousins embraced. Sam didn't smell any booze or marijuana on him, but for once he didn't really care. He was too upset. Ted didn't fail to notice his distress and asked what happened. After pushing Ted's car to the side of the driveway, Sam led him up to the house and explained. "All I wanted to do was be generous to good people who've been good to me," he said. "Tell me, how that's a bad thing?"

"They're just jealous, man," Ted said. "They probably don't even realize it. Now me, I'd love a trip to Vegas. From what I hear that's the place to party."

Sam took Paul and Diane's envelope out of his pocket and handed it to his cousin. "Have a good time," he said.

"Are you serious?" Ted asked, opening the envelope.

"Totally," Sam said. "Take a friend, if you'd like."

Ted silently thumbed through the thousand in cash. "Dude, this is too fucking cool," he said.

"At least somebody will enjoy it," Sam said. "Here's the house."

"Look at that place!" Ted exclaimed upon getting a good look at it. "Sweet!"

"Thanks," Sam said. "Come on in, I'll show you around."

They entered the house. Chloe had started barking the moment they approached the front door. Once inside, she inspected Ted and jumped on him, demanding attention. Ted whistled when he saw the inside of the house. Sam explained about finding Susan and how she and Tracie had designed the interior. "Man, I'm glad you finally found her," Ted said. "I know it's what you always wanted. You going to see her today?"

"She went to California to visit my sister," Sam said. "She goes every year."

Sam led Ted down to the man-cave. "Now this is what I'm talking about!" Ted said, checking the place out. On the far wall was a eighty-inch widescreen TV, complete with a home theater system. To the right was a rack filled with movies and music. On the left was a full wet bar, which drew Ted's attention immediately. The only furniture was a leather couch and four bar stools. The back wall was dominated by a huge neon sign that said 'Vipers.'

"Still rooting for those bums, huh?" Ted asked as he stationed himself behind the bar. "You mind?"

"Not today," Sam said, seating himself at the bar. "There's beer in the fridge. Grab me one, will you?"

"Sure," Ted replied, pulling out a bottle of Foster's and opening it for Sam. "As for me, well, let's see what you've got back here."

Sam guzzled the beer as Ted rummaged through his liquor. Ted came up with a bottle of tequila. "Got any lime?" he asked.

"Beats me," Sam said. "Check upstairs, maybe Tracie has some in the kitchen."

Ted hurried to investigate as Sam guzzled down the beer and got himself another. As he opened the bottle, he wondered for a moment what Tracie would say if she saw this. She didn't object to alcohol, but she did object to drowning one's sorrows. She would probably be pretty upset with him. He decided that it was a good thing that she wasn't there because he didn't want to fight, and he did want to drink. He opened the bottle.

Within a couple of hours Sam had put away half a dozen bottles, which he lined up on the bar. Ted, for his part, found the lime he was looking for and was amusing himself with tequila shots. "Wish I had some coke," he said.

"There's some in the fridge," Sam said.

Ted nearly collapsed in hysterics. "Not soda, you moron!" he said.

"Oh, that," Sam said, wondering how he could have possibly misunderstood. He decided it didn't matter and opened yet another beer. He was starting to feel it now, which was fine with him. "I don't want that shit in my house."

"Hey, when's your old lady and the kids going to be home?" Ted asked.

"Dunno," Sam said. "The kids are spending the rest of the week at her folks' house. I don't know when Tracie's coming back."

"No kids for the rest of the week?" Ted replied. "Bet I know what you two will be up to!"

He started laughing again. Sam didn't find it that funny. He was still sober enough to know that Tracie would probably want nothing to do with him once she found out this. Again, though, he found that he really didn't care. Everything he'd been through in the last few months was starting to come crashing down on him, and he just wanted to shut it all out. The beer was helping with that.

"Hey, I've got an idea," Ted said. "Why don't you and Tracie come with me to Vegas?"

Sam thought a moment. "You know," he said. "I was about to say no thanks but you might be on to something there. Let me see if she's interested."

He called his wife. "Are you okay?" Tracie asked when she took the call.

"Great," Sam said. "So what happened after I left?"

"After you left, Dad lit into both of them," Tracie said. "I haven't seen him that angry since I was a kid. He actually swore. Dad doesn't to that. I had to send the kids into the other room. Mom had a few choice things to say, too. Dad told them to leave his house."

"Did he really?" Sam asked, surprised. "I don't want him to fight with his brother."

"He didn't, really," Tracie said. "He just told him off. Uncle Paul didn't say anything. When Dad told him to leave, he and Aunt Diane got up, got their stuff, and left. They didn't say a word."

"Wow," Sam said, taking another pull from his beer. "Hey, guess who's here?"

"Who?"

"Ted," Sam replied enthusiastically. "We're having a little party here."

"You're drinking?" Tracie asked.

"Yep," he said. "So if you see a broken-down car in the driveway, it's Ted's. Don't have it towed. On the other hand, maybe we should have it towed. I'll get him a decent car."

"Sweet, man," Ted said. "Thanks."

"Sam, I thought we weren't going to be giving Ted anything unless he cleaned up," Tracie said.

"Hey, he didn't bring any dope with him," Sam said.

"You know what I mean," Tracie said.

"Don't start with me, honey, not today," Sam said.

"Okay, I won't," she said, sounding reluctant.

"Ted had a great idea," Sam said. "Why don't the three of us go to Vegas? We'll have a great time."

"I don't think that's a very good idea," she replied. "I don't think I'd have a very good time with Ted around."

"Ah, lighten up," Sam said.

"What did you say?" Tracie asked, incredulously.

"I said lighten up," Sam said. "Ted's okay."

"Sam, you've been drinking, so I'm not going to try and make you see reason right now," she said. "I'm not coming home for a while. When I do, I want Ted gone and I want you sober, or at least sleeping it off. This isn't what we're supposed to be doing when there's trouble."

"But if feels so good," Sam said.

"It won't stay that way," Tracie said.

"After everything we've been though the last few months, I think I've earned the right to cut loose for a while," Sam said, starting to get angry. "You don't want to go, fine. Ted and I will go without you."

He hung up and opened another beer. "Ted, I'm going to call my charter service and get us a plane.

Get ready for Vegas."

THIRTY-TWO

SAM AWOKE SLOWLY. He opened his eyes; saw the light coming through a window, and immediately shut them again. His skull was pounding and he was pretty sure he smelled vomit somewhere nearby. Shielding his eyes, he opened them again and tried to make sense of his surroundings. He was in someone's living room. A half-eaten pizza lay in an open box on floor next to him, and there were empty liquor bottles everywhere.

As his eyes focused on the pizza box, it slowly dawned on him that he was lying on a sofa. He gently tried to get up but his head and stomach convinced him that wasn't a good idea, and he lay back down again. Near the pizza box, he saw some torn cloth which he realized was his shirt. Looking around some more, he saw his pants lying on a baby grand piano. Only then did it penetrate the fog in his brain that he was completely nude.

That realization made him jerk upright, which he regretted as a wave of pain and nausea soared through him. He didn't remember taking his clothes off. In truth, he wasn't sure how he'd gotten into this room, wherever it was.

He found his underwear nearby and put them on. Then, he mustered the strength to get up and retrieve his pants. It was slow going, but he finally made it. As he put them on he saw Ted passed out on another sofa. Unlike him, Ted was still fully clothed. Sam didn't have the heart to wake him.

Checking his pockets he found his wallet and saw that it was empty of cash. His credit and debit cards were still there as was his driver's license, so he hadn't been robbed. Then he remembered what happened to his money; he'd gambled it all away playing blackjack yesterday. In fact, he seemed to recall signing a line of credit with the casino and losing even more money.

The memories started to come back. He'd spent most of the day after Christmas gambling. He'd actually signed for a million-dollar line of credit in the casino and played high-stakes blackjack. If he remembered correctly, he'd lost over one hundred thousand dollars. Though he had plenty of credit left he decided to quit for a while when Ted showed up with a couple of girls he'd met in the bar.

The four of them started drinking together and one of the girls tried to get friendly with him. He seemed to remember keeping her at arm's length, but she was persistent and he finally allowed her to cuddle with him in the back of the limo. That was the last thing he remembered. What had he done?

Sam found himself in need of a bathroom. Getting up again was a little easier this time, but not by much. He looked around and followed a short hallway until he found what he was looking for. As he relieved himself he saw a woman lying in the bathtub. It was the woman who'd been hanging on Ted. She was completely nude. Embarrassed for gawking, Sam found a towel and laid it on her. The action woke her with a start.

"Ugh!" she exclaimed. "What the hell am I doing in my bathtub?"

"I have no idea," Sam replied. "In fact, I'm not even sure where I am."

"My house," the woman said. "What was your name again?"

"Sam," he said. "And you?"

"I'm Melissa," she said. "Can you help me out?"

Sam pulled her out of the tub, making sure the towel kept her covered. Melissa found the toilet and promptly threw up. Sam waited until she was done, then helped her back to her feet. "You okay now?" he asked.

"I'm better," Melissa said. "I wouldn't say okay, but better. Where's Jackie?"

"Who?" Sam asked.

"Jackie, the girl who spent the whole night trying to get into your pants," Melissa said. "She's a friend of mine."

"I have no idea," Sam said. "We'd better look around."

Jackie was found in Melissa's bedroom, sleeping. To Sam's relief, she was fully clothed. That still didn't explain what had happened to his clothes, but at least he hadn't slept with her. "Jackie was so high that we put her to bed early," Melissa said. "You seemed relieved about that."

"I'm married," Sam explained. "I don't want to..."

"Don't worry, you didn't," Melissa said.

Sam sighed in relief. Melissa slipped on a robe and led Sam back to the living room where Ted was still out cold. "Look at this mess," Melissa said, sitting down. "At least the furniture is still intact."

"I can help you clean up," Sam said. "Listen I, uh, have to ask you something. It's kind of personal."

"You've already seen me naked," Melissa said. "That's pretty personal."

"I woke up without my clothes on," Sam explained. "And I don't remember how that happened."

Melissa laughed. "You were pretty drunk," she said.

"Yeah," Sam affirmed.

"I seem to remember stripping for you and your friend."

"Stripping?" Sam asked, shocked. "Why?"

"I think I must have told you that I used to dance," Melissa continued. "You guys asked for a show and I was drunk enough to do it. That's how I wound up naked. As for you, you decided to put on a show yourself."

"I stripped for you and Ted?" Sam asked, dumbfounded.

"Yeah," Melissa laughed. "You ripped your shirt apart and everything. It was pretty funny."

"Oh, man," Sam moaned. "I've been acting like an idiot."

"This is Las Vegas," Melissa said. "People act like idiots here all the time. Don't worry about it."

"Thanks," Sam said. He hoped Melissa was remembering the evening's events correctly. The last thing he wanted was to be unfaithful to his wife. How was he going to explain this to Tracie? Would she forgive him? He had no idea, and part of him didn't want to find out. But he knew it was time to face up to what he'd done, and that's what he was going to do.

Sam went over to Ted and shook him. "Wake up, party boy," he said. "Time to go home."

Ted didn't stir. "Ted?" Sam said. "Ted, come on, man."

Ted still didn't move. Sam lightly slapped his face. His skin felt cold. "Ted!" Sam exclaimed, slapping him a little harder but still to no effect. He checked for a pulse.

There was none.

"No!" Sam said. "Call 911! Now!"

THIRTY-THREE

LATE THAT AFTERNOON, Sam was released from the Clark County Detention Center, his silent wife at one side and Aaron Charlton on the other. If this had happened back home, the reporters would have been all over them. Here, Sam was not well known, so they were able to leave the jail in peace. Sam's head hung low as the three of them entered a waiting limousine that took them back to Caesar's Palace, where he still had a suite. He barely noticed his surroundings as Tracie led him into the suite and sat him down on a sofa. Aaron tried to talk to him about his legal situation, but it was clear that his client wasn't listening right then, so he retired to his own room.

Once he was gone Tracie sat next to Sam on the sofa. As she looked at her husband, she found herself at a crossroads. She was furious with him for his behavior over the last two days, and a good part of her wanted to let him know precisely how angry she was. But she could see his grief over Ted's death, and that brought out her nurturing side. She couldn't decide whether to hug him, or slap him across the face. The two options were running neck and neck.

Sam was in shock over the events of the last few hours. Once the police arrived, everyone in the house was arrested on suspicion of drug possession. Sam had watched from the backseat of a squad car as his cousin's body was brought out on a stretcher and loaded into a coroner's van. He only dimly remembered being questioned by the police, processed at the jail, and being put in a cell with several other men. They'd allowed him his phone call, and that was when he called Tracie and told her everything. She and Aaron reached Las Vegas in short order and got him out of jail.

Finally, Tracie spoke. "Are you hungry?" she asked.

Sam said nothing. "Sam, talk to me," she said. "Please?"

"What am I supposed to say?" Sam replied. "It's bad enough that I've been acting like an ass, but Ted died because of me. If I hadn't brought him out here..."

He broke down in tears. Tracie put her arms around him. She would get on his case later.

In the end, the Las Vegas authorities cleared Sam of any wrongdoing and said he was free to go. He had his lawyer make the arrangements to have Ted's body taken back to Port Mason for burial while he and Tracie flew home. He and Tracie passed much of the flight in silence. They had yet to discuss Sam's behavior after the incident at Christmas. Actually, they'd said very little to each other at all.

They flew private charter, sitting on opposite sides of the cabin. Sam was thinking about Ted and everything they'd been through together. He was also thinking about his marriage and how badly he'd damaged it. He didn't want to lose Tracie. He didn't want to lose his kids. She hadn't said anything about leaving him, but it was on his mind. Why had he done it? There was no good answer.

About half an hour from home, Tracie finally spoke. "Can we talk now?" she asked. "This silence is driving me nuts."

Sam swiveled his chair to face her. "Somehow, I don't think 'I'm sorry' is going to cut it, is it?"

"It goes a long way," Tracie replied. "Since I know you mean it."

"I am sorry," Sam said. "For everything. You can light into me if you want. It's what I deserve."

"Yes, it is," Tracie agreed. "But I'm not going to do it. I do have a question for you, though."

"What is it?"

"Why?" she asked.

Sam had no reply, which was fortunate for him, because his wife didn't really want to hear the answer. "I have been proud to be your wife for fifteen years," she said. "And I'll tell you why. It's because you've always been a good man. You didn't drink too much; you didn't run around with the wrong crowd; and you were a good example for our children. In two days you destroyed all of that. I'm madder at you now than I am at Uncle Paul and that's saying something.

"Before you say anything," she continued. "Let me tell you why I'm so mad. It's not because you went to Vegas with Ted. It's not because of all the drinking I'm sure you did. It's not even, and I can't believe I'm saying this, because you threw away a hundred thousand dollars gambling. I can live with those things. What I'm really upset about was that you didn't turn to me when you were upset and, more importantly, you didn't turn to God."

Again, Sam wisely kept his mouth shut. "When we gave our lives to Jesus, we agreed to pray together about our problems," Tracie said. "You didn't do that. You didn't even give it a chance. Instead you started drinking and listening to someone you had no business listening to. Then, instead of staying home and facing your problems, you ran away. You ran away from me."

Now she was crying. Sam took her hand. Tracie allowed him to but was still crying. Sam felt like crying himself, which wasn't something he often did, but he kept control of himself because he had something to say.

"I'm not going to argue with you," he said. "Because you're absolutely right about everything."

Tracie looked at him with some skepticism, but at least she was looking at him. "I'm not trying to tell you what you want to hear," Sam continued. "I'm telling you the truth. I'm guilty of everything you said. I ran away. I wish I hadn't, and not just because of what...what happened to Ted."

"Why?" Tracie asked. "Why did you do it?"

"I don't know if I have a good answer for that," Sam said. "I can't even say that it seemed like a good idea at the time. Everything just got to me. It wasn't just what happened with your uncle, it was everything that's happened since Anderson Braddock showed up. I felt like it was all crashing down on me. I'm not saying that as an excuse, it's just what happened. And if you think for a minute that I don't feel like a piece of shit over it, you're dead wrong."

Now it was Tracie's turn to be silent. "I'm sorry," Sam said. "I know that's not enough but it's all I can say. I'm sorry and I love you. All I wanted to do today was get back to you, even if you told me you never wanted to see me again."

"Oh, honey, I'm not going to do that," Tracie said, grabbing him into a fierce hug. "I want the man I married back. I think he is."

"You're right,"

They prayed for guidance. They prayed that her aunt and uncle would get over their anger. They prayed for each other and their children. They prayed for Ted, for his salvation. When they were done they held each other for the rest of the flight.

THIRTY-FOUR

TRACIE FORGAVE SAM, but he was a long way from forgiving himself. He should have known better. He should never have taken Ted to Las Vegas in the first place. What had he been thinking? He might as well have bought Ted drugs at home and been done with it.

The worst part was having to call his aunt and uncle and breaking the news to them. Sam hadn't spoken to his Uncle Brian in years. He'd called and left messages from time to time but they weren't returned. The situation saddened him, but he really didn't know what else he could do about it.

This lack of contact had nothing to do with Ted, and everything to do with a rift between Brian and Sam's late father, Kevin, going back to a dispute over their mother's estate. The two brothers had vehemently disagreed over how to dispose of her assets. Kevin was executor of the will and, in that capacity, decided to sell off her rental properties and split the cash with Brian. Brian didn't want to do that and accused Kevin of trying to loot the estate. A terrible series of arguments ensued, and at one point Brian tried to contest the will. When it was all over, the two brothers never spoke again.

Though not part of the fight between his father and uncle, Sam didn't feel comfortable talking to Brian, and as a consequence, didn't have occasion to speak to him until his own mother's death. On that occasion, Brian called him and asked if he would be welcome at the funeral. As it had only been a year since the end of the estate fight Kevin still wanted nothing to do with his brother, and Sam had to tell him not to come. That was the last time Sam spoke to his uncle. When Kevin Harman died a few years later, Sam tried to reach out to Brian but never heard back.

When Sam tried to call about Ted, he again got his uncle's answering machine. He certainly didn't reveal Ted's passing that way so he called his cousin Katherine, Ted' sister. He dreaded that call even more than calling his uncle. Though they hadn't been close in years, Sam was always fond of Ted's younger sister. Having to tell her that Ted was gone was very nearly unbearable. Katherine was naturally devastated, but despite Sam's explanation of how Ted wound up in Las Vegas, she refused to blame him, saying that Ted had been on this road for a long time and that something like this was bound to happen. It was poor Katherine who had to break the news to her parents.

One week after Ted's death, Sam sat in the front row at Roselawn Cemetery as his cousin was laid to rest. Next to him were Ted's parents, Brian and Renee, and his sister, Katherine. Tracie sat to his left, holding his hand tightly as Marty Lovell led the small gathering in the final prayers. Sam could barely pay attention to his pastor and friend, his eyes focused on the casket before him and his thoughts consumed by the memory of his cousin.

Sam refused to leave the cemetery until the casket was placed in the vault and lowered into the grave. Only then did he stand up, toss a flower into the grave, and walk slowly towards the funeral home limousine. Tracie still held his hand and walked beside him. Neither said anything. Once they were in the limo with Ted's family and driving out of the cemetery, Sam tried to speak but no words came. He had no idea what he was supposed to say.

"You arranged everything beautifully, Sam," Aunt Renee said. "Thank you."

"Yeah...I..." he looked at his aunt and uncle. What was he supposed to say?

For his part, Brian Harman stared out the window as the car took them home. Sam could see a solitary tear run down the face that reminded him so much of his father. Like Kevin, Brian was a reserved man and not given to emotional displays, except under the most extreme duress. Losing his son, even after many years' estrangement, was taking its toll. It was a pain Sam prayed he'd never have to understand.

Katherine, who'd been crying since the funeral home service, leaned across and threw her arms around Sam. "Stop blaming yourself," she sobbed. "You didn't do anything wrong."

"Yes I did," Sam replied. "I took him there. I should have known better. I did know better."

Aunt Renee was crying again, too. "He could just as easily have died here," she said.

"But he didn't," Sam said. "And it's my fault.

Nothing can change that."

"No, nothing can change that," his uncle said, still staring out the window.

"Brian!" Renee scolded.

"Sam's right," Brian Harman said. "Nothing can change what happened to Ted. And you're right, he could have just as easily died here. And maybe if we'd known more about addiction when Ted was young, we could have gotten him to turn himself around. And maybe, just maybe, if he hadn't seen me smoking pot all those years ago, he wouldn't have been so interested in trying it for himself."

"What?" Sam asked. "What are you talking about?"

"Didn't you ever wonder how Ted got started?" Brian asked, looking at Sam for the first time.

Renee looked like she knew the whole story. Sam, Tracie and Katherine sat there dumbfounded as Brian told them the tale. "Renee and I were full-fledged hippies in the late sixties," he said. "We lived out of a VW bus, protested the war, protested the establishment and got high a lot. Hell, we were at Woodstock. We didn't get married until after we found out Renee was pregnant with Ted. Even after that, we didn't give up the lifestyle for a while.

"Eventually, though, we both realized that being anti-establishment was all fine and well, but it didn't pay the bills," he continued. "So I got a real job, we found a house, and settled into middle-class life like your dad. But I didn't give up everything. I tried to keep it quiet, just doing it every once in a while after the kids were in bed. One night when he was fifteen, Ted spied on me. I didn't know it until he was caught that first time. When I demanded to know where he got the idea of smoking pot, he said he got it from me."

"It's why we had so much trouble getting him to stop," Renee added. "He would just say he wasn't doing anything we hadn't done ourselves."

"In fact, he'd been stealing from my stash," Brian said. "Just a little bit here and there so I wouldn't notice. After that, I quit. It wasn't worth watching Ted destroy himself. Whenever I tried to challenge him to quit, he just laughed at me. He'd say there would be plenty of time for that when he was an old man."

"You know how stubborn he could be," Renee said. "The more we pushed one way, the more he'd go the other just to spite us. Sam, we tried everything."

"I know," Sam said. "I tried too."

"You see, there's plenty of blame to go around," Brian said. "Yes, the trip to Vegas was the last straw for him, but you didn't know that. No one could have known what would happen. And it could just as easily have happened here. You blaming yourself isn't going to bring him back."

"It's not that easy," Sam said.

"I know it's not," Brian said. "Because I'm going through the same thing. We'll both carry this for the rest of our lives. What we're going to have to do is learn to live with it. If you're half the man Kevin was, you will."

"What about you?" Sam asked.

Brian went back to looking out the window. "I've been learning to live with it for almost twenty years," he said. "I guess I'll have to keep on learning."

THIRTY-FIVE

A FEW DAYS later, Sam went back to work. When he saw Sandy Ward in his outer office he immediately knew something was wrong, and not just her shared grief over Ted's death. "What's going on?" he asked.

"It's Bill Dodd again," she said. "He knows about Ted."

"Oh, no," Sam said. "That means the whole city knows. Get Jenna down here. Aaron, too. We've got work to do."

Sam and Tracie sat down in his office with Jenna Vanderberg and Aaron Charlton to listen to Bill Dodd's latest podcast. To say that it was unkind was a gross understatement.

"Well, friends, Sam Harman's at it again," Dodd said. "This time, he's tried to cover up a post-Christmas adventure in Las Vegas that cost him the life of his own cousin. You heard it right, folks, a man died and Harman tried to whitewash it, but our investigators have uncovered the truth and we're going to tell you everything. More after the break."

Tracie paused the playback "Are you sure you want

to hear this?" she asked Sam.

"I need to," Sam said. They resumed the playback.

"This is a sad tale, folks," Dodd said. "For reasons we don't yet know, Sam Harman chartered a flight to Vegas on Christmas day for himself and his cousin, Ted. Ted Harman was twice convicted for drug possession and had an arrest record going back to high school for drug-related offenses. In fact, his last turn in the county jail was the result of his copping a plea and turning in two marijuana growers. Who knows what else he was up to?

"Let's get back to the main story. Sam and Ted had themselves a fine old time in Sin City," Dodd continued. "According to our sources, Sam blew over one hundred thousand dollars gambling. That may be small change to someone like him, but that's still a lot of money to regular working folks like you and me. Ted seemed to prefer spending his time looking for drugs and loose women. On the morning of the 27th, Sam found his cousin dead in a woman's home where they'd apparently spent the night. The woman, one Melissa Aubrey, is a former exotic dancer with two arrests of her own for prostitution. We'll let you folks do the math on that one."

Sam stopped the playback and looked at Tracie. "I swear I didn't know she was a prostitute," he said. "And I swear I didn't sleep with her."

"I believe you," Tracie said.

"We need to hear it all, Sam," Aaron said.

He resumed the playback. "When the police arrived they arrested Sam and put him in the local jail, but guess what? His high-priced lawyer showed up and he was back on the street within hours. According to the Las Vegas authorities they had no evidence to charge Sam so he got off scot-free. Wonder how much money that cost him?"

"Why that son of a--" Aaron began, but a gesture from Sam silenced him.

"Now, I can't prove that any money changed hands, folks," Dodd said. "But I also can't prove that it didn't, so again, I'll let you be the judge. As for this lady of the evening, we did manage to get hold of her earlier, but the only thing she was willing to tell us was that Sam Harman didn't have sex with anybody at her house. Then she hung up. I should add that Miss Aubrey is facing a cocaine possession charge herself. I guess she didn't make enough of an impression on Sam for him to get her off the hook, too. Looks like Sam didn't do quite as good a job of cleaning up after himself as you would think.

"What a blow to the image Sam Harman has tried to project," he continued. "He's wanted us to think he's an honest, family man who supports his church and helps those less fortunate. Well, we see now that he has another side. Your calls, after the break."

"I suppose this bastard is already off the air?" Sam asked.

"Sam, your language," Tracie said.

"Sorry," Sam replied. "But I've had it with this guy. I--"

The intercom buzzed "Sam," Sandy said. "The school called, they're holding for you on line two."

"I hope one of the kids isn't sick," Tracie said.

"I hope that's all it is," Sam said, picking up the phone. "Sam Harman."

"Mr. Harman, this is Paige Kochman, the principal

here at Blessed Savior's," was the reply. "I'm going to have to ask either you or Mrs. Harman to come down here and pick up Sam Jr."

"What's the problem?" Sam asked.

"He punched another boy in class today," she said. "We're going to have to suspend him for the rest of the week."

Within an hour Sam and Tracie were at Blessed Savior's. Sam Jr. looked sullen and angry as he was led into the principal's office. "Would you like to tell your parents what happened, or should I?" Paige Kochman asked.

When the boy didn't reply, the principal took the initiative. "According to his teacher, Richie Crawford made some rude comments about you, Mr. Harman," Kochman said. "Neither your son nor Richie will give me the specifics of what was said, but immediately after the comments were made, Sam Jr. hit him. His mother took him to the emergency room because we think his jaw was broken."

Sam looked at his son in astonishment. Yes, he'd grown quite a bit in the last few months but he hadn't suspected Sam Jr. of being that strong. "You broke a kid's jaw?" Sam Sr. asked.

"He had it coming," his son said.

"Samuel Brian Harman Junior, don't you dare say things like that," Tracie snapped. "There are going to be some serious consequences for this."

"What did he say, son?" Sam asked.

Sam Jr. shook his head. "You can tell us," Sam said.

"I'll—I'll tell you, Dad," Sam Jr. said. "But that's

it."

"You don't get to negotiate this," Tracie said. "You'll tell all of us, and you'll do it now. You're in enough trouble as it is. Don't make it worse."

"Wait a minute, honey," Sam said. "Maybe we should do it his way."

"Sam..." Tracie began.

"It'll be okay," Sam said. "Would you both give us a minute?"

Mrs. Kochman and a very reluctant Tracie left the office. "Okay, let's have it," Sam said. "What did Richie say?"

"He...he said you ran around with hookers," Sam Jr. said. "And that it was all over the radio."

"Looks like Bill Dodd has a wider audience than I thought," Sam said.

Sam Jr. looked stunned. "It's true?"

"No," Sam said. "Not exactly. I'll explain in a minute. Is that all he said?"

"No," Sam Jr. said softly. "He said...he said Mom must be..."

It was clear that his son didn't want to repeat this part, but Sam wanted to know. "Just between us," he said. "I promise."

"He said that Mom must be a lousy lay if you're going to hookers," Sam Jr. said. "That's when I did it. That's when I hit him. I would have hit him more if Mr. Matheny hadn't pulled me off him. I'll do it again if I see him. He can't go around saying things like that about my mother."

Sam embraced his son. "I'm sorry you had to hear that," he said. "Now it's my turn to tell you something."

With that Sam related the entire tale of his trip with Ted to Las Vegas, even the part about his doing a striptease. His son chuckled a bit at that part of the story, but sobered quickly when Sam finally gave him the details of Ted's death. "I did some very stupid things," Sam said. "And my cousin is dead because of it. But that doesn't give people the right to go around saying things like that about your mother. I can't condone you breaking another kid's jaw, but I'm not going to condemn you, either. If somebody had said something like that to me, I'd probably want to hit him too."

"So what are you going to do with me?" Sam Jr. asked.

"I don't know," Sam said. "I'll have to talk to your mother about that. Don't worry, I'll keep my promise. I won't tell your mom what was said. Part of me is proud of you for standing up for her. I'll try not to make it too bad."

"Okay," Sam Jr. said.

Sam called Tracie and the principal back into the office. "Tell the Crawford family that we'll foot all his medical bills," Sam said.

"I'm sure they'll be glad to hear it, Mr. Harman," Kochman said. "But Sam is going to have to apologize to Richie. And Richie is going to have to apologize to him, too. They're still in the same class, after all, and they'll have to get along from now on."

"As long as Richie keeps his mouth shut about things he doesn't understand, Sam will keep his fists to himself," Sam said. "Right, son?"

"Okay, Dad," Sam Jr. said. He clearly wasn't happy about it, but he seemed to understand that this was how it would have to be.

"And I expect there will be punishment at home?" Kochman said.

"That's our business," Sam said before Tracie could say anything. She didn't look too happy with him for undercutting her like that, but in the interest of presenting a united front didn't say anything. Sam would do his best to explain it later without breaking his promise to his son.

One thing was certain; Bill Dodd had a lot to answer for.

THIRTY-SIX

SAM KEPT HIS word and did not reveal what his son had told him. When his irritated wife pressed for details all he would say was that his son 'defended your honor' and that, in his opinion, suspension from school was sufficient punishment. Though she tried, Tracie couldn't get anything more out of either her husband or son and eventually she gave up. She did not, however, agree that suspension was all the punishment Sam Jr. deserved. Violence was unacceptable under any circumstances, and Sam Jr. was grounded for a month. To make the sentence a bit more bearable, and because he couldn't help but be proud of his son, Sam secretly bought him a $100 iTunes gift card.

The next item on Sam's agenda was the planned golf trip to Florida. Because of Ted's death, Sam seriously considered postponing or canceling the trip altogether but Tracie talked him out of it. The trip would be good for him, she argued, so why shouldn't he go? As usual, he admitted she was right. He took his friends to Florida during the third week of January.

The four-day trip had been very busy, so there wasn't a lot of conversation on the chartered flight home. Most of the guys dozed in their seats. Sam was at his laptop, having received the latest version of the film script from Scott Willably. He was reading and making notes when Marty sat down in the chair opposite him.

"Sam, you really outdid yourself on this trip," his friend and pastor said. "How much did it set you back?"

"You'll never know, Marty," Sam replied, grinning.

"I thought you'd say that," Marty said. "Still, I want to thank you. This was really very generous of you."

"I did it because I wanted to," Sam said. "Maybe after I finish shooting The Path, we can all go again. We can hit the California courses this time."

"Sound great," Marty said. "But if you don't mind, I'd like to talk about you for a minute. How are you really doing with all this?"

"All things considered, not so bad. Sam said. "The whole thing with Ted...I never thanked you for doing his funeral. You did a great job."

"Thank you," Marty said. "You still blame yourself for what happened, don't you?"

Sam sighed. "Yeah, I suppose so," he said. "I'm the one who took him there. I'm responsible."

"Yes you are," Marty said, which surprised Sam. "I'm not going to dispute that or condone what you did. What I'm concerned with is how this is going to affect you from now on. We all sin, Sam, we all make mistakes. What I think you're forgetting is that God forgives sin, but we have to go Him and ask for that forgiveness. And as you do that you have to forgive yourself."

"I don't know if I can do that yet, Marty," Sam said.

"I feel such...such great guilt. I loved him like a brother and I...I…"

He was close to breaking down. "You did what you did, but you don't have to keep punishing yourself for it," Marty said. "I can tell you're not ready to forgive yourself, but I want you to ask God to forgive you. He will because Jesus already paid the price for your sin. Go to Him, Sam. Right now."

Sam did as he said, bowing his head and praying silently. Marty put a hand on his shoulder and prayed for him as well. When they were done Sam discovered that the minister wasn't quite done with him.

"Your life seems to be turning into a larger-than-life adventure," Marty said. "I've often wondered, though, what you've been doing for God in all this. You haven't been back to church since that business with Art and Owen."

"I wasn't sure if that was a good idea after what happened," Sam said.

"Of course it is," Marty said. "You belong there. People still ask me when you're coming back. We miss you. And don't forget your kids. They need to be in church. You all do. The longer you stay away the greater the chance that you'll walk away from God. Going to Las Vegas like you did proves my point. You need to come back."

"You're right," Sam said. "Okay, I'll talk to Tracie about it, but I'm sure she'll be on board."

"I think you're right," Marty said. "When you come back we'll get you plugged right back in again. It'll be good for you and for the church."

"I'm still planning on resurfacing the parking lot,"

Sam said. "And if there are any other projects you need funded, just let me know."

"I'm not talking about money," Marty said. "You've been more than generous and I appreciate that. But what I'd like to see you do is get more involved with the church. You should already know that being part of a church is more than showing up on Sunday and dropping money in the collection plate. It's a commitment to a larger family, the family of the Lord. I guess what I'm really driving at is that I'm concerned about your walk with God. Have you been reading your bible like you used to? Are you praying like you used to?"

The look on Sam's face answered Marty's question for him. "That's what I was afraid of," he said. "You've surrounded yourself with your wealth and with material things. You spend thousands of dollars on trips like this. I'm not saying you shouldn't enjoy your money, but you need to be mindful of God's desires for you. You have to keep your focus on spiritual things, and I don't mean by giving more money to the church. God wants your time and talents as well as your treasure."

"I'm making that movie," Sam pointed out. "It's a Christian film with a Christian message."

"I've read the script," Marty said. "And I think it's a great idea. But let's both be honest. You're not just doing it to spread the gospel. You're doing it because you've always wanted to make movies, and now you can afford to do it. God needs to be at the center of everything you do, especially now. My question to you is: is He? Are you putting Him in the center?"

Sam didn't say anything. "I'm not trying to rebuke

you, Sam," Marty said. "I don't think this has happened intentionally. My chief concern is for your immortal soul. You know that, don't you? I want to see you in heaven someday, and I don't want your money jeopardizing that. Do you understand me?"

Sam nodded thoughtfully. "I understand," he said. "And you're right, we've been falling away. We didn't mean to."

"I know," Marty said. "But now that you understand what's been happening, what are you going to do about it?"

"I'm not sure," Sam admitted. "I need to talk to Tracie about this."

"Jan already is," Marty said. "I admit it; we kind of ganged up on you. I imagine they've already had their conversation on this topic. We've both been concerned."

"I might have known," Sam said. "What do you think I should do?"

"Honestly?" Marty replied. "I think you should go on a mission trip. You've funded several, and it's appreciated, but I think it's time for you to step it up to the next level. We still have spots open for our trip to the Dominican Republic in April. You should go. Ideally, you and Tracie should both go, but I know that might be a problem with the kids."

The suggestion took Sam by surprise. Yes, he'd paid for every mission trip the church had sponsored since coming into his inheritance, but he'd never given any thought to going himself. He remembered, in a time before the money, Tracie mentioning that she'd like to go someday, when they could afford it. Now they could. He would have to think about this.

Friends of his had gone on these trips and come back with some amazing stories of conversions, acts of faith, and giving amongst the poorest of the poor. Maybe Marty was right, maybe it was time for him to step up.

They talked about the possibilities for the rest of the trip home. When they landed, their wives were waiting for them at the general aviation terminal. Tracie was talking to Jan when Sam walked in. "How did it go?" she asked.

"Great," Sam said. "We even met Arnold Palmer."

"I meant your talk with Marty," Tracie said.

"It was good," Sam said. "He told me some things I needed to hear. How'd you do with Jan?"

"Really well," she replied. "Are you ready to go back to church?

"Yeah," he said. "You?"

"Definitely," she said. What do you think about the mission trip?

"I think we should go," Sam said. "How about you?"

"I'm in," she said. "I already talked to Mom and Dad about taking the kids. It's all arranged on this end."

"Okay," he said. "Let's do it."

THIRTY SEVEN

SAM'S MISADVENTURE IN Las Vegas could have destroyed his marriage. Instead, it strengthened it. They were virtually inseparable for weeks, which reminded him of the early days of their relationship. He'd missed the togetherness of those early days and was thrilled to have that feeling again. They took a bit of a step back from their busy lives and simply enjoyed being with each other. The pain and guilt over Ted's death slowly began to ease.

One thing that still bothered Sam was the incident that prompted the whole mess; the clash with Tracie's aunt and uncle. The incident weighed heavily on Sam into February. To make matters worse, Carl and Paul hadn't spoken since. This was very troubling since the brothers had always been close. Sam didn't want to drive a wedge into his wife's family

The situation hurt Tracie even more than Sam. She and her uncle had always been close. Though they teased each other mercilessly, Sam knew there was a deep bond of love between them. To see that relationship threatened because of his money was, to say the least, upsetting. And what if somebody died waiting to make things right? Sam learned that lesson from the spat between his own father and uncle. He was determined not to see it happen to the Pruitt family.

In early February Sam decided it was time to straighten things out. Tracie was in meetings with several of the charitable foundations they supported, so Sam left the office early and drove for an hour and a half until he reached the small town of Collier. Paul and Mary lived on farmland just outside the tiny burg. At one time they had farmed nearly 1,000 acres but decided a few years earlier that it was time to retire. They rented almost all of their acreage to other farmers and lived quite comfortably from the profits and their other investments.

Though retired as a farmer, Paul Pruitt found plenty around their property to keep him busy. They still raised a few head of cattle and kept chickens for their eggs, which were normally distributed to the family. With both of their children living out of state, Sam wondered who was getting the eggs now.

When Sam pulled into their long driveway he saw Paul coming out of his workshop. In addition to farming Paul was a very good carpenter and had made a few of pieces of furniture for Sam and Tracie over the years including a beautiful kitchen table, which they still used today, and a pair of end tables, which now graced Sam's man-cave.

When he saw Sam's car he stopped cold. Sam pulled over to the side of the driveway, as he always did, and got out. "What are you doing here?" Paul asked as Sam approached.

"Came to talk to you," Sam replied.

"We've got nothing to say to each other," Paul said.

"Actually, we have plenty to say to each other," Sam said. "And you know it. Believe it or not, I come in peace."

"Where's your wife?" Paul asked.

"At the office," Sam said. "She doesn't know I'm here."

"Why are you here?"

"To see if we can work out this problem you seem to have with me," Sam said.

"You can't buy me off, Sam," Paul said.

"I left my checkbook at home," Sam said. "I'm not here to bribe you."

Paul looked like he was thinking hard. Finally, he said, "Well you came all this way you might as well come into the house. Diane probably has coffee on."

Diane looked as shocked to see him as Paul had but didn't react with any hostility. They sat around the kitchen table over coffee. Diane offered him a slice of pie. Though it pained him to do it, he turned it down. Both Tracie and his doctor had been getting on to him about his weight and eating habits.

"Okay, so what is it you want with us?" Paul asked.

"I want to put things right between us," Sam said. "The way we all left things at Christmas...we can't let it stand. Tracie's unhappy and so am I. We always got along before. Something about me having money has really offended you. I'm not entirely clear what I did wrong but I think maybe you should tell me."

"Throwing money around the way you do and you have the nerve to ask me that?" Paul asked. "Look at yourself. Fancy suit, BMW, how much did that overcoat cost you? And how about that diamond necklace you put around Tracie's neck? And that fancy watch you're wearing? Buying your kids designer clothes and shoes? Constantly being on the news for giving money away to this and that? It's sickening."

"Why?" Sam asked. "Because I'm taking advantage of what I have or because I didn't share it with you?"

"I don't want your filthy money," Paul said.

"Hank Curtis was a ruthless businessman," Sam replied. "But he made his money relatively honestly. None of his businesses were illegal."

"At least he earned it," Paul said. "Unlike you."

"It's my fault he left it to me?" Sam said. "I never even heard of him until his will came out. I didn't ask for it. I still don't understand why you're so hostile, Paul."

"Sam," Diane said. "I understand you didn't ask for this. But those expensive gifts you gave out at Christmas were just too much."

"They were obscene," Paul added.

"Why, because you couldn't match them?" Sam replied. "And if we'd kept to the same kinds of gifts we used to give, what would you have said?"

Neither had a reply for that. "Let's say I'd kept a much lower profile and not spent anything," Sam said. "You'd probably think I was a cheapskate, not sharing with anyone. And as for the publicity around my giving money away, that was only for the stuff I couldn't keep quiet. We've given a lot more that wasn't reported in the press. Believe it or not, we do those things because we think they're the right thing to do, not for personal glory or publicity.

"Now maybe hitting Carl and Mary with that stuff with the rest of the family around wasn't the best decision we could have made," Sam admitted. "But we gave it to them because we wanted to. Because we knew they'd probably never get them for themselves even though they can afford it.

"Let me ask you something," Sam said. "Do either of you have any idea how generous Carl and Mary have been with us over the years?"

They shook their heads. "They've helped us out of a couple of serious financial jams," Sam said. "We probably could have managed something on our own, but they gave us the money to solve those problems. We didn't ask them to, and it wasn't easy for me to accept the money. But they did it out of the goodness of their hearts. All I was trying to do was show them the same kindness they always showed me. If that really offends you, I'm sorry."

Paul and Diane were silent but Sam could tell they were at least thinking about what he'd said. That was at least some kind of progress, he reflected. He didn't share his real opinion; that they'd decided upfront to condemn him for the money no matter what he did. It saddened him to see people he'd never thought capable of such base behavior acting like this. He could see their likely point of view, though. They'd worked hard all their lives and were now able to sit back and enjoy the fruits of that labor with the satisfaction that they'd 'made it' on their own. Having had to do it the hard way must have made it difficult to see someone they knew, someone they'd treated like family, have it drop into his lap.

"We worked hard for what we have and we're proud of that," Paul said.

"As you should be," Sam agreed. "I know I didn't

earn what I have but my birth father seems to have thought that I deserved it anyway. The fact is that I have that money now and I do use it. I have investments and we've given a lot to charity. Do you know why I never came to you and offered you money? Because I knew you'd never accept it. I knew it the minute Carl turned down a similar offer. You two are cut from pretty much the same cloth, you know."

"It's the way we were raised," Paul said.

"I was raised to believe that you help those around you," Sam said. "Especially family. That's all I've tried to do."

Paul looked like he had something to say but Sam wasn't finished. "I could have built myself a real mansion," he said. "But I don't want to live in that kind of house. My security people don't like it but I still drive myself around. We still use those pieces of furniture you made for us years ago. Tracie and I still cook our meals. One of us takes the kids to school every day and picks them up afterward. I've had a look at how a lot of rich people live. I don't begrudge it to them, but it's not for me."

Paul and Diane said nothing. "Look, if you don't want anything to do with me, I'll understand," Sam said. "But don't punish your brother and don't punish Tracie. I know they both miss having you around."

"Carl threw me out of his house," Paul said.

"I don't want to get you honked off again, but you did give him pretty good reason," Sam said.

"Maybe," Paul grudgingly admitted.

"So can we at least call a truce?" Sam asked. "You don't have to come around to my viewpoint, you know. We can agree to disagree. I'll promise never to give you an expensive gift again."

"You don't have to promise that," Diane said quickly with a smile.

Even Paul chuckled at that. "Well, I said what I came to say," Sam said. "I guess I'd better be on my way."

He got up to leave but Paul stopped him. "Can you let a stubborn, opinionated old farmer apologize first?" he said. "I still don't hold with some of the things you've done, but I suppose I could have handled it better. And we've missed you folks, too."

He stuck out his hand and Sam took it. Diane came over and hugged him. As soon as she did his cell phone rang. "Hello?" he said.

"Sam, where are you?" Tracie demanded.

"I'm at your uncle's," he said. "I think we've got things patched up."

"You went out there without telling me?" she asked, sounding a bit angry.

"It seemed like a good idea at the time," Sam said.

"We'll discuss that later," Tracie said. And Sam had no doubt that he was in for a lecture. But Tracie really wasn't concerned with that. There was a bigger problem. "You've got to get back to the office as soon as you can," she said.

"Why?"

"Your ex-wife is here and she won't leave until you talk to her."

Sam didn't like the sound of this.

THIRTY-EIGHT

WHENEVER SAM THOUGHT of his recent dealings with his ex-wife he thought of the term 'slippery-slope.' Despite his declaration that he wouldn't offer her any assistance beyond helping with a new job and the weekly checks for her son, he never escaped the feeling that Becky would be back with her hand out in the near future. He also knew that he was more than likely going to cave in and give her that help, despite his protests to the contrary. It wouldn't be confined to one more request for help either, he knew. His fondest wish was that Becky would simply go away and never bother him again.

When he arrived at the office he found her waiting in the lobby. "What are you doing here?" Sam asked even though he already knew the answer.

"I need your help," Becky said.

"I thought I told you--"

"Yeah, I know," Becky cut him off. "But will you at least hear me out? Please, Sam?"

Sam gestured for her to come into his office. When the door was shut he offered her a chair and sat down behind his desk. "So did you lose your job?" he asked.

"No, I didn't," she replied testily. "I'm trying hard, Sam, I really am. The job is actually pretty good, all things considered. They're nice people over there."

"Dad always thought so," Sam said. "So what's the problem?"

At that question Becky burst into tears. Sam was taken aback; Becky had never been prone to crying when he'd been married to her. "Sam, I have cancer," she sobbed.

Sam's jaw dropped open and he sagged back in his chair. "Oh, no," was all he could manage to say at first.

"It's cervical cancer," she said. "I hadn't had an exam for years, or they would have caught it sooner."

"Why...why didn't you have the exams?" Sam asked, knowing that although Tracie hated her 'yearly' she always had it done.

"I couldn't afford it," Becky explained. "Until you got me that job I didn't have medical insurance. They—they said it's pretty advanced."

"Becky...Becky I'm sorry," Sam said. "If you need help with the medical bills just send them here and I'll take care of them."

"That's not the only reason I'm here," Becky said. "The cancer has spread. They said they can't do anything for me. I have maybe a year."

She broke down into tears again. Sam went over and held her while she wept. They stayed like that for a while as Becky got it all out of her system. "I'm sorry," she said when she finally pulled back. "I'm crying all over your suit."

"That's what dry cleaners are for," Sam replied, giving her a tissue. "Does your son know?"

Becky shook her head. "No," she said. "I don't know how to tell him. I really don't know what to do about anything. That's why I came to you. I need help with this. I need someone to help me deal with this."

"What about your family?" Sam asked.

"Come on, Sam, you remember them," she said. "You think they're going to help? All they'll do is complain about me being a burden."

"So you came to me," Sam said.

"Not my first choice," she admitted. "But in spite of everything I know I can trust you. Isn't that weird?"

"Yeah," Sam said. "Will you be okay by yourself for a couple of minutes? I need to talk to Tracie."

"Sure," Becky said. "How bad does she hate me?"

"I don't think she hates you," Sam said. "I think she's just...mad because of how hurt I was after..."

"After I cheated on you," Becky said. "I guess I can't blame her for that."

"Let me go talk to her," Sam said. "I'll be right back."

He went through the door that connected their offices. Tracie was sitting at her desk, staring at her computer screen, but Sam could tell by the look on her face that she wasn't really paying attention to it. She didn't even notice him come in. "Hey," he said softly.

She jumped a bit in her chair. "Sorry," Sam said. "I didn't mean to startle you."

"I guess I was a little preoccupied," she said. "What happened with Becky?"

Sam told her everything. "Oh, no," Tracie said. "Oh, that poor woman. And her son, what about him?"

"I don't know," Sam said. "I'm going to help her, though, whatever she needs."

"Absolutely," Tracie said. "Maybe we can find her a doctor who can help."

"Yeah, maybe," Sam said. "I'm glad you're on board with this."

"How could I not be?" Tracie replied. "It's one thing to be angry over what she did to you, but that doesn't mean I wished this on her. No, we'll do whatever we can for her. Let's get to it."

Not only was Tracie on board with helping Sam's ex-wife she actually took a leading role. The first thing she did was go into Sam's office and hug her, promising that the Harmans would do everything thing they could for her. This brought a new round of tears from Becky, which provoked them in Tracie and even caused Sam's eyes to moisten a bit.

It was Tracie who arranged for Becky to be examined at the M.D. Anderson Cancer Center in Houston. She also arranged home nursing care and insisted that Becky quit her job and focus on taking care of herself and her son. The Harmans would take care of everything

But Tracie's most important contribution to the situation was getting Becky to go to church for the first time. She was reluctant, which was to be expected given her lack of a religious upbringing, but out of gratitude for everything Sam and Tracie were doing, she agreed to go. After attending a few times, and after discussions with both Pastor Marty and his wife, Jan, she accepted Christ as her savior. Tracie started taking her to a weekly bible study and connected her with a faith-based cancer support group.

For her part Becky was overwhelmed by the support she received from Sam and Tracie. Though the examination at the cancer center in Houston only confirmed the previous prognosis, the fact that someone was there for her made the whole situation a little easier to bear. For the first time she really regretted what she'd done to Sam and even screwed up the courage to ask for his forgiveness, which he gave. After all those years it felt good for both of them to let go of the bitterness they'd taken from their ruined marriage. Though she knew she was dying, Becky Dunlap never felt more alive.

At the same time Sam was getting to know Becky's son, Kyle. He seemed to be a good kid, though he was a bit cool towards Sam at first. That was understandable; he was, after all, his mom's ex-husband. When the Harmans had Becky and Kyle over for dinner one night, though, the ice was broken in the kids' playroom as Kyle and Sam Jr. bonded over the Wii. As Sam got to know Kyle better, he realized that for all her faults, Becky had done a good job raising her son. He didn't smoke, drink or use drugs and he tried hard in school. Sam found he liked the kid.

One night not too long after Becky's return from Texas, Sam and Tracie lay in bed reading. Sam couldn't focus on his book, though, and kept putting it down. "What's wrong?" Tracie asked.

"I keep thinking about Kyle," Sam said. "And what's going to happen to him after Becky's gone."

"You set up that trust fund for him," Tracie said.

"I'm not thinking about his financial situation," Sam said. "I'm thinking about where he's going to end up. I shudder at the thought of him going to live with Becky's mom."

"Becky said she and her mom don't get along," Tracie said.

"Depends on the day of the week," Sam said. "Or at least it used to. She's either mad at Becky for not taking care of her, or she's trying to run her life. Sometimes she can be the sweetest person in the world but when she isn't in that kind of mood, watch out."

"What are you thinking, Sam?" Tracie asked, although she had a pretty good idea where this was going.

"What if he came to live here?" Sam asked.

"Are you serious?" she replied.

"Yes," Sam said. "You know, when I sent that ambulance chaser packing, Becky asked me if it would be so hard to be a father to Kyle. At the time I refused. Of course that was before I got to know him. I like him, honey, and I want him to have a good life. I don't think he'll get that with Becky's family. He will with us."

Tracie sighed, as if in relief. "Becky will be glad to hear that," she said.

"What?"

"Becky asked me a week ago if we'd take Kyle," she explained. "I said I'd talk to you about it, but she didn't want me to. I think she was afraid she was asking too much after everything else we've done for her."

"She has changed," Sam said, admiringly.

"By leaps and bounds ever since she accepted Christ," Tracie agreed. "I tried to tell her you'd be okay with it if I asked, but she said she would either ask you herself or let you volunteer."

"Well I'm volunteering," Sam said. "We'll tell her tomorrow."

Tracie threw her arms around her husband. "This is so good of you, Sam," she said. "She's been so worried about him."

"Like I said, he's a good kid," Sam said. "He's had it pretty rough at times, and he's going to have an even tougher time when Becky...when she's gone. We should do whatever we can for him. And that's exactly what we're going to do."

THIRTY-NINE

THOUGH SAM HAD been very candid, and public, about his disdain for politics in general and politicians in particular, the latter was undeterred from constantly seeking his favor. Deep pockets, he observed, drew out everyone. As he ramped up pre-production on *The Path* in early March, he found himself flooded with calls and emails from members of the city council, all of whom were up for re-election the following month. Despite Sandy Ward's best efforts the messages got through to him, and he frequently dealt with the respective alderman personally.

He was promised all sorts of incentive to donate to their campaigns. Thanks to Bill Dodd, who Sam hadn't forgotten about, his space activities through Lunar Exploration Technologies were well known and several aldermen said they could help with zoning variances for his planned spaceflight control facility. That was, of course, assuming Sam was willing to support them in their bids for re-election. And some of the challengers to the incumbent aldermen also solicited him, making similar promises.

Sam had long known that politics in Port Mason

was a dirty business, but since becoming wealthy he truly came to appreciate the depth of corruption in the city. State campaign finance laws put severe limits on what he could directly contribute to politicians but, as they all pointed out, there was no law stopping him from setting up his own political action committee, which would be free to spend as much as it wanted so long as there was no actual coordination with specific campaigns. The first time this was suggested Sam seriously considered having his security team physically remove the alderman in question.

No political action committee was formed, however, and Sam tried to focus on making his movie. The politicians still found ways to annoy him. The twelfth ward covered the southwestern edge of the city, including the woods where Sam planned to do most of the shooting. The woods were in Agnew Park and, therefore, under the jurisdiction of the city, which required a permit be issued for any commercial use of its land. Sam's scouting of the park convinced him that it was absolutely perfect for The Path, so he applied for a permit. This brought him into the sphere of the politicians.

Alderman John Olivero had represented the area for eight years and was running for a third term, the last allowed by a term-limit ordinance passed in an unusual moment of good government by the council twenty years earlier. When he heard about Sam's permit application he smelled an opportunity and Olivero was the consummate opportunist. It was an open secret that he planned to run for mayor next time around. That would require generous amounts of money. Where better to get it than from Port Mason's resident billionaire? He contacted Sam and suggested they meet to discuss the permit.

Sam reluctantly invited Olivero to lunch at Ashley's, a popular establishment on the riverfront but not one usually patronized by the political crowd. It was a nice, family place that the Harmans absolutely loved. Sam chose it for two reasons. First, he wouldn't be caught dead in the downtown spots the politicians liked to frequent, and second, they had a shrimp scampi to die for. As a precaution against his own temper, Sam brought Tracie along. He had a feeling this meeting wasn't going to go well.

Olivero, a lawyer in his mid-fifties, was a veteran of the city's political battles. Before joining the city council, he'd been active in the local Democratic Party for years and even claimed to have known Sam's father when they'd both been precinct committeemen. Sam didn't say anything, but he seemed to remember his father making some unflattering comments about John Olivero. He set that aside and kept his best face on as they sat down to lunch.

"I understand you retain Leonard and Spengler as your legal counsel," Olivero said. "They're a good bunch."

"We think so," Sam said cautiously, taking a sip of water. He hadn't had a drink since Ted's death, and in any event was not part of the 'three martini' lunch crowd.

Olivero was, though he preferred Manhattans. He took a generous swallow from his glass. "They're a fine firm," he said. "Best in the city, and I'll say that even if they are one of my chief competitors. Aaron

Charlton handles your stuff, right?"

"Yes."

"I've dealt with Aaron before," Olivero said. "Sharp as they come, in and out of the courtroom. If I needed my own lawyer, he's the guy I'd want."

Sam wasn't one for small talk and wanted to get right down to business, but he'd been cautioned by Aaron not to rush into things with Olivero. "Give him time," his attorney said earlier. "Let him make the first move. What he wants from you is far more than you want from him."

As usual, his lawyer was proven correct. When the salads were served Olivero broached the subject. "How much are you putting into this movie of yours?" he asked.

"Five million," Sam said.

"You really think there's money in this kind of movie?" the alderman asked.

"Not the kind of money from a major feature, if that's what you mean," Sam said. "But we'll be able to make our money back and then some. It'll mostly be through home video sales. That's where the Christian film market makes almost all of its money."

"Interesting," Olivero said. "Got any big-time stars?"

"No," Sam said. "We're going to use local talent. I've been going to a lot of community theater play over the last couple of months, plus a couple of productions at the University. We've got some great talent in this town. All they need is a place to shine."

"'A place to shine,' I like that," Olivero said. "Mind if I steal that for a campaign slogan?"

Sam nodded his acquiescence. Olivero beamed like

he'd made a new best friend. "And I understand you're also using local personnel for your production crew and all that?"

"That's right," Sam said.

"I like that you're going local," Olivero said. "Usually when a movie company comes to town they bring in all their own people, Hollywood types who treat us like dirt. But I can see that you're not that kind of guy. And you've certainly put plenty of money into this community, even if it does benefit the mayor."

"Yes, well, that was just a by-product," Sam said. "We would have done what we did no matter who was in office."

"I get that, Sam, I really do," Olivero said. "And in spite of everything you've done, I haven't heard so much as a whisper of you wanting anything in return. That's really admirable."

"Thank you, "Sam said.

"Now about your permit application," Olivero said. "Under city ordinance, it has to be approved by the full council, but they nearly always follow the recommendation of the Tourism and Development committee, on which I am the ranking Democrat. I would be happy to endorse your application, before both the committee and the full council."

"That's very kind of you," Tracie said.

"I wish I could say I was doing it out of the kindness of my heart," Olivero said. "But this is Port Mason, and as you know, nothing in this town comes for free. I'm sorry to have to say that but it's true. I'm afraid I'm going to have to ask for something in return."

"We don't make political contributions," Sam said,

firmly.

"And I respect that," Olivero said. "I wasn't planning to ask for one. But there is something you can do for me. Even though my ward is considered one of the better parts of town, the recession hit us hard and people are hurting. What we need is economic development. That's where you come in.

"I know the other aldermen want you to build your space center in their wards," he continued. "And I do, too. I also know you already own some property in my ward. Quite a bit, in fact."

"You're talking about the six lots on Kennedy Street, aren't you?" Sam asked.

"That's right."

"And you want me to commit to building the space center there in exchange for my permit," Sam said. "Does that about sum it up?"

"Sure," Olivero said. "Not a bad deal. Those lots you own are the best in the city anyway. Where else would you put the place?"

"Can we think it over?" Sam asked. "I'll get in touch with you about it tomorrow."

"No problem," Olivero said. "I'd like to make this happen as soon as possible, though."

"We know, there's an election coming up," Sam said. "I'll call you tomorrow."

After lunch Sam and Tracie drove back to the office in Sam's car. For once the stereo was turned off. Sam needed to think clearly. "Why does there always have to be a deal?" he asked. "Why can't someone just get what they want with no strings attached?"

"People are basically greedy, hon," Tracie said.

"Politicians included. Sometimes I think they're the greediest of all. Maybe not for money, but for power and influence. At least he didn't ask for money."

"I almost wish he had," Sam said. "That would have been easier to turn down."

"Sam is it really that tough a decision?" she asked. "You told me weeks ago that the Kennedy street property was perfect."

"I know," he said. "But the whole idea strikes me as...dirty. And I wonder if it's illegal?"

"I don't think he'd be that brazen," Tracie said. "I don't like the idea of making dirty deals either, but you were planning to build there anyway. You and I both know it. It's not like you'd really be giving in."

"Yeah," Sam sighed.

"How badly do you want to make the movie?" she asked. "Especially after all the time and effort you've already put into it?"

"You know what it means to me," he replied. "Okay, we'll make the deal. I just hope this doesn't come back to bite us."

FORTY

MANAGING THREE BILLION dollars was not an easy job. Sam and Tracie learned this very early on, so they put together what they considered a crack management team to do the job for them. These people handled their investments, cash flow, and the nuts and bolts of their business activities. To discourage theft they paid handsome salaries with full benefits and a few extra perks thrown in like company cars and use of a company condo in the Florida Keys. They were also generous with vacation time, family leave, and so forth. In spite of all this, they both knew that sooner or later someone was going to rip them off. It still came as a shock when it actually happened.

In late March Sam rented conference space at the Fairmont Hotel to begin the process of casting his movie. He spent two weeks on the search for talent, videotaping auditions during the day, and poring over those tapes at night. By the end of the month he settled on his final cast and set about securing their services. He also established a schedule for rehearsals in April and the actual shoot in May. He invited the cast up to the office after they all signed on for an initial read-through of the script. After it was over Sam went back to his office to go over the latest financial reports from the growing family empire to find one of his accountants waiting for him.

Oliver Shroyer was a CPA and partner in Port Mason's best accounting firm, Vanderslik & Wright. In his late fifties, Shroyer was the firm's senior partner and personally handled Sam and Tracie's affairs, leading a team of hand-picked associates. The day-to-day accounting was handled by three CPAs directly employed by Harman Family Enterprises; Vanderslik & Wright was in charge of monitoring these accountants and performing quarterly audits of the books. Almost all of Sam's personal dealings with Shroyer took place on the phone, via email or over the occasional lunch. This was only the second time Shroyer had visited their offices and the first time he'd done so without an appointment.

"Sam, we've got a problem," he said without preamble. "You should probably have your wife sit in on this."

Sam quickly summoned Tracie and the three sat down in Sam's office. "There is a significant amount of money missing," Shroyer said. "We found out about it this morning."

"Define 'significant,'" Sam said.

"Thirty million dollars," Shroyer said.

"What?" Sam exclaimed. "How do you lose thirty million dollars?"

"You don't," Shroyer replied. "I suspect the money was stolen."

"You found out about it this morning?" Tracie asked. "It's two in the afternoon."

"I wanted to be sure it wasn't a correctable error on our part before coming to you," Shroyer explained. "Whoever is responsible has been authorizing relatively small payments from the accounts you set up to finance your space activities. I believe the payments in question were sent via wire transfer to a series of shell corporations. From there the money was wired to foreign banks."

"And once out of the country the money is nearly impossible to trace," Sam said. The moving of money through the global financial system was part of the crash course in money management Anderson Braddock had put him through the previous summer. By keeping the money moving through a series of offshore accounts in countries without stringent financial reporting laws it, was not difficult for an embezzler to cover his or her tracks. By now the money would be tucked away where it was likely never to be found. For all they knew, it could be back in the United States, sufficiently 'laundered' to hide all trace of its origin and ready for investment in any legitimate enterprise.

"That's right," Shroyer said. "It was the small amounts that kept us from noticing it before. The only reason we caught it now was because the last transfer took place on Friday just as the banks were closing and it was for ten million dollars."

"Wait a minute," Sam said. "Nobody can move that much money out of Harman Family Enterprises without either my authorization or Tracie's, and I know neither one of us did it. How did they pull that off?"

"That, I'm afraid, is for the authorities to

determine," Shoryer said. "I would strongly suggest you call the FBI and report the embezzlement immediately. The sooner their financial crimes unit is on the case the more likely you are to recover the money."

"One of our accountants should have caught this," Tracie said. "Unless..."

"Unless one of them is the thief," Sam finished. "I was just thinking that. I remember Braddock telling me that a good accountant can steal more than the best bank robber. Tracie, get George in here. And Tim while you're at it, maybe we've been hacked. I'll call the FBI."

Once again Sam and Tracie's notoriety served them well; a small team of FBI agents were at their office within twenty minutes. Tim Druse was abruptly dismissed from his work on Sam's computer by an FBI technician, who essentially picked up where he'd left off in trying to determine if they'd been hacked. George Conran, their chief accountant, found the records of the transfers quickly and also reported that one of his subordinates, Melody Lindquist, had called in sick that morning. Calls to her home were not answered. FBI agents were dispatched to her residence.

The theft of the thirty million dollars stung Sam. Sure, compared to the vastness of his fortune it may seem like a relatively paltry sum, but it wasn't the amount that hurt so much as the fact one of his own employees had done it. He'd gotten to know Melody a bit since she came to HFE, or thought he had. She seemed to be an engaging, smart, and business savvy woman intent on making her mark. When she started she told Sam that her eventual goal was to open her own accounting firm. Sam respected that sort of ambition and privately considered investing in such an endeavor if she ever proposed it.

He pulled her file and reviewed the background check he'd ordered from Steve Bennett. She graduated at or near the top of her class throughout high school, college, and graduate school before earning her CPA. After that she spent three years at the same accounting firm as George Conran before Sam and Tracie lured them to Harman Family Enterprises. No known boyfriends, never married, clean criminal record. There was absolutely no reason to suspect her of being an embezzler.

The technician examining Sam's computer discovered what Druse already suspected. A computer program had been introduced into the main server that cracked all the passwords and authorization codes for the Harman family accounts. This revelation set both the FBI agents and Sam's own people scrambling to find out if any more money was missing. Thankfully, nothing more had been stolen, but as a precaution, all electronic banking activities were suspended until this matter was resolved and the program removed from the systems. Sam and Tracie spent the rest of the afternoon on the phone with their various banks, changing passwords and restricting access to prevent any more theft.

While they were doing this, word arrived that Lindquist was not at her condominium and there was no sign of her car. An alert was put out to the local police, and within an hour the car was found at the airport. It was eventually determined that Lindquist had taken an early flight to Miami, where she was last seen getting into a limousine. The limo was hired for cash, no names provided, though the driver did remember dropping her off at a charter service's hangar. Unfortunately, this driver had a nasty drinking habit and couldn't remember which hangar he'd dropped her at.

From there the trail went cold. Sam considered it enough evidence to convince him of who'd stolen the money, but the question of how the computer program got into their systems was unanswered. He didn't believe for a moment that Druse had done it. For one thing, he was still here. For another, he knew Tim was smart enough not to leave any traces of the software. The FBI was not so easily convinced, and Druse was taken in for questioning.

Tracie went to pick up the kids that evening but Sam stayed at the office while the FBI conducted their investigation. The agent in charge was Blake Elmore, a fifteen-year veteran of the Bureau with, as he put it, extensive experience in financial crimes. This experience, combined with the evidence gathered so far, led him to believe they'd probably seen the last of both Melody Lindquist and Sam Harman's money. Sam took this surprisingly well, only swearing once.

"I understand you're angry, Mr. Harman," Elmore said. "But you yourself pointed out that by moving the money through foreign banks, a good embezzler can cover his or her tracks very well. We'll keep at it, of course, but there are plenty of countries who will not cooperate with us when it comes to banking records. They make too much from money laundering to risk it."

"Great," Sam said. "So what do I do, just write it off and hope I can get a tax deduction?"

Elmore smiled. "I guess," he said. "That's between you, your accountant, and the IRS."

"Her background check came back clean," Sam said, tapping a file folder from Bennett Investigations that lay on his desk. "But I suppose even the most upstanding citizen can be tempted."

"That's exactly right," Elmore said. "If it weren't the case, I'd be out of job. But seriously, you shouldn't blame yourself or, for that matter, anyone else. This is the work of a thief and that's where the blame belongs."

"I don't suppose this can be kept quiet for long," Sam said.

"We'll try," Elmore said. "But I won't lie to you; things like this do have a way of getting out."

Once the agents were gone Sam sat back in his chair and closed his eyes. What was next, he wondered?

FORTY-ONE

THE PRIVATE GULFSTREAM V made its way across the United States on its way back from the Dominican Republic. The mission team from Chester Avenue Christian Church sat quietly in the cabin, tired from ten days of constant work and ready to get home. Sam was particularly quiet; his mind awash with images of the things he'd seen during his visit. Marty had been right about one thing; he was coming home a changed man.

He thought he'd seen poverty in the welfare district when helping his cousin Ted out of one jam or another, but what he'd seen there was nothing on what he'd seen in the Dominican. Many of these people literally lived on pennies a day. He met children who spent their days in the fields working instead of in school because their parents couldn't find work. It was a sobering experience. Sam understood more than ever just how blessed he was. He resolved to do more for people in those conditions.

But what really struck Sam, even more than the poverty, was the joy these poor, simple people had in their lives. He saw it in the churches, when people would give what little they had even though they really couldn't afford it. He saw it in the streets in the middle of the worst poverty. He saw it in the schools he visited. These people wanted for so much but didn't seem to complain. They praised God in the midst of their poverty. Sam had never seen anything like it. He was already thinking about things he could do for those people.

Finally, the plane reached Port Mason. As they taxied to the general aviation terminal, Sam saw several black SUVs parked nearby and several men and women wearing dark blue windbreakers standing beside them. The plane came to a stop and the attendant opened the hatch, at which point the people in the windbreakers stormed into the aircraft, drawing guns as they did so. "DEA!" their leader shouted. "Nobody move! Keep your hands in front of you!"

The members of the mission team, terrified by the sudden appearance of the Drug Enforcement Administration agents, looked around nervously. Some let out small cries of fright. The man who'd spoken moved slowly up the aisle until he came to where Sam and Tracie were seated. His gun was not quite pointed at them, but it was not quite pointed away, either. "Samuel Harman?" he asked.

"Yes," Sam replied, gripping Tracie's hand tightly.

"Stay right where you are and keep your hands on your knees," the agent said. "Mrs. Harman, I'm going to have to ask you to step away."

"I'm not leaving my husband," Tracie replied.

"Tracie, do what he says," Sam said quietly, withdrawing his hand from hers and placing it on his knee, as he'd been instructed.

His wife reluctantly got up and moved away from

him. "Burks," the intense DEA man said. "Escort these people off of the plane one at a time. Make sure they're searched and get their information. You know the drill. Start with Mrs. Harman, here."

"Yes sir," a young woman said. Tracie was escorted to the front of the plane, where Burks frisked her and went through her purse, seizing her cell phone and travel documents. Tracie was then shown off the plane. It went like that for the rest of the mission team, including an incredulous Marty and Jan Lovell, both of whom gave Sam questioning looks as they were led away.

Once everyone was off, the lead agent backed away a step and instructed Sam to get out of his seat slowly and with his hands in the air. Sam did exactly as he was told, his heart racing. As soon as he was on his feet two other agents covered him with their weapons while their leader spun Sam around and frisked him, relieving him of the contents of his pockets. Then he was handcuffed. "Bring in the dog," the leader said, pushing Sam back down into a seat.

A German shepherd was brought onto the plane. Guided by a handler, the dog began sniffing every nook and cranny in the main cabin before moving aft to the baggage compartment. DEA agents started pulling out suitcases and bags for the dog to inspect. Sam tried to look behind him but he was roughly shoved away. He said nothing, thoroughly intimidated by the agents and their weapons. Suddenly, the dog started barking. "Got a hit," the dog's handler said.

"Open it up," the lead agent said.

Sam heard the sound of a suitcase being unzipped.

The barking increased. "Check the rest of them, just to be sure," the lead agent said.

He reappeared in front of Sam, holding a clear plastic package secured by brown packing tape. The package contained a white substance. Sam felt the color drain from his face. He said nothing.

"Care to tell me what this is, Mr. Harman?" the lead agent asked. "There are nine more just like it in your luggage. If it's what I think it is, you've got about two hundred thousand dollars worth on this plane. Kind of small time for someone with your money, isn't it? Or was this just a trial run to see if you could get away with it?"

"I don't know what you're talking about," Sam replied, softly. "I packed those bags myself. All that should be in there are my clothes."

"Well it not all that's in there, now, is it?" the agent said, angrily. "As much as you have, and you think you need to do a little drug smuggling on the side?"

Burks came back on to the plane. "Mike," she said. "We didn't find anything on the other passengers."

"That's okay," Mike said. "I think we have who we came for. How are you guys doing with those bags?"

"Just about done," a voice replied. "Daisy hasn't found anything else."

"That beast is called Daisy?" Sam asked.

"Shut up," Mike said. "You're under arrest."

Sam was led off the plane by Mike, surrounded by a trio of DEA agents. Tracie and the mission team watch in shock as he was led to one of the SUVs and put inside. The vehicle quickly drove off even as more agents boarded the plane. Reunited with her cell phone, she quickly called Aaron Charlton and told him what little she knew. Then she got her car from long-term parking and headed to the federal courthouse downtown. She called her parents and filled them in, asking them not to say anything to the kids until she knew more.

She was remarkably calm, given what had just happened to her husband. It has to be a mistake, she repeated to herself silently, over and over. She also prayed that God would protect Sam and deliver him from what she knew had to be either a gross misunderstanding or...or a setup. Tracie veered across the road, ignoring angry horn blasts, and headed towards the river.

FORTY-TWO

SAM WAS HANDCUFFED to a table in an interrogation room. Mike and the agent named Burks were with him. Mike sat across from Sam, staring at him intently. The DEA agent was intense, his arms folded across his chest but not saying anything. Sam also said nothing, well aware of his right to remain silent. He was sure Tracie had called Aaron; he only hoped the lawyer got here soon. Mike didn't look like the type to give up easily.

"I know it's a cliché," Mike said. "But there really are two ways to do this, easy and hard. You follow me?"

Sam nodded. "Good," Mike said. "Now, let's try the easy way first. Why would someone as wealthy as you try to smuggle ten kilos of cocaine into the country? Assuming you paid two grand apiece, that's only a one hundred eighty thousand dollar profit. For a guy like you that's chump change. So what was it? The challenge? The thrill of trying to get away with it? Tell me."

"I suppose telling you that I have no idea where the drugs came from or how they wound up in my bags would be useless," Sam said.

"Very," Mike said.

"Even if it's the truth?"

Mike looked skeptical. Given the circumstances, Sam couldn't blame him. He closed his eyes briefly and prayed for strength. When he was done, he found Mike's expression unchanged. Sam took a deep breath and spoke calmly. "I don't know how ten kilos of cocaine came to be in my bags," he said. "I have never dealt in drugs, nor would I ever deal in drugs. That sort of thing killed my cousin recently and there's no way I would be part of it. That's all I have to say until I see my lawyer."

Mike stood up, leaned forward, and put his hands on the table. "You want to lawyer up, go ahead," he said. "But we've got the dope in your bags, and I'll bet your prints are all over the packages. I don't care how much money you throw at this, you're not walking away. Your only hope for a slightly lenient sentence is to tell me who you bought the drugs from and how to find them."

Sam said nothing. "Fine, the hard way, then," Mike said. "We are going to go through every detail of your life. We are going to tear your house apart from top to bottom, even if your kids have to watch. You're going to do a perp walk for the TV cameras which, I'm told, are lining up outside as we speak. You're going to the county lockup today, and from what I hear, the folks down there aren't too fond of you."

That statement made Sam gulp a bit. He knew what the DEA agent was talking about. Former Sheriff John McCreary, the man Sam had thoroughly embarrassed just after the election the previous fall, was still very popular among the employees of his old office. Since the swearing-in of new Sheriff Clinton Landry, there had been reports in the press of considerable unrest among deputies and jail employees. Landry had completely reorganized department's command structure, putting out several long-term supervisors and replacing them with people who had few, if any, ties to the old administration. He was also aggressively recruiting new deputies to replace the ones who were either in prison or on their way there after the evidence room scandal.

Sam, now friendly with a few county board members, heard privately that Landry was opening up records to outside investigators and ordering deputies to submit to interviews with the State Police. While all these things fulfilled campaign promises, they also made Landry very unpopular within his own department. These friendly board members warned Sam that some of these disgruntled people held him at least partly responsible for the current state of affairs, since he'd refused to support McCreary for re-election.

"So, you don't want to go to county?" Mike asked. "I don't blame you. But that's exactly where you're headed if you don't tell me what I want to know. Where did you get the drugs? Who was your contact in the Dominican Republic? How did you plan to distribute the cocaine?"

Sam still said nothing. Mike was starting to get angry, or at least was pretending to be. The 'good cop, bad cop' scenario came to mind. He was about to say something more when the door opened, and Aaron Charlton entered the room. "I'm Mr. Harman's attorney," he said. "No more questions until I talk to him. Understand? Now could we have a minute?"

Mike and Burks left the room. Once the door was closed Sam spoke. "Is Tracie OK?" he asked.

"She's fine," Charlton said. "You're the only one who was arrested."

Sam sagged in his chair. "You got here just in time," he said. "I think they were about to get nasty."

"I came as soon as I could," Charlton said. "Did you tell them anything?"

"Only that the drugs weren't mine," Sam said. "That agent, Mike, he said he was sending me to county. Can they do that?"

"I'm afraid so," Charlton said. "You worried about McCreary's old friends?"

"You could say that," Sam said. "Can you get me out of here?"

"I'll be honest, Sam, I don't think that's going to happen," Charlton said. "Trying to bring that much cocaine into the United States is a major felony. You're looking at twenty years minimum, if convicted. With your wealth I know they'll classify you as a flight risk."

"So what do I do?" Sam asked.

"Leave everything to me," Charlton said. "I've already told our criminal defense unit to get ready. We're going to hit hard on this, that I can promise."

"Tell Tracie to keep away from the house," Sam said. "They said they were going to tear the place apart."

"Like hell they will," Charlton said. "I'll file a motion with the judge requesting that I be present to insure your property isn't damaged. But you're right;

Tracie and the kids shouldn't be there."

"So when do I go to court?" Sam asked.

"That's up to the DEA," Charlton said. "But I can't imagine they'll waste any time."

"Is Tracie here," Sam asked.

"She's coming," Aaron said. "She said something about getting you some extra help."

Steve Bennett looked up from his computer as Tracie Harman was shown into his office. Bennett Investigations had grown in the months since Sam came into his fortune. He and his uncle now had an associate to handle the voluminous number of background checks ordered by the Harmans, and being linked to Sam had been good for their other business so if a Harman showed up without an appointment, that person got in to see them right away.

"Sam's been arrested," Tracie said without preamble. She told Bennett what little she knew so far. Only then did the events of the day catch up with her. She started to cry. "He's not a drug dealer," she wept. "It has to be a setup."

"And you want me to find out," Bennett said. "I try to avoid meddling in law enforcement's business. The feds can be particularly touchy about that."

"I know," Tracie sobbed. "But he's your friend, isn't he? You know him. You know he wouldn't do something like this."

That argument carried a fair amount of weight, not only because it was true but also because she hadn't tried to pressure him. No offer of an exorbitant fee. No threat to cut off their business ties. It was a simple plea from a wife trying to save her husband. Though never married, Bennett understood that kind of devotion. There were people in his life he would gladly die for. He couldn't blame Tracie Harman for trying. "What do you want me to do?" he asked.

"Find out if Jerry Curtis had anything to do with this," Tracie said. "He hates Sam. He has to be the one who sent that nasty email after that protester was killed. He said awful things on the radio. He has more money than we do and who knows what kind of contacts."

The mention of Jerry Curtis changed everything. While tracking Sam down for Anderson Braddock, Bennett had been given a complete rundown on the Curtis family, including a very complete file on Jerry. He knew things about the man that Tracie didn't, which made her belief about a setup at least plausible. As far as Bennett was concerned, the man belonged in jail.

"Okay," he said. "That I'll do. The DEA won't be looking at the Curtis family so anything I do on that front won't be seen as interfering. In fact, if they do get wind of it they'll probably laugh and go back to prosecuting Sam. I'll need an advance on my fee to book a flight to Houston."

"I'll give you ten thousand dollars right now," Tracie said, taking out her checkbook. "And I'll get you your own plane."

FORTY-THREE

SAM WAS LED into the courtroom in handcuffs, which remained on until he was next to his lawyer at the defense table. As the bailiff undid the restraints, Sam looked at Tracie, seated in the front row between Marty and Jan. The three held hands, and Sam could tell from the looks on their faces that they had been praying right up to the moment Sam entered. More than anything he wanted to reach out and hold his wife, but he'd been warned that no contact would be permitted. Instead he tried to smile, and then turned to face the bench.

When asked later Sam, wouldn't remember much of the hearing. He was still in a state of shock over the day's events. In the end Sam was charged with several felonies and ordered held without bail since his wealth made him a flight risk. He did remember the tears in Tracie's eyes as the handcuffs were put back on and he was led away.

The events following the hearing, on the other hand, would remain with Sam for the rest of his life. DEA agents took charge of him again and led him past a horde of reporters to an SUV that transported him to the Port Mason County Jail. The agents signed custody of him away and left him with a pair of jail guards, who couldn't seem to wipe the smiles off of their faces. Once the agents were gone the guards grabbed him by the arms and shoved him through a door. He stumbled and fell. They laughed as they hauled him to his feet.

A team of five guards watched and laughed as he was forced to strip. As he stood there essentially on display, he had a growing sense of dread over what was to come. His fears were confirmed when the man in charge said "Cavity search."

An hour later, Sam was thrown to the wolves. The cavity search had taken quite a while for some reason. Sam had thrown up twice during the 'procedure' and then ordered to clean up his own mess. Finally he was dressed in an orange prison jumpsuit with flip flops and shown to his cell. Three other men were in there, and they looked like they'd been waiting for him. Sam didn't like the look of them. They were all big and well muscled, their expressions hard. The man Sam pegged as their leader cracked his knuckles. The guards laughed and forced Sam into the cell.

The door slid shut. The guards walked away. Sam was alone with the three other prisoners. "I don't suppose I could persuade you guys to leave me alone," he said.

The three men laughed. "You think you're better than the rest of us, rich man?" the leader said.

The punch came so quickly that Sam was on the floor before he had any idea of what was happening. He was kicked in the abdomen which would have made him puke again, if he'd had anything left in his stomach. Before he could catch his breath he was pulled up to his feet and shoved up against the wall. The three men were grinning. Sam didn't understand. The guards were one thing--he'd embarrassed McCreary and possibly cost him the election. He could understand why they'd mistreat him. But he didn't even know his cell mates. What had he ever done to them?

Then it hit him. "Tell me what you're getting to do this," he said. "I can do better, I guarantee it."

"Think you can buy us, rich man?" the leader said. He hit Sam in the left bicep. Sam groaned in pain. He struck again in the same spot. Sam sagged against the wall. Another punch came, this one in the jaw. One of Sam's teeth felt loose. He fell to the floor again.

"T, hang on," one of the other prisoners. "Maybe we should listen to him."

T whirled on his compatriot. "We made a deal," he said. "Now shut your hole and pick him up."

"One hundred thousand dollars," Sam gasped. "For each of you."

That made T stop short from kicking him again. "Are you serious?" one of the others asked.

"Yes," Sam said, struggling to his feet.

"T-Bone," the man said. "That's a hell of a lot of money."

"If he pays," T-Bone said. "You think we can trust this guy?"

"The next time I talk to my lawyer, I'll tell him to have three certified checks drawn," Sam said. "One hundred thousand apiece. You have my word."

Half an hour later two guards came back into the cell block. They stopped in front of Sam's cell. What they saw completely shocked them. Sam was sitting on a bunk with T-Bone, laughing at something while the big man dabbed at the blood on Sam's mouth. The other two men were casually leaning against another bunk, looking relaxed and happy. "What the hell's going on here?" one of the guards asked.

"Just making new friends," Sam said. "You put me in with some really cool guys here, thanks a lot."

The two guards looked confused. "So you've never been to Vegas, T-Bone?" Sam asked.

"Shit, man, I've never been out of Port Mason," T-Bone said.

"You've missed out," Sam said. "Tell you what, when you guys get out of here give me a call. I'll fly you out there myself."

One of the guards' jaws dropped. The other got angry. "You're not here to make friends, T-Bone," he said. "I thought we had this worked out."

"We made a better deal," T-Bone said.

The angry guard pulled out his radio. "Open number 12," he said, getting his baton ready. "I think you need to go to solitary, Harman. You're stirring things up in here."

"He's not going anywhere," another voice said.

Sheriff Clinton Landry, flanked by two jail guards Sam hadn't seen before, entered the cell block. The county's top lawman looked angry, and Sam felt his spirits rise. "You two are relived," Landry said. "And suspended, along with your pals. Now get your asses out of my jail!"

The two guards left. Landry approached the cell

door. "I'm sorry about this," Landry said. "Your name didn't reach my desk until twenty minutes ago. I got there as soon as I could. Are you alright?"

"It was a little rough at first," Sam admitted. "But I think we've reached an understanding, right guys?"

"Sure, Sam," T-Bone said. "We've got your back."

"Still, maybe I'd better put you in segregation," Landry said. "I'm still not sure which guards can be trusted around here."

"We've got his back," T-Bone said, more forcefully.

"It'll be all right, Sheriff," Sam said. "In fact, my new friends here have some interesting things to tell you."

The next morning, former Sheriff John McCreary was arrested by his successor and charged with bribing county officials. Seven jail guards and the captain in charge of the jail were also arrested. Sheriff Landry, faced with a sudden manpower shortage, had to ask the state department of corrections to take some of his most dangerous prisoners until he could get his staff back up to full strength. For their own safety, McCreary and his compatriots were held in segregation.

Sam Harman was still in jail, his bail status unchanged, but he was becoming rather popular behind bars. He put out the word that if anyone was offered money to harm him he would triple it, no questions asked. He was sure that some of the inmates who claimed to have been offered money to hurt him were lying, but for once he didn't care if he was scammed. He had a strong sense of self-preservation, and even if he paid off every inmate in

the county jail he would consider it a bargain.
  Now if could just get himself out of this place.

FORTY-FOUR

IT WAS JUST past dark when a Lear Jet landed at Ellington International Airport in Houston and taxied to the general aviation terminal. Steve Bennett watched from his seat as the terminal grew closer and decided that this was definitely the way to travel. The plane stopped at a hangar marked "Wallace Charters, Ltd." The pilot opened the cockpit door and moved to the hatch, which he opened. Once the ladder was in place he nodded to Bennett. "You can deplane now, sir," he said. "I'm sorry to rush you but we're flying to Dallas to pick up another charter and we're running a little late."

"Busy night for you guys," Bennett said, collecting his bag.

"Comes with the job," the pilot replied. "Thanks for flying with us."

"Thank Tracie Harman," Bennett said. "She's footing the bill."

Almost as soon as his feet hit the pavement, the ladder was retracted and the hatch shut. Seconds later the plane taxied away from the hangar, leaving Bennett alone on the tarmac. Nobody was around to greet him, and the hangar seemed to be shut down for the night. Bennett didn't like this and reached into his jacket to make sure his .40 caliber Beretta was ready. He also checked the ASP collapsible baton he carried on the back of his belt. There was an advantage to flying on a private plane, he reflected. He was fully armed and ready for trouble.

He tried the door to the hangar, which was locked. He started walking down the tarmac to the next hangar, from which he could see light. As he passed the gap between the two he thought he heard something and threw his bag towards it with his left hand, while drawing his gun with his right. The gap area was dark but he heard the thump as his bag hit something followed by a grunt. He ran across the gap, put his back to the wall of the next hangar, pulled out the baton, and waited.

He heard the footsteps and crouched low, extending the baton just as the man raced around the corner. The would-be attacker tripped on the baton and fell to the pavement. Bennett quickly kicked him in the belly and leaped over him, turning to face the gap area again and keeping himself in the light. He understood that this made him an easier target, but he was betting that this goon (or goons as he suspected) wanted to keep this assault as quiet as possible; and therefore preferred to stick to the shadows. Bennett never liked playing by the other guys' rules. By staying in the light he would force them to come to him.

It didn't take long. As the first attacker groaned on the pavement (had Bennett gotten him below the belt? He couldn't be sure.), a second emerged slowly from the side of the hangar. Like Bennett the thug was armed, his gun up and ready. It was a standoff, and Bennett still didn't know if there were any more lurking in the shadows. This was one of the times he missed being a cop. If this had been a police matter he would have had backup. He mentally kicked himself for not bringing his uncle along.

The man with the gun slowly advanced. Bennett stood his ground. The thug stopped next to his partner. "Hey," he said, his accent pure Texas. "Can you get up?"

Moaning, his partner replied, "Give me a minute. Bastard got me in the balls."

"Why don't you put that gun down, and we can have a nice, civilized conversation," Bennett suggested.

"I don't think so," the man said.

Bennett said nothing. He was playing for time. Someone, he reasoned, was bound to see what was going on and summon the police. He only had to wait. Unfortunately, the gunman had figured that out, too. "I think my friend and I will be going," he said. "You can explain to the airport police why you're standing on the tarmac with a gun in your hand."

Keeping his gun trained on Bennett, he used his free hand to help his partner up. The two backed slowly away. Bennett made no move to go after them, but kept his gun up. They reached the corner of the hangar, slipping quietly around the side. As soon as they were out of sight Bennett ran back to the hangar, pressing his back to the wall and keeping his gun up and ready. There was, after all, a very good chance that they would come back around to take a shot at him. Instead, his bag flew out of the darkness and landed on the tarmac. Bennett didn't go to retrieve it, as much as he wanted to. He had a flashlight in there, and he wanted a peek in that dark area but wasn't stupid enough to walk into that kind of trap.

He waited there for five minutes before moving again. He stepped slowly towards the corner of the hangar, slipping the baton back into its holster. Before he reached it he heard the sound of an engine. He turned to see a car approaching him. It clearly wasn't the police, there were no flasher bars. He turned his gun on the car, which screeched to a halt.

The door opened slowly, and a man got out with his hands raised. "Mr. Bennett," the man said. "I'm David Lambert. Do you remember me?"

Bennett slowly lowered his gun. "Yes," he said. "You work for Braddock, don't you?"

"Yes sir," Lambert confirmed. "He sent me to meet you. I'm sorry I wasn't here sooner, but we just learned you were coming."

"Put your hands down, I'm not going to shoot you," Bennett said, holstering his gun. He went over and got his bag.

"Mr. Braddock was afraid there might be some…unpleasantness upon your arrival," Lambert said, opening the trunk for Bennett's bag. "I take it he was correct."

"Yeah, you could say that," Bennett said, tossing his bag in the trunk. "But if he was worried about that, why did he send you?"

Lambert opened his suit jacket to reveal the gun concealed there. "I perform a number of functions for Mr. Braddock," he explained. "Including bodyguard and expediter."

"So you're a handy guy to have around," Bennett said.

"Yes sir," Lambert said. "My instructions are to take you to Mr. Braddock immediately."

"I assume that means he has some idea of what's going on around here?" Bennett asked. Lambert nodded. "Okay, let's go."

As they drove away from the airport, Lambert handed Bennett a file folder. Inside were five photographs. Bennett recognized two of them immediately as the two men who'd tried to get the jump on him. "So you know these guys?" he asked, holding up the two photos.

"Only too well," Lambert said. "The blond one is Stu Peart. Your basic hired muscle; long on fighting skills but not too bright."

Bennett nodded. Peart was the one he'd tripped and kicked. "And his partner?" he asked.

"Boss," Lambert corrected. "His name is Alvin Koontz, and he is to Jerry Curtis what I am to Mr. Braddock."

"I take it the rest of these guys are on this goon squad?" Bennett asked.

"Yes," Lambert replied. "They also double as Jerry's drinking buddies. That's how he met all of them. Koontz is the most dangerous of the bunch. Smart as a whip."

"I noticed," Bennett said, giving Lambert a rundown of the confrontation. "You might want to check out those pilots, too. They dumped me at that hangar and hightailed it out of there, even though there was no one to meet me."

"The misfortune of flying with Wallace Charters," Lambert said. "Despite the name, Jerry owns the company. The Harmans would be well advised to stop using them."

"I'll be sure to tell them," Bennett said. "Do you know if Sam used them for that trip to the Dominican Republic?"

"He's used them exclusively ever since he came into his inheritance," Lambert said. "Mr. Braddock only recently learned that they're owned by Jerry. He'll give you the details. Do you see anyone following us?"

Bennett had been checking the mirrors every now and then out of habit and hadn't seen anything. "I don't think so," he said.

"Me neither but I've learned to be careful where Jerry's involved," Lambert said.

"This might be an easier job than I thought," Bennett said. "It sounds like you guys have already done a lot of the legwork I was planning to do."

"You'll earn your fee, Mr. Bennett," Lambert said. "Dealing with Jerry Curtis is not easy, I can promise you that. Be glad you came here armed."

"I've seen the file," Bennett said.

"Then you know how dangerous he is," Lambert said. "I think I'd better leave the rest to Mr. Braddock."

FORTY-FIVE

WHEN LAMBERT USHERED him into Braddock's home study, Bennett was shocked by the change in the man since that fateful meeting the year before when the old lawyer told Sam Harman about his inheritance. He'd looked old then, yes, but there was still a fire in him that gave him a vigorous aura. That fire was gone now. Anderson Braddock looked deflated, as though he had finally been brought down by the burdens he carried. Bennett wondered if he was ill. He certainly looked it.

"You'll have to excuse me for not standing," Braddock said. "But I have a harder time getting around these days. The less stress I put on these old bones the better."

Bennett noticed that Braddock was in a wheelchair. "I think it best if we get right to business," Braddock said. "Have a seat. David, get that infernal oxygen tank over here."

Bennett sat down in front of the desk while Lambert wheeled an oxygen tank over from the corner and handed Braddock the tubing that fitted into his nostrils. Braddock took a few deep breaths. "Sorry about that," he finally said. "Never smoked a single cigarette in my life, but I guess I've spent so much time around industrial chemicals that the effect is the same. I don't have cancer, just reduced lung capacity. Enough about me, let's talk about our friend Sam Harman and his trouble with Jerry Curtis.

"I told Sam that Jerry wouldn't let this go without a fight," Braddock said. "But I have to admit that setting him up on drug charges wasn't what I expected him to do. I suspect Alvin Koontz's fine hand in that. Did David tell you about him?"

"Actually, he met me at the plane," Bennett replied, outlining the encounter.

"I'm sorry David wasn't there sooner," Braddock said. "But I only learned you were coming here an hour ago."

"How'd you find that out?" Bennett asked.

"One of Jerry's boys actually works for me," Braddock said. Bennett looked to Lambert, who seemed just as surprised at the news as he was. "I was able to slip him into Jerry's circle right after Sam inherited his fortune. I knew even then that Jerry would be out for revenge. The only reason he went along with Sam's deal was because his brothers pushed him to."

"He's nuts," Bennett said. "He doesn't seriously think anything he does will get the money back, does he?"

"No, he's not that stupid," Braddock said. "I think he just wants to make Sam's life a living hell. I always knew Jerry had a dark side, but ever since I placed my man in Jerry's group I've learned that it's a lot darker than I thought. I knew he used prostitutes but didn't suspect that he was also their pimp. He runs nearly half the streetwalkers in the Houston area, according to my source. His gang, for lack of a better term, handles the nuts and bolts of the operation but he gets all the profits. He's only recently moved up to dealing in drugs."

"Why haven't you turned him over to the cops?" Bennett asked.

"Right now all I have is my source's word for it," Braddock explained. "That's not the same as actual evidence."

"Even an anonymous tip would get the local police looking at him, wouldn't it?" Bennett asked.

"The Curtis name still means a lot in Houston," Braddock said. "I'm not saying he has cops on the take, but it wouldn't surprise me. I won't even bore you with the politics involved."

Bennett knew from personal experience that there were always a few willing to sell their badges. People like that gave all cops a bad reputation. "Still, you should call it in," Bennett said. "Maybe go straight to the DEA."

"I appreciate that you want to do the right thing, Steve," Braddock said. "But the first priority has to be stopping Jerry from ruining Sam Harman's life and reputation. I promised Hank Curtis that I'd look after the boy. I have to keep that promise."

"So how do you know Jerry's behind this?" Bennett asked.

"I can't prove anything," Braddock said. "But he's the only logical suspect. He has the means and the motive."

"Tracie Harman hired me to find out if Jerry was behind Sam's arrest," Bennett said. "From what you told me she might actually be right. We need something solid for the police or the DEA to nail him and get Sam out of jail. Can your man provide that?"

"Not yet," Braddock said. "The problem is that Jerry is not very trusting. My man has never been to whatever facility Jerry uses as his base of operations. If we could locate that place, we'd have him."

"And hopefully get whatever evidence we need to free Sam," Bennett said. "I think it's time for the direct approach."

FORTY-SIX

SINCE SAM'S ARREST, Tyler Security had increased its presence on the Harman property and begun patrolling the woods nearby. The security command post, tucked away behind the five-car garage where Sam stored his classic automobiles, was on full alert around the clock. Stan Tyler himself took charge of the situation, putting every available body he had on the property. Things seemed to be a secure as Tyler could make them, given the circumstances.

The five masked men slowly approaching the property were not deterred in the least. For the last two days, they'd camped out deep in the woods between the Harman property and the neighboring Pruitt land, hiding out in an abandoned shed Carl Pruitt once used for storing hay. From there they'd watched as the security people set up e a perimeter around the Harman property with motion detectors and irregularly timed patrols.

They waited until late Saturday night for the go-ahead signal. Brandishing M4 assault rifles, the same type used by the U.S. Army, they moved quickly through the woods and, ignoring the motion detectors and rushing the main house. As the alarm sounded and floodlights came on, they opened fire; shooting out any window they could see. They charged through the pool area, firing as they went. Glass shattered everywhere, and Chloe started barking frantically.

The security team responded immediately. Three armed men charged out the back door of the main house while two more emerged from Sam's garage, firing their pistols. One of the attackers went down but the rest turned their guns on the security people and quickly and mercilessly cut them down.

Leaving their fallen comrade behind the attackers headed around for the front of the house, shooting out every window and causing considerable damage to the brickwork. When they reached the attached garage, two of them assumed covering positions while the other two entered through a service door. There was only one car inside, Sam's BMW 550i. The team leader removed a small object from his belt and attached it to the gas tank, then signaled his partner to follow him out.

Stan Tyler led a team of three from the command post towards the main house. They found the house and garage teams lying in their own blood. They started to tend to their fallen comrades when they heard more gunfire from the front of the house. Tyler recognized the sound of the assault rifles. Why did the bad guys always have better weapons? "You two, go around that way!" Tyler ordered, indicating the garage. "Jack, we'll--"

His voice was cut off by an explosion in the attached garage. They all staggered back from the blast, one of them nearly falling into the pool. Chloe ran out the open back door. Since she knew all the security people by now, she stopped in front of them, whimpering as she looked around. Tyler reached down and scratched behind her ear. "Easy, now," he said. "You're okay."

The radio crackled. "Unit 1 to base!" a voice shouted. "We're taking fire! One man down!"

"Jack, put the dog in the big garage!" Tyler ordered. "You two, come with me."

They entered the house. The walls were riddled with bullet holes. The kitchen cabinets were virtually demolished, as were their contents. Glass, porcelain and plastic pieces were strewn everywhere. Tyler led his people to the front of the house and found more damage. Just how much ammunition did these people have? Through the shattered bay window, he could see that attackers were now pinned down by his people on that side of the property. Dropping to the floor, he and his team crawled across the destroyed living room until they reached the windowsill. They had a perfect shot at the four attackers.

In spite of his years as a police officer, Tyler had never taken a human life. Only twice had he discharged his weapon outside of a firing range or training course, and only one of those shots had hit its intended target. But he was superbly trained and showed no hesitation as he raised his weapon and fired on the attackers from behind. Combined with the fire from the two men he had with him, the attackers should have been cut down in short order.

So his surprise was understandable when they got up again, turned, and fired on him.

One of Tyler's men fell. Tyler himself took a round to the chest. *They're wearing Kevlar*, he thought dimly before passing out, *we should be wearing Kevlar*.

By the time the police arrived it was all over. The house was burning from the explosion of Sam's car. The security team suffered six dead and four wounded, including Stan Tyler who was airlifted to St. Mary's Hospital with life-threatening injuries. While being tended by the paramedics aboard the helicopter, he came to and asked if the dog was all right. Then he passed out again. He died seconds later, a seventh casualty.

Though the fire department arrived quickly, the damage to the house was devastating. The attached garage, guest bedrooms and utility area were completely destroyed, with the rest of the house suffering severe smoke and water damage. Later, when examined closely, it was determined that the house was structurally unsound and a total loss.

The attackers were, of course, long gone by the time the police arrived but they did catch one lucky break. The attacker who'd been wounded in the pool area was still alive, though he'd taken a round in the head. He was taken to St. Mary's, where he was kept under tight guard. He carried no ID and was not in any condition to answer questions, but the DEA and the State Police went to work trying to identify him, hoping it would lead them to whomever was responsible for this.

Because she didn't want her children exposed to any of the controversy surrounding Sam and the drug charges, Tracie had moved the family to the Presidential Suite at the Fairmont after his arrest and hired extra security to keep unwanted visitors out. Because the entire security team at the house was either dead or wounded, Tracie didn't learn of the attack until she woke up the next morning and watched the early news. She quickly turned the TV off before the kids heard it, but she didn't account for her news-hound eldest son who always checked the top stories on his iPad when he got up. Sam Jr. came into the master bedroom holding the device and looking completely shocked.

"Mom?" he asked. "Are they really dead?"

Tracie held out her arms for him, cradling him as she hadn't been able to do in years. "They killed Mr. Tyler," the boy sobbed.

"I know, honey, I know," Tracie cried. Stan spent a lot of time at the house looking after his most important clients and they had all grown very close to him. No one ever expected something like this to actually happen.

Soon Kristen and Noah came into the room, having no idea what was going on. Tracie tried to explain it to them as gently as she could, but nothing could prevent them from bursting out in tears at the news of Stan Tyler's death. Upon learning of the damage to their home, Noah asked if Chloe was alright. Nobody knew the answer to that. When Tracie got hold of herself, she led her family in prayers for the slain. Then she thought about Sam, still sitting in jail. Did he know yet? What was this doing to him? She bowed her head and started praying again.

It wasn't long before the DEA and the Police were at

the door of their suite. Though they did have the decency to report that the family dog was alive and well, they weren't here to simply bear news. Tracie was grilled for a good hour about any knowledge she might have of her husband's activities. She was outraged, naturally, but truly had nothing to tell them. As she patiently endured the questioning, she hoped against hope that Steve Bennett would come up with something.

Sam was roused early and led to an interrogation room. Mike, the DEA agent, was there along with a uniformed officer of the State Police by the name of Schmidt. Only now did he learn that Mike's last name was Hagen. At first he told them that he wasn't talking without his lawyer present. After Hagen explained that Charlton was on his way, he told Sam about the attack on the house and the casualties. Sam was grateful he was sitting down. He supposed he must have looked white as a sheet.

"Who would want to shoot up your house?" Hagen asked.

"Jerry Curtis," Sam said. "He's the only person I know who hates me that much."

"We've heard about your alleged troubles with him," Schmidt said. "Since we have one of the gunmen in custody, maybe he can corroborate your 'theory.'"

"Assuming these aren't your drug dealing buddies out to make sure you don't talk," Hagen said.

"I'm not involved with drug dealers," Sam said. "I told you that before."

"Says the man who tried to smuggle ten kilos of cocaine into the country," Hagen replied. "Tell me another one, Harman."

Aaron Charlton made his entrance. "I hope you're not asking my client questions yet," he said. "I've already spoken to your superiors once about that, Agent Hagen."

"Save it, Counselor," Hagen replied. "We're trying to find out who's running around with military assault rifles, shooting up drug smugglers' homes."

"I heard about that," Charlton said. "Surely you're not blaming Sam. He was here, in case you didn't notice."

"Maybe it's a message that someone doesn't want him to talk," Hagen said. "Like, oh I don't know, your pals in the Dominican Republic who sold you the cocaine?"

Another DEA agent entered the room and whispered something into Hagen's ear. "Well so much for getting an answer out of our prisoner," he said. "He just died on the operating table. Your security guys riddled him pretty good."

"They were protecting my home," Sam said. "I just thank God that Tracie took the kids to the hotel. Please tell me they're under guard."

"City and state police are there," Schmidt said.

"Thank you," Sam said.

"It's not out of the goodness of our hearts," Hagen said. "Your wife is a material witness."

"You leave Tracie alone!" Sam snapped.

"Give me a good reason," Hagen replied. "Tell me what I want to know."

"I don't know anything about drugs!" Sam said. "How many times do I have to tell you people that?"

"This interview is over," Charlton said. "My client

has nothing further to say to you gentlemen."

Sam was led back to his cell. Once the door was closed and the guard gone, T-Bone handed Sam a note. "This got passed down," he said.

Sam opened the note. It said: Plead guilty. If you don't, the next time we go after your family.

He sat down on his bunk, putting his head in his hands. He prayed for deliverance from this ordeal. He prayed for the safety of his family, and he prayed that Steve Bennett would get to the bottom of this.

FORTY-SEVEN

NEWS OF THE attack on the Harman home did not take long to reach Steve Bennett. The brutality of the attack, not to mention the deaths, shook the private investigator to his core. He'd known Stan Tyler for years. The man was a close friend of his uncle's. They'd served on the police force together. Bennett's shock quickly gave way to rage. If Jerry Curtis was behind this, he was going to pay. It had just become personal.

That evening Bennett and David Lambert walked in to a bar on the Houston waterfront. The place was a dive that catered mostly to longshoremen, sailors and prostitutes. They looked around, found who they were looking for and walked over to them. It was a group of five men sitting at a table playing poker. There was an impressive looking pile of cash in the pot. Bennett took a wad of bills out of his pocket and flashed them. "Is this a private game or can you guys deal me in?" he asked.

Alvin Koontz looked up from his cards with a detached expression. He noticed Bennett, Lambert, and the fact that they had inserted themselves between the table and the door. To his left, Stu Peart fixed Bennett with a gaze that would have killed were that sort of thing possible. The other three matched the photographs Lambert had shown Bennett the night before. Bennett knew which one the spy was but did nothing to draw attention to him.

"Your money looks good to me," Koontz said. "Let me win this pot and you can have a seat."

The hand was over in a few moments and true to his word, Koontz won with a full house. As he raked in his winnings Bennett grabbed a chair and sat down, putting his money on the table in front of him. "Five card draw," Koontz said, dealing a new hand. "Ante's ten bucks."

Bennett dropped a ten in the center of the table. The others followed and picked up their cards. Stu Peart didn't look at his, he just stared at Bennett. "No hard feelings?" Bennett asked. "I was aiming for your stomach, just so you know."

"Al, why are you letting this bastard sit with us?" Peart asked, not taking his eyes off Bennett. "How about we take him out back and teach him a lesson."

"I hate clichés," Bennett said. "Besides, the way you performed last night you could use a lesson or two, yourself."

Before Peart could react Koontz put a hand on his arm. "No need to be hostile," he said. "At least not in public."

"My thinking exactly," Bennett said, looking at his hand. He had two sixes, the rest was garbage. He threw those down. "I'll take three."

Koontz dealt him three new cards. He'd picked up more garbage. That was okay, he wasn't really here to play poker. "So why did a couple of nice guys like you try to ambush me last night?" he asked.

"Why would I want to discuss that with you?" Koontz asked.

"It would be the friendly thing to do," Bennett said. "The bet's to me? I'm in for fifty."

The man to Bennett's left swore and tossed down his cards. "Love that poker face," Bennett said. "Seriously, Al, I'd like to know what I did to honk off two people I've never even met."

"I'm sure you would," Koontz said. "But life is full of mysteries. Think of this as one of them. I'll see your fifty and raise you another fifty."

Another player folded. "I don't know how much you know about me, Al, but solving mysteries is my job," Bennett said.

"You can't solve them all," Koontz said. "Your best bet would be to go home."

"That wouldn't be very good for my reputation," Bennett said, throwing another fifty into the pot. "Call."

"Sticking around wouldn't be good for your health," Peart said.

"Settle down, Stu," Koontz said. He displayed his cards. He had three jacks.

Bennett tossed down his pair of sixes as Koontz raked in the cash. He tossed down another ten dollars for the next hand as Koontz shuffled the cards. "Tell me something, Al, what does it take to get a meeting with your boss?"

"What boss?" Koontz said. "I'm an independent businessman."

"I know you own this bar," Bennett said. "But if you'll forgive me for saying so, I'm surprised it rakes in enough for you to be driving that brand-new Camero out back."

"You just caught us on a slow day," Koontz said, starting to look more intently at Bennett.

"Of course I did," Bennett said, smiling. "But surely a man like you is…what do the rich folks say…diversified?"

Koontz said nothing. Bennett noticed that he hadn't started dealing the cards just yet. He took a look around the room and noticed a couple slipping through door behind the bar. The girl was dressed in a skirt that left almost nothing to the imagination and a halter top that displayed more cleavage than it concealed. Bennett, who was an experienced street cop, knew the look all too well. He wondered if there was a special room in the back or if they were just going to do it in the storeroom. "This place might be more profitable than it looks," he said.

"Looks can be deceiving," Koontz said. "I've been thinking, maybe your money isn't any good after all. Why don't you and your friend get out of here?"

"And here I thought we were all ready to be pals," Bennett said.

"You're not as funny as you think you are," Koontz said. "And you're not as smart, either. I'd bet my last five pots that you're wearing some kind of wire. So why don't you and your friend get out of here before I decide we need to find out exactly where that wire is, okay?"

"If that's the way you want it," Bennett said, getting up. "Give Jerry Curtis my regards, will you?"

"And who's Jerry Curtis?" Koontz asked.

"He's a billionaire who runs hookers and sells

drugs," Bennett said. "I thought you might know him. Guess I was wrong. Enjoy my money."

Bennett and Lambert left the bar. "Son of a bitch," Peart said. "You should have let me take care of him."

"Shut up," Koontz said, crawling under the table.

"What are you doing?" Peart asked.

"I said shut up," Koontz repeated. A moment later he came back up with a small black disc. He looked at it for a moment before crushing it under his boot.

"Is that what I think it was?" Peart asked.

"Yeah," Koontz said. "Go outside and look around. Make sure he's not watching the bar."

"What are you going to do?" Peart asked.

"Visit Jerry," Koontz said. "This guy has balls, I'll give him that. We need to find out more about him."

Bennett and Lambert were driving away when Peart and the rest of the gang came outside. They drove several blocks from the bar before stopping. Bennett pulled out a small device that was the size of an average cell phone. "Well, they found the bug," Lambert said. "Just like you said they would."

"Koontz found it," Bennett said. "He's the brains of the outfit. Now let's see if he took the bait."

They'd planned all along for the bug to be found. It would pain his uncle that they'd deliberately wasted an expensive piece of equipment but the Harmans were footing the bill so he wouldn't be upset for long. They weren't keeping the bar under surveillance for one simple reason. They didn't need to. While Bennett and Lambert were in the bar an associate of the latter slipped a small GPS tracking device on the undercarriage of Koontz's car. All that remained to be seen was whether or not Koontz would go to see Jerry Curtis.

Almost immediately the dot that represented Koontz's car started moving across the screen of Bennett's hand held tracker. "He's moving," Bennett said. "South."

"Towards the docks," Lambert said, looking at the screen. "Like we expected."

"He's probably trying to shake any potential tail," Bennett said. "Good thing this has a five mile range. We can follow him while staying out of sight."

Koontz was thorough, Bennett gave him that. He must have driven around Houston's waterfront area for almost an hour before coming to a stop. Bennett and Lambert followed the action from a McDonald's parking lot. Once Koontz's car stopped, they sprang back into action. Ten minutes later they found the Camaro parked outside a warehouse. A drive around showed that there were lights on. The problem was that there were several warehouses nearby, also with lights on. There was no guarantee that the one Koontz parked in front of was the one they wanted, but Bennett had a gut feeling that it was. He trusted his instincts. "Let's pay them a social call," he said.

"You're going to just waltz in there and ask to speak to Jerry?" Lambert said. "Are you nuts?"

"I like the direct approach," Bennett said.

"He's likely to kill you," Lambert pointed out.

"Maybe," Bennett said. "But maybe Koontz will keep Jerry under control. He doesn't strike me as the type to let things get out of hand. You being there will help. He knows you work for Braddock. The moment he sees you he'll be wondering how much Braddock knows. He may be the one person Jerry's afraid of."

"If you're such a gambler, how come Koontz beat you at poker?" Lambert asked.

"I'm pretty sure he was stacking the deck," Bennett said. "Besides, it was only one hand."

Lambert didn't see any of Jerry's known cars but Bennett pointed out that he probably had a special car he used for his criminal operations, no doubt registered to someone else. As they approached the warehouse on foot, Bennett turned on a special device that doubled as a wristwatch. It could record up to two hours of video and audio. The door was locked but there was a doorbell which Bennett rang. Nobody came to answer.

Bennett assumed they were under surveillance even though he didn't see any visible cameras. He tried the doorbell again. This time there was a buzz followed by a loud click. He tried the door again and this time it opened. "This is where it gets tricky," Bennett said, drawing his gun. "You got my back?"

"Yeah," Lambert said, drawing his own.

They entered the building.

FORTY-EIGHT

JERRY CURTIS WATCHED on a security monitor as Steve Bennett and David Lambert entered the warehouse. "They followed you," he said to Alvin Koontz.

"Shit," Koontz said. "He planted that bug to throw me off. He must have put a tracker on my car."

They were in the warehouse's office, which doubled as the headquarters of Curtis' criminal empire. One entire wall was covered with LCD monitors that displayed images from the security cameras that covered every square inch of the building's interior and the entire surrounding block. The images were in full color and looked as crisp as broadcast quality television.

Along the adjoining wall was a complex computer workstation, presided over by a young man in his twenties. Dennis Roberson once worked for Curtis Enterprises in its computer division until Jerry discovered he was using company computers to hack into places he had no business being. Though Roberson hadn't actually stolen anything, his activities could have hurt the company and Jerry wouldn't have that. He fired Roberson then turned around and offered him a million dollars a year to oversee computer operations for his private ventures. Roberson immediately accepted and had been a great help hiding in all the money Jerry made from his various criminal activities, as well as undertaking a few personal projects for him.

Roberson turned from his workstation to face them. "The DEA just identified the dead dude from the attack on Harman's house," he said. "They're looking for known associates now."

An enraged Curtis stalked across the room and hit one of the four men standing there. "Asshole!" he shouted. "You let those rent-a-cops get the drop on you and look what's happened!"

"Jerry, settle down," Koontz said. "It's not their fault. How were we supposed to know there were so many of them? We're lucky we didn't lose the whole team."

"But if the DEA traces them here, they'll trace them to me," Jerry said. "That wasn't part of the plan."

"Hey, boss," Roberson said, looking at the monitors. "What about those guys?"

Curtis and Koontz looked at the screen. Bennett and Lambert were in the warehouse proper now and were making their way through the stacks of crates. Curtis grabbed the man he'd hit and threw him up against the wall. "I hired you morons because you're supposed to be pros! Prove it now! Get down there and kill those bastards!"

A look of alarm crossed Koontz's face. "Jerry, I don't think that's a very good idea," he said. "If they disappear more will come looking for them."

"If that bastard half-brother of mine thinks his

private detective scares me, he's dumber than I thought," Curtis said. "Now you guys get down there!"

The four men took their M4 assault rifles from a gun locker and left the room. "As long as Bennett doesn't report back this can still work," Curtis said. "There will be no way to tie those drugs to me. Harman will spend a long time in jail."

"Is it really that important?" Koontz asked.

"Of course it is," Curtis replied. "That asshole is giving away money that ought to be mine. Maybe I can't get the money back but I can get him. Besides, you see that guy with Bennett? He works for my father's lawyer. I always hated that old son of a bitch. Getting rid of him will tell Anderson Braddock to stay out of my business."

"That's a lot of heat to bring down," Koontz said.

"You let me worry about that," Curtis said, going to the gun locker. He pulled out another M4 carbine and checked to make sure its extended magazine was fully loaded. He stuffed two additional clips into his back pockets. He stared at Koontz. "What are you waiting for?" he asked.

Reluctantly, Koontz went to the locker and got a Heckler & Koch UMP submachine gun. He loaded the weapon and joined Curtis before the bank of monitors. "We'll see how those hired guns of yours do," Curtis said. "If Bennett and Lambert get past them, it's our turn. I kind of hope they do."

Bennett and Lambert worked their way slowly through stacks of crates. They could see the office area on the other side of the warehouse. There were lights on but they couldn't see any signs of movement. "You realize this is a trap, don't you?" Lambert asked.

"Of course it is," Bennett replied. "That's why you're here, to watch my back."

"We don't even know what kind of firepower they have," Lambert pointed out.

"True," Bennett admitted. Then he noticed something. "Hey, look at this."

It was a stack of long, flat green crates that Bennett recognized from his time in the army. There were six crates in this stack and he saw another six stacked behind it. Though they were all locked Bennett didn't have to look inside to figure out what they contained. "Hand grenades," he said. "It has to be."

He took several pictures on his cell phone to document the finding. "I wonder what other toys Jerry Curtis has in here," he said, looking around at the other crates in the warehouse.

"We probably shouldn't be poking around too much," Lambert said. "Let's just find Curtis."

"Right," Bennett replied.

They continued moving through the warehouse, constantly looking around for signs of an ambush. When they reached the middle of the building, they spotted something new. Several tables had been set up with what Bennett recognized as all the things one needed to process cocaine from its pure form to the cut variety commonly sold on the streets. Nobody was working in the area at the moment, but everything looked ready to resume production at a moment's notice. Bennett photographed everything.

"Let's double back," he said. "See if we can catch

them trying to sneak up on us."

Lambert nodded his agreement and they headed back the way they came. As they neared the stack of grenade crates Bennett froze in his tracks. The top crate was open and seemed to be partly empty. "Uh-oh," Bennett said. "Cover me."

He dashed over to the crate with Lambert close behind, watching his back. Bennett reached into the crate and pulled out one of the grenades. "Flash-bangs," he said, examining it. "M84 stun grenades. If you hear anything hit the floor shut your eyes and cover your ears."

Lambert nodded and they moved on after helping themselves to some of the M84s. Bennett resolved to use them only if necessary. Though intended as a non-lethal weapon he knew flash-bangs could be deadly under the right conditions. They'd been known to start lethal fires, and he'd heard of a cop in North Carolina who'd accidentally detonated one and later died from his injuries.

As they cleared the last set of crates a shot rang out. Lambert cried in pain and fell to the floor, clutching his leg. Because of the way the shot echoed in the cavernous, warehouse Bennett couldn't figure out where it came from. As he squatted down to check Lambert's wound, another shot was fired, ricocheting off of the concrete floor in front of them. Bennett looked and this time he saw a shadow dart behind a crate. He pulled one of the M84s, pulled the pin and rolled it down towards the crate. He plugged his ears and shut his eyes.

Even thus protected, the sound was deafening and he could see the light from behind his eyelids. He didn't hesitate, though, running after the blast as soon as it went off. He had maybe five seconds before his target recovered enough of his senses to react. He spun around the corner with his gun up only there was nobody there. Cursing at his own foolishness he raced back towards Lambert. A string of gunshots followed him.

He reached Lambert without taking a hit. A small pool of blood had formed underneath the wounded leg. Lambert was on his cell phone. "I've had enough of this shit," he said. "Can we please get out of here now?"

Bennett helped Lambert to his good leg. They made fairly good progress towards the door but just before they reached it a string of gunfire shattered the glass. They dropped to the floor. Bennett saw a figure rise from behind one of the crates. He raised his gun and fired twice. The man jerked and fell. At the same time Lambert dropped another one who tried to ambush them from around a corner. Bennett opened the door. "Crawl out of here," he said to Lambert. "I'll try to draw their fire."

"You are crazy," Lambert said. "Let's just go and let the cops raid this place."

"I'm not letting Jerry Curtis get away," Bennett said. "Now go!"

Before Lambert could protest any further Bennett ran off, a hail of gunfire following him.

FORTY-NINE

IN THE OFFICE Jerry Curtis watched with growing rage as two of his hired guns went down. "Military grade weapons and they're cut down by a couple of handguns," he said in disgust. "What a perfect waste of good money those guys were."

"Jerry, maybe we'd better clear out of here," Koontz said. "Lambert was on his cell phone before he got out. The cops have got to be on their way by now."

"Fuck," Curtis said, switching the selector on his gun from SINGLE SHOT to FULL AUTO. "Come one, we'll deal with this."

Koontz reluctantly followed him out of the office. As he shut the door, a wide-eyed Dennis Roberson began furiously tapping away at his computer.

Steve Bennett was no thrill-seeker. He didn't enjoy rushing into firefights and getting shot at. But he did have a strongly developed sense of justice, and he wanted to see someone pay for what had happened to Stan Tyler. It was this that drove him to go back into the warehouse when the far safer plan would have been to run for it and let the local law handle things. He didn't want to see Jerry Curtis escape. This might also be Sam Harman's only chance at freedom. He had to see it through himself.

He went on the offensive. First he tossed a flash-bang over a stack of crates and plugged his ears. When it went off, it was followed by a string of gunfire. None of it hit near him but it did give him a direction. Off to the left, he thought, and slowly started heading that way. His Beretta 96D secure in the traditional two-handed grip, he kept low and watched for any sign of an attacker. He had no way of knowing that he and Lambert had cut the assault team in half. He also didn't know that Jerry Curtis and Alvin Koontz were now in the hunt.

Then he caught a break. He spotted a streak of blood on the floor and followed it until he found a wounded man trying to pull himself to his feet. Bennett came up behind him and placed the barrel of the gun against the back of the man's skull. "I'm betting you know what a forty-caliber round can do to your brain at this range," he whispered. "So ease back down to the floor and lie on your stomach."

The man did as he was told. Bennett took out a pair of plastic flexi-cuffs and applied the restraints to the man's wrists. "How many of you are there?" he asked.

"Four," was the reply. The man was clearly in serious pain.

"So two left," Bennett said. "What about Curtis?"

"Last time I saw him he was in the office with Koontz and the computer geek," he said. "Get me some help, man."

"Up yours," Bennett said. He spotted the nearby assault rifle and smiled. Like a gift from heaven, he thought to himself as he holstered the Beretta and picked up the rifle. He took his prisoner's ammunition and checked the weapon. The clip was almost full and he had two spares. Things were starting to look up.

Then he had an idea. "Call out for help," he ordered. "Now."

Staring down the barrel of his own rifle must have been too much for the wounded man because he cried out in pain almost immediately. "I'm hit!" he shouted. "Somebody, help, I'm hit!"

"Shut up!" a voice called out. "Or I'll kill you myself you useless piece of crap!"

"That must be Jerry Curtis," Bennett said. The wounded man nodded. "Good, say something nasty to him."

"Jerry you dumb fuck!" the man shouted. "You got me shot!"

"Don't tell me you're actually enjoying this," Bennett said.

"I should never have taken this job," the man said. "Jerry, if you don't get me some help I'll shoot your worthless ass!"

Bennett thought he heard something and raised his hand to silence his prisoner. He saw a foot step cautiously from behind a large crate. He raised the rifle and waited. He didn't recognize the man who stepped out. When the man stepped into full view, he knew at once that he'd been caught. Without a word he set his rifle down and lay down next to his comrade. Bennett cuffed him as well, just in case. "I'm glad you boys are so cooperative," he said.

"I'm not getting myself killed for that guy," his new

prisoner said.

"Smart thinking," Bennett said. "Now, both of you stay quiet. That trick won't work again."

He moved out of the area. The two cuffed men looked at each other. "We should have asked for more money," they both said.

Jason Penrod was the leader of the small group hired by Jerry Curtis to intimidate Sam Harman, and he was regretting taking the job more and more each minute. A small-time criminal who made a career out of holding up mom-and-pop stores and gas stations, Penrod had done two stretches in jail for armed robbery before hooking up with a drug dealer who needed an enforcer. The work was easier, paid better, and he found he was good at it. Over time his reputation grew into murder-for-hire, which was how he'd wound up working for Jerry Curtis. He had killed twice for the billionaire and when he was offered one hundred thousand dollars to shoot up a house in Port Mason he figured it was easy money and said yes.

He hadn't counted on losing one of his men, who happened to be a good friend. Working with a team had seemed like a good idea at the time, but now he wished he'd selected people he didn't know. He wanted to quit and just go home, but he knew Jerry Curtis would kill him for even suggesting it. As things stood right now he was tempted to kill Jerry himself and run for it.

Penrod turned a corner, rifle ready, only to find himself face to face with Alvin Koontz. Jerry's right hand man looked nervous. Penrod could relate. Then

Koontz hit him with a shocker. "Jerry's gone completely nuts," he said. "I've had enough of his shit. You want to get out of here?"

"He'll kill both of us," Penrod said.

"Let Bennett and him duke it out," Koontz said. "I've got a ton of money hidden away outside the country. Want a piece? Just help me get out of here. I'll give you ten million dollars."

That prospect definitely outweighed the benefits of staying. "Let's go," Penrod said.

Bennett heard the two men talking and even though he had the drop on both of them he decided not to bother. Two less meant it was down to him and Jerry, which was just how he wanted it. He watched the two men run across the warehouse floor. In the distance, he could hear sirens. The police were on the way. He hoped they were coming in force.

"Where are you two going?" Jerry Curtis yelled.

"We've had enough of this shit," Koontz said. "The cops are almost here. It's over."

He was answered by gunfire. Both men went down. Rather than take off through the maze of crates, Bennett slung the rifle over his shoulder and started climbing them. It wasn't easy, the crates were big and they were stacked well enough that hand and footholds were a little hard to find. But Bennett was in as good of physical condition as he had been as a cop. Plus, free-climbing was a hobby of his and compared to that, this was actually a bit easier.

"Hey, Jerry!" he shouted from the top of a stack. "You know it's over, right? The cops will be here any minute! When they find out what you've got stashed away in here you're going to jail!"

Bullets struck the crate. He dropped to his stomach, hoping that Jerry was shooting from the floor. None of the rounds seemed to come near him. He readied his own rifle and, seeing a shadow moving across the floor, fired at it. He didn't hang around for his opponent to fire again, quickly getting to his feet and jumping to another stack of crates. He almost didn't make it, smacking into the side of the stack and barely grabbing hold, losing his rifle in the process. He dangled by a few fingers before he managed to swing his other arm up and grab hold. His foot found purchase, and he pushed himself up on top of the crate. He made a mental note not to try anything that dumb again and drew his Beretta.

The sirens were groing louder. The cavalry was here. "You hear that, Jerry?" he asked. "They're coming for you!"

"Like hell!" Jerry replied, standing up to fire. Bennett jumped down to a lower stack as Jerry cut loose with the rifle. One of the bullets grazed Bennett's left hip as he hit the top of a crate. He rolled over in agony, managing to keep a grip on the Beretta. More gunfire raked the crate, chipping the wood all around him. Despite the pain he rolled off the crate and onto the floor. He immediately regretted it for two reasons. First, he was back in the crate maze and didn't know where he was. Second, the impact sent a new shockwave of pain though his hip. He crumpled to the floor, looking around for Jerry Curtis. With his good leg he started pushing himself across the floor.

Then he heard a familiar sound from his police

days: the sound of a door being battered down. "Police!" a voice shouted. "Nobody move!"

Bennett looked around but didn't see anyone near him. "He's got an automatic rifle!" he shouted. "Be careful!"

Almost as soon as the warning was out of his mouth, the rifle barked again. He heard a cry of pain. He hoped the officer was wearing Kevlar but knew that Curtis could well be using armor-piercing rounds. Bennett tried to get to his feet, using one of the crates for support. For a flesh wound this one sure hurt, but he managed to stay up. Then he heard a click and realized Jerry was reloading. The sound was very close, behind him. He turned and pulled out his last flash-bang, pulled the pin, and threw it in that direction. "Fire in the hole!" he shouted, plugging his ears again.

He heard the bang, counted to three, then opened his eyes. He could see the back of Jerry Curtis' head on the other side of a crate. Ignoring the pain in his hip, Bennett leaped over the crate and crashed into Curtis. They both fell to the floor. Bennett rolled away, saw the rifle, and kicked it with his good foot. It skidded away but unfortunately he had put too much weight on his left foot and he fell to the floor again. He tried to grab his Beretta from its holster but a pair of hands grabbed his wrist and pulled it away. Then a meaty fist crashed into his jaw. He tried to roll with it but still took most of the blow. Dazed, he tried to reach for the gun but just as his fingers touched the butt it was yanked out of his reach.

Jerry Curtis stood over him, holding his gun. He cocked back the hammer. "Nobody beats me," he said.

Before he could pull the trigger two cops came running around a corner with their guns drawn. "Drop the weapon!" one shouted. "Now!"

Jerry didn't seem to hear him. He pulled the trigger. Bennett took the round in his abdomen. Before Curtis could fire again, though, the cops opened fire. He fell to the ground, dropping the Beretta. The cops kicked it away and began handcuffing him. Bennett was dimly aware of one of them calling for an ambulance, but he passed out before he could even hear the reply.

FIFTY

STEVE BENNETT AND Jerry Curtis were rushed to the nearest hospital but only Bennett survived; Curtis died of his wounds in the ambulance. The round that struck Bennett perforated his small intestine but emergency surgery saved his life and the doctors believed he would make a complete recovery. Within twenty-four hours he was agitating to get out of the hospital, but the doctors wouldn't hear of it. The police officer Jerry shot survived, but just barely.

It took a while for the Houston police to sort everything out, but in the end they reached the right conclusions. Jerry Curtis' warehouse had been a hotbed of criminal activity. In addition to the drug operation, he was housing prostitutes in the building, some as young as sixteen. They would sleep on cots in the warehouse during the day then be taken to various parts of Houston at night to 'work.' The women were expected to look and be at their best at all times, so he supplied them with free drugs to keep them 'up.' If one of them failed to bring in enough money or stopped being her 'best,' they were removed from the company of the others, never to be seen again. Houston police would eventually hold Curtis responsible for seven missing women who were now presumed dead.

The authorities went through every crate in the warehouse and were astonished by what they found. Jerry had been running weapons to Mexico, supplying all sides in that country's drug cartel wars. A large shipment of assault rifles was scheduled to be smuggled out within days.

The police learned all of this from the one surviving insider. Dennis Roberson was caught trying to sneak out the back door with a laptop. He quickly offered to spill the goods without even asking for a deal in return. With Alvin Koontz dead, he was the only link between Jerry Curtis and the incredible finds in the warehouse. On his laptop were all of Jerry's criminal records, including his offshore banking activities. It was discovered that he transferred five million dollars to former Port Mason County sheriff John McCreary at the same time Sam Harman was arrested. This was the source of the money used to try and make Sam's life in jail miserable.

He also revealed that the computer program used to bilk Sam out of thirty million dollars was his creation. Melody Lindquist was hired by Jerry to embezzle the money. When she fled to Miami, she didn't take a flight out of the country. Instead, she flew by private jet to Houston where Curtis was waiting for her. Rather than pay her the promised fifteen million dollars, Curtis raped and tortured her until she revealed the account numbers and passwords needed to access the stolen money, then slit her throat and watched her bleed to death. Roberson captured the entire scene by way of the warehouse's surveillance system.

He also had recordings of Curtis bragging about his efforts to make Sam Harman's life a living hell, using the stolen money to finance the whole thing. On the recordings, he boasted openly about how he used his charter flight company to plant the ten kilos of cocaine found in Harman's luggage. This evidence was enough to convince the DEA, and Sam Harman was released from jail two days later to a happy reunion with his family. Their home destroyed, they remained at the Fairmont hotel, surrounded by what was left of Tyler Security and local police officers.

The recordings also revealed who had thrown that bottle at Sam's head during the protest outside his office when Brian Vogel was killed. Alvin Koontz had been conducting surveillance on Sam when he came upon the protest. When Sam came out he called Jerry, and sent him live video of the whole thing via cell phone. Since Koontz was posing as a wino he had the bottle in his hand, so Jerry ordered him to throw it. He didn't seem to have any involvement in the death of Brian Vogel, though. That mystery remained unsolved.

It was a shaken and remorseful Sam Harman who arrived at his property a few days later with his wife to survey the damage. Half of the house was a burned-out skeleton. All around the grounds were little flags where bullet casings had been retrieved and bodies found. They slowly and silently walked around the remains of their home, unable to comprehend what would drive someone to do this. Sam felt no remorse over his half-brother's death, Jerry had brought that on himself, but he was wracked with guilt over the eleven other deaths now tied to his inheritance. It was too much to take, and he sat down heavily on the ground.

Tracie knelt next to him, saying nothing. They had known many of those who died. There would be funerals to attend, and they planned to go to all of them. They both wept over the deaths. All because one man felt cheated out of money he probably would never have spent. Sam wept bitterly and it wasn't long before Tracie did as well.

"Why did I take that money?" Sam asked. "It's brought us nothing but trouble. If you count Ted, and I do, thirteen people have died because of this. Tracie, it's not worth it."

"What do you want to do?" Tracie asked.

"I don't know," Sam said. "Part of me just wants to walk away. Give it all to charity and go back to some kind of honest work. But I don't know. That wouldn't bring anyone back. And it would be like letting Jerry win. But how much more misery is this going to put us through?"

"The money didn't do all this," Tracie said. "Jerry Curtis did."

"Because of me," Sam said. "Because...because I exist. Because I took something he thought should be his."

"Jerry hurt a lot of people," Tracie said. "And if he hadn't been stopped, he would have hurt a lot more. I hate to say this, honey, because I want to believe the best of everyone, but I think he was just plain evil. He had a rotten heart, and he liked to hurt people. He hurt those poor girls he forced into prostitution. He hurt people with his drugs, and with the guns he sold.

None of that had anything to do with you."

Sam said nothing. "Honey, I'm not going to tell you what to do," Tracie said. "If you want to give it all up, I'll be there with you. If you want to keep it, I'll be here. I love you, not your money."

Slowly, Sam stood up. He held his wife's hand and walked over to the big garage. It had escaped the ravages of the fire and his cars were intact. He now owned a 1965 Ford Mustang convertible, an 1957 Chevrolet Impala convertible, a 1968 Chevy Camaro, and the pride of his collection, a new Aston Martin DBS worth over two hundred thousand dollars. This was what people had died defending. Not his family, who hadn't even been here. This. Possessions. Mere things. It wasn't worth it.

But could he take all this away from his family? Could he let Jerry Curtis win?

"What are you going to do?" Tracie asked.

"I don't know yet," Sam said. "Before I decide, though, we have some things to do."

FIFTY-ONE

THE HARMAN FAMILY arrived in Houston the day Steve Bennett was released from Methodist Hospital. Sam had flown Bennett's family to Houston to be with him during his hospital stay and now put them up in the best suite at the Four Seasons hotel, taking a separate suite for his own family. His guilt over the serious injury done to his friend was considerable, and he was determined to do everything he could to make it up to him.

For his part, Bennett wasn't the least bit mad at Sam. He was mad at himself for letting Jerry Curtis get the better of him. "I know I'm smarter than that," he said, relaxing in the suite after Sam apologized profusely for getting him hurt. "I'm not as sharp as I used to be. Got to do something about that."

"I don't suppose I could talk you into a safer line of work," said Ann Bennett, Steve's mother.

"Not likely," Bennett admitted. "I like what I do too much. I think I might start wearing Kevlar when on the job, though."

"You might want to reconsider going back to work," Sam said, taking an envelope out of his pocket. "After you take a look at this."

Bennett opened the envelope and gasped at what he found inside. "Ten million dollars?" he said. "You can't be serious."

"I am," Sam said. "And you'd better take it."

"Mr. Harman," Bennett's father, Jim, began.

"Please, Sam," Sam said.

"Sam," Jim said. "It's too much, even after what happened to him."

"It's not like I'm going to miss it," Sam said. "And he earned it."

"I don't know what to say," Bennett said. "Thank you doesn't seem to be enough."

"I'm the one thanking you," Sam said. "You risked your life for me. I'm not going to forget that."

He rose to leave. "Sam," Bennett said. "I know you blame yourself for what happened. I probably would too. But you didn't do anything wrong. Jerry Curtis was the villain here, not you."

Sam nodded in agreement but knew that it would be a long time before he got over this. He took his leave of the Bennett family and left the hotel. The limo he'd hired drove him to the Curtis estate. Several limos and other expensive cars were parked out front, and the family's security team was out in full force. He wasn't sure if he would be admitted to the mansion, but he knew he at least had to try and explain his role in Jerry's death.

To his surprise, Bill Curtis personally greeted him at the door and welcomed him into the house. "Mama's been hoping you'd come to visit," he said.

"I'm surprised you didn't have me thrown off the grounds," Sam replied.

"Sam, what happened to Jerry was his own fault, not

yours," Bill said. "I know Mama feels the same way."

"What about Nick?" Sam asked.

"Well, let me worry about Nick," Bill said. "He and Jerry were always close and I'm afraid he's not taking it very well. He's flying in from Monaco. Maybe the flight will calm him down."

Bill led him past a room where several family members were sitting or talking quietly. "Mama's in her private suite," he explained. "She'll see me, and Nick when he gets here, but the only other person she'll see is you."

They went up a flight of stairs, coming to a stop halfway down a corridor. Bill knocked softly. "Mama," he said. "Sam's here."

"Well get him in here," Sallie Curtis replied. "I'm not getting any younger."

Except for being dressed in black, Sallie Curtis looked the same as she had the last time Sam saw her. "I ain't gonna bite, boy," she said. "Get in here and have a seat."

Sallie was sitting in an easy chair and beckoned Sam to sit in the chair next to her. "Bill, let's have a drink," she said. "Sam? What'll you have?"

"Uh, bourbon and water, I guess," Sam said.

"Make that three," Sallie said. Bill fixed the drinks at a mini-bar. When he brought them over Sam started with a small sip, thought about it and then went for a bigger gulp.

"That's more like it," Sallie said, downing a third of her own drink. "You know I don't beat around the bush, Sam, so you'll believe me when I tell you that what happened to Jerry wasn't your fault. He got himself in to that mess and paid for it. So I don't want you blaming yourself, you hear?"

"I hear," Sam said. "I'm not sure I agree with you, but I understand what you're saying."

"Jerry was a tough boy to bring up," Sallie said. "That temper of his...well it got him into plenty of trouble. Hank spoiling him didn't help, either. He had every advantage anybody could ask for, and he threw it away on drugs, women and who knows what else. I've cried for him, Sam, and I'll miss him for the rest of my days, but in the end he's responsible for his death, not you. What he was trying to do to you was horrible. I don't blame you for fighting back."

"All those people, though," Sam said. "They died because I took that money. I've been thinking, about walking away from it. Just giving it all up."

"Don't be stupid, boy," Sallie said. "Keep the money. Hank wanted you to have it and that's that. Don't argue with me, you'll lose."

Sam didn't know what to say to that, so he said nothing. "You stay here for the funeral," Sallie commanded. "And quit wasting your money on hotels. I told you before when you come here you stay with me."

Sam nodded. "I'll call Tracie," he said. "But maybe it would be better if I didn't go to the funeral."

"Nonsense," Sallie said. "You're a Curtis, you belong there. If I say you're going, then you're going and nobody's going to say otherwise."

"For what it's worth, Sam, I agree with Mama," Bill said. "This isn't your fault, even though I can see you're going to blame yourself for a while. Do yourself a favor, though, and stop. Guilt won't change what happened to your friend, and it won't change the choices Jerry made. At least you know that this family doesn't blame you and that we welcome you...as one of us."

And with that Bill Curtis embraced his half-brother for the first time.

That night Sam and Tracie lay in bed in the Curtis mansion holding hands. The funeral would be the next day, and Sam wasn't looking forward to it. His name was making headlines again. He didn't look up the Port Mason news on his laptop; he didn't want to hear what they were saying about him now. He was sure he never wanted to see his name in the headlines again.

"So did you make a decision?" Tracie asked.

"Yeah," Sam said. "I'm going to keep the money. Sallie will kill me if I don't."

Tracie laughed. After a moment, Sam did too. "You know, that's the first time I've seen you smile since you got out of jail," she said. "I was starting to wonder if you still remembered how."

"Haven't had much to smile about lately," Sam said.

"I know," Tracie said. "But God doesn't want us to be miserable. You know that, don't you?"

"Yeah," Sam said. "Wish the rest of the world felt that way."

"You're going to get through this," Tracie said. "Just trust God to take care of it. Besides, now that we're keeping the money we have a house to rebuild."

"True," Sam said. "We'll make it just like it was."

"No, we won't," Tracie said. "It's going to have to be bigger."

"Oh, right, Kyle will be living with us," Sam said. "So we tack on an extra bedroom. No big deal."

"Actually, we need one more room," Tracie said. "And it has to be ready in about seven months."

"Why?" Sam asked. The look on Tracie's face gave him the answer. "Oh, wow," he said. "Are you sure?"

"What is it with you men?" Tracie asked. "You always have to ask if we're sure."

"Must be in our DNA," Sam said. "How far along are you?"

"Now that question doesn't bother me," Tracie said, smiling. "The doctor says I'm about eight weeks pregnant. She also says that everything is fine."

"Wow," Sam said. "Another baby."

"You okay with this?" she asked.

"Okay?" Sam replied. "Honey this is wonderful!"

"Really?" Tracie asked.

"Yes, really," he said, taking her in his arms and kissing her deeply. "Have I told you today how much I love you?" he asked.

"No, you haven't," Tracie replied. "But then again, I haven't told you, either."

"I do love you," Sam said. "More and more each day."

He kissed her again. They didn't get to sleep for a while after that.

FIFTY-TWO

THEIR CHILDREN TOOK the news of the new baby very well. Kristen squealed with delight and immediately started suggesting names, but only girls' names. Noah was excited too because he was going to be a big brother. Sam Jr. seemed to take it in stride but wasn't nearly as excited as the other two. His parents understood, this was probably getting to be old hat for him. He was also getting to that age where he was too cool to get worked up about that sort of thing. Sam wasn't too sure he liked the idea of his oldest son getting that grown up, but he also knew there wasn't anything he could do about it.

Sam was a little concerned that he was getting too old to be having babies but again, he had little choice in the matter now. Though he would take whatever God gave them, he admitted to himself that another little girl would be nice. As in her previous pregnancies, Tracie was absolutely glowing, though he knew that would change as the pregnancy progressed. It didn't matter to him; she was and always would be beautiful to him.

Three days after Jerry Curtis' funeral the Harmans flew home. To Sam's surprise and relief there was no press waiting for them, just Tracie's parents. The kids broke the news of Tracie's pregnancy before either Tracie or Sam could. The Pruitts were delighted, of course, and they celebrated by going to dinner at Ashley's.

While eating, Sam caught the eye of Amanda Clark, who was having dinner with a well-dressed gentlemen he assumed was her boyfriend. Moments later he realized that her date was one of the Mayor's aides. Sam smiled to himself, thinking that she was on the job after all. Then he noticed she didn't have a notebook on the table. They also touched hands a lot. Rather than coming over to ask a bunch of questions, she simply waved and smiled. Sam smiled back and nodded. Then he got the attention of the waiter and sent a bottle of wine to their table. No sense in not maintaining good relations with the press, he thought.

Amazingly enough, none of Sam's most recent troubles affected his movie plans. Even as his old house was being torn down and foundations laid for its replacement, he was rolling cameras on The Path. Production went even better than Sam expected, and principal photography was completed by the end of May. The process of making the film kept him busy for months, allowing him to put some emotional distance between himself and Jerry Curtis situation. When editing was finished and the film completed, Sam felt like himself again.

One problem that just wouldn't go away was radio host Bill Dodd. As soon as Sam was released from jail, Dodd was on the air crying about another cover-up. Sam was starting to develop a thicker skin about Dodd but still wished there was a way he could put the man in his place. At the end of June, while he was taking a short break from editing The Path, that way finally presented itself.

One morning Bill Dodd began his morning show with the guest he'd been trying to get for nearly a year. "Friends, I have a special treat for you this morning," he said. "Our guest is none other than Port Mason's own resident billionaire, Mr. Sam Harman. Sam, welcome to the show."

"Thanks for having me," Sam replied.

"Sam we have a lot of ground to cover so I'll get right to it," Dodd said. "A lot of people, myself included, are wondering if the whole story about your arrest on drug charges is ever going to come out. The story about your half-brother is a little too fantastic to believe, don't you think?"

"Funny you should bring that up," Sam said. "Because you're right, one part of the story hasn't come out yet. I'm going to give you an exclusive, Bill. How about that?"

"This ought to be good," Dodd said. "So what do you have for us?"

"Well the DEA and the FBI are still going over Jerry Curtis' financial records," Sam said. "It's a pretty complicated mess, but they did find a tidbit that should be very interesting to your listeners."

"What's that?" Dodd asked.

"The fact that last year you were paid one million dollars by my late half-brother," Sam said.

Dodd's face went white and for once words failed him. "And it gets better," Sam said. "Jerry had a computer specialist working for him. This guy didn't trust Jerry one bit, and he kept excellent records of everything Jerry did. It was a kind of insurance policy in case Jerry ever turned on him. He even bugged Jerry's phone. You remember that day last year when Jerry called in to this show and said all that nasty stuff about me? Well there's a recording from Jerry's phone that shows you and he planned out the whole thing. I have a copy right here, courtesy of my new friends at the FBI. Would you like to hear it?"

Sam offered him a compact disc. "You can fake anything these days," Dodd said.

"True, but how do you explain the million dollars?" Sam asked. "You spin that for your listeners any way you want. I don't care. I'm posting this on my company's website this afternoon. Anyone who wants to listen to it can log on and download it. Take care, Bill."

Sam left the studio. On his way out of the building he stopped in the station manager's office and dropped the CD on his desk. "You should listen to this," Sam said.

That afternoon WXLR announced that Bill Dodd had been fired. Sam smiled. There was some justice in the world after all.

EPILOGUE

IN OCTOBER BECKY Dunlap succumbed to her cancer; her son, Sam and Tracie at her bedside. In her memory, Sam and Tracie donated ten million dollars to cervical cancer research. Though deeply grieved by the loss of his mother, Kyle found a new family in the Harmans and quickly came to love them as though they were his flesh and blood. Sam and Tracie treated him like a son, and they had many good years together.

The Harmans rebuilt their home from the ground up, adding new bedrooms for Kyle and their new baby. More security conscious after the attack on his home, Sam ordered a security fence built around his property. Stan Tyler's son, Pat, inherited Tyler Security and continued to provide protection for the Harman family.

Sam kept his financial promises to T-Bone and the rest of the inmates at the Port Mason County Jail who helped him after his arrest. Though several burned through the money quickly and returned to their old ways, T-Bone decided to start his life over again and used his money to get an education and rebuild his life.

Bill Dodd wasn't concerned over his firing at first. After all, he had a million dollars in his pocket. Unfortunately for him, this million was traced back to Jerry Curtis' drug operation and subsequently seized by the DEA.

Former Sheriff John McCreary was indicted for numerous crimes including bribery, extortion, conspiracy and theft of government property. The day the indictment was handed down he was found dead in his home, an apparent suicide. The funds paid to him by Jerry Curtis were eventually traced back to the money stolen from Sam Harman.

Sam actually got most of the embezzled money back. Thanks to hard work by the FBI's financial crimes unit, all the money was tracked back to Jerry Curtis. Twenty-five of the original thirty million was returned to Sam, who used it to found a new drug treatment center in Port Mason. It was named the Theodore Harman Clinic for Addiction and Recovery.

Mayor Eric Hawkins was re-elected to a second term though it was widely acknowledged that the Harman grants played a considerable role in his victory. Sam refused to take any credit and turned down the Key to the City when it was offered to him a month later. He never changed his position on giving money to political campaigns.

Within a year of Jerry Curtis' death, Sallie Curtis and Anderson Braddock both passed away. In a surprising turn of events, Sallie left Sam her voting share of Curtis Enterprises, more than doubling his fortune. This time around the Curtis family didn't object and Sam was even granted a seat on the board of directors. He even bought a condominium in

Houston to use when he visited.

The Path received great acclaim in the Christian Film community and even earned a mention or two from the mainstream critics who panned its religious message but praised its suspenseful elements and direction. The film earned $30 million, mostly from DVD and Blu-Ray sales. .

Steve Bennett recovered fully from his injuries, and despite his windfall, continued working with his uncle at Bennett Investigations.

Moved deeply by his experiences in the Dominican Republic, Sam set up a foundation to sponsor missionary trips there. He also began looking for ways to invest in the tiny country, hoping his money could help improve the lives of at least some of the people there.

In November the much-anticipated launch of Lunar Exploration Technologies *Prospector* probe took place on board a Proton rocked from the Baikonur Cosmodrome in Kazakhstan. The launch itself was a success but ten days later on its final approach to the moon Prospector's guidance system failed and the probe crashed into the lunar surface. With Sam's continued financial support LET resolved to try again

Art Bryant, the former church elder, and Owen Gorman did start a new church, calling it the True Believers Tabernacle.

Sam and Tracie remained members of Chester Avenue Christian Church. Not only did they provide tremendous financial support for the church, but they used it as a means to funnel money to other faith-based causes both in the community and around the world. Sam was even offered a seat on the Board of

Elders, which he declined because he didn't consider himself qualified. "Writing checks doesn't confer the spiritual maturity needed in an elder of the church," he said at the time. "And while you can call me many things, 'mature' is not one of them."

In December, the new baby was born. Sallie Rae Harman weighed seven pounds, two ounces and was twenty one inches long. Though delighted with their new baby Sam and Tracie agreed that four kids (five, counting Kyle) was definitely enough. Sam had a vasectomy shortly after learning of Tracie's pregnancy.

Sam Harman never joined a country club.

ACKNOWLEDGEMENTS

Nobody writes and publishes a novel without help and I'm no exception. The Inheritance would not have been possible without the assistance of the following. My thanks go to:

Almighty God for giving me the skills and desire to write.

Angela, for her love, support, encouragement, and excellent proofreading.

Josie and Jimmy for being the two greatest kids a dad could hope for and for understanding when I kicked you out of the office so I could write.

My parents, Robert and Barbara Gonko, for always believing in me. I wish you were here to see this.

My brother, Todd, his wife Jessica, and KatieMae, Madi, Jesse and Nate.

Vi Shaughnessy, my 'second mother.'

Richard and Phyllis Holloway for being the best in-laws anyone could hope for.

Karen Harman for insight on the manuscript and letting me borrow her last name.

Bobby Brooks for the cover art.

All my Facebook friends for the messages of encouragement. There are too many of you to list here but you know who you are.

Pastor Stan and Rosann Summers and the rest of my extended family at Koke Mill Christian Church. Again, too many names to list here but you know who are.

Finally I want to thank YOU, the reader, for picking up this book and (I hope) enjoying it. I'm working on the next one. Hopefully you consider that good news.

ABOUT THE AUTHOR

The Inheritance is Robert Gonko's first published novel. He lives in Illinois with his wife, Angela, and his children, Josie and Jimmy.

CONNECT WITH ME ONLINE
Blog:
http://robertgonko.wordpress.com

Facebook:
https://www.facebook.com/robertgonkoauthorpage

Twitter:
http://twitter.com/rgonko2

Made in the USA
Charleston, SC
05 April 2013